R

Red Fairy Book

nH DiDi

ul

Red Fairy Book

collected and edited by
ANDREW LANG

illustrated by
MARC SIMONT

with a foreword by
MARY GOULD DAVIS

LONGMANS

LONGMANS, GREEN AND CO LTD
48 Grosvenor Street, London W.1

*Associated companies, branches and representatives
throughout the world*

THIS EDITION FIRST PUBLISHED 1950
NEW IMPRESSIONS 1954, 1956, 1959, 1961, 1963, and 1967

PRINTED IN GREAT BRITAIN BY
LOWE AND BRYDONE (PRINTERS) LIMITED, LONDON, N.W.10

To

MASTER BILLY TREMAYNE MILES

A PROFOUND STUDENT

YET

AN AMIABLE CRITIC

NOTE

As this edition has been set in a larger, more readable type, a few of the original stories have been omitted.

Foreword

To WRITE a few words of introduction to the first four of the Andrew Lang Fairy Books is a simple act of friendship. We are not likely to forget the pages from which the Marquis of Carabas made his first bow to us! We are eager to tell our children and our grandchildren that it was in these books that we first met 'Cinderella' and 'Jack and the Beanstalk' and 'Rumpelstiltskin.' It was in 1889 that the *Blue Fairy Book,* the first of the series, appeared. It was a period when realistic stories dominated the world of children's books. 'Novels of childhood' by Mrs. Ewing and Mrs. Molesworth and other writers were offered to the children as their only fare.

The publishers admitted that the *Blue Fairy Book* was an experiment. Its success was immediate and it turned the tide from realism to the old folk and fairy tales. After the publication of the *Blue* the children demanded others, and the *Red,* the *Green* and the *Yellow* followed. 'The children are pleased,' said Andrew Lang, 'and they are so kind as to *say* that they are pleased. The editor does not care very much for what other people may say.' More than fifty years later it is certainly safe to state that hundreds of modern women have taken their first taste of romance from these pages, hundreds of modern men their first thrill of adventure.

Andrew Lang and his staff of helpers went far afield to find the stories that are in these books. Taking the whole series, practically every literature in the world is represented. One has only to read his biography to know that it was a labour of love. Student, scholar, lover of history and romance, he left no stone unturned that might reveal a new tale for the children. Because they are ageless, they need for a new generation only the courtesy of a modern dress; clearer type, new illustrations where the old ones seem outmoded and slight editorial changes.

They have been, are and will always be, books that it is a joy to share with boys and girls, and that boys and girls are sure to find for themselves. Fathers and even grandfathers will testify that they leaped from these fairy tales to science and invention, mothers and grandmothers that in them they found the natural transition from 'The Sleeping Beauty' to the real romance. It is a part of the inheritance of childhood to have read them, and no collection of books for children is complete without them.

To Andrew Lang belongs the honour of having made a very great contribution to the preservation of the literature of the world. In bringing together from the four corners of the earth these characteristic stories, he has helped to lay the foundation stones of a united world. The love of fairy tales is common to all peoples. To English-speaking children it was Andrew Lang who opened the door of Fairyland.

MARY GOULD DAVIS

New York
March, 1948

Preface

In a second gleaning of the fields of Fairyland we cannot expect to find a second Perrault. But there are good stories enough left, and it is hoped that some in the *Red Fairy Book* may have the attraction of being less familiar than many of the old friends. The tales have been translated, or, in the case of those from Madame d'Aulnoy's long stories, adapted: by Mrs. Hunt from the Norse, by Miss Minnie Wright from Madame d'Aulnoy, by Mrs. Lang and Miss Bruce from other French sources, by Miss May Sellar, Miss Farquharson, and Miss Blackley from the German, while the story of 'Sigurd' is condensed by the editor from Mr. William Morris's prose version of the *Volsunga Saga*. The editor has to thank his friend, M. Charles Marelles, for permission to reproduce his versions of 'The Pied Piper,' of 'Drakestail,' and of 'Little Golden Hood' from the French, and M. Henri Carnoy for the same privilege in regard to 'The Six Sillies' from *La Tradition*.

Lady Frances Balfour has kindly copied an old version of 'Jack and the Beanstalk,' and Messrs. Smith and Elder have permitted the publication of two of Mr. Ralston's versions from the Russian.

Andrew Lang

Contents

Illustrations

xv

Red Fairy Book

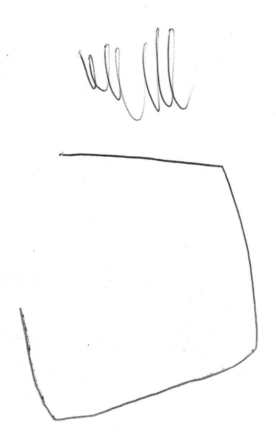

Twelve Dancing Princesses

NCE UPON A TIME
there lived in the village of Montignies-sur-Roc a little cowboy, without either father or mother. His real name was Michael, but he was always called the Star Gazer, because when he drove his cows over the commons to seek for pasture, he went along with his head in the air.

As he had a white skin, blue eyes, and hair that curled all over his head, the village girls used to cry after him, 'Well, Star Gazer, what are you doing?' and Michael would answer, 'Oh, nothing,' and go on his way without even turning to look at them.

One morning about the middle of August, just at midday when the sun was hottest, Michael ate his dinner of a piece of dry bread and went to sleep under an oak. And he dreamt that a beautiful lady, dressed in a robe of cloth of gold, came and said to him:

'Go to the castle of Belœil, and there you shall marry a princess.'

That evening the little cowboy told his dream to the farm people. But, as was natural, they only laughed at the Star Gazer.

The next day at the same hour he went to sleep again under the same tree. The lady appeared to him a second time, and said:

'Go to the castle of Belœil, and you shall marry a princess.'

In the evening Michael told his friends that he had dreamed the same dream again, but they only laughed at him more than before.

'Never mind,' he said to himself, 'if the lady appears to me a third time, I will do as she tells me.'

The following day, to the great astonishment of all the village, about two o'clock in the afternoon a voice was heard singing:

> 'Raleô, raleô,
> How the cattle go!'

It was the little cowboy driving his herd back to the byre.

The farmer began to scold him furiously, but he answered quietly, 'I am going away.' He made his clothes into a bundle, said good-bye to all his friends, and boldly set out to seek his fortune.

There was great excitement through all the village, and on the top of the hill the people stood, holding their sides with laughing, as they watched the Star Gazer trudging bravely along the valley with his bundle at the end of his stick.

It was well known for full twenty miles round that in the castle of Belœil lived twelve princesses of wonderful beauty, as proud as they were beautiful, and so sensitive and of such truly royal blood, they would have felt at once the presence of a pea in their beds, even if the mattresses were laid over it.

They had twelve beds all in the same room, but what was very extraordinary was the fact that, though they were locked

'Oh, how pretty our garden boy is.'

in by triple bolts, every morning their satin shoes were worn into holes. No noise was ever heard in the room, yet the shoes could not wear themselves out alone!

At last the Duke of Belœil ordered the trumpet to be sounded and a proclamation made that whoever could discover how his daughters wore out their shoes should choose one of them for his wife.

On hearing the proclamation, a number of princes arrived at the castle to try their luck. They watched all night behind the open door of the princesses, but when the morning came they had all disappeared, and no one could tell what had become of them.

When he reached the castle, Michael went straight to the gardener and offered his services. Now it happened the garden boy had just been sent away, and though the Star Gazer did not look very sturdy, the gardener agreed to take him, as he thought his pretty face and golden curls would please the princesses.

The first thing he was to do, when the princesses awoke, was to present each one with a bouquet. So Michael placed himself behind the door of the princesses' room, with the twelve bouquets in a basket. He gave one to each of the sisters, who took them without even deigning to look at the lad, except Lina, the youngest, who fixed on him her large black eyes as soft as velvet, and exclaimed, 'Oh, how pretty he is—our new flower boy!' The rest all burst out laughing, and the eldest said that a princess ought never to lower herself by looking at a garden boy.

Now Michael knew that all the princes had disappeared, but the beautiful eyes of Princess Lina inspired him with a violent longing to try his fate. Unhappily he did not dare to come forward, being afraid he should only be jeered at, or even turned away from the castle on account of his impudence.

Then the Star Gazer had another dream. The lady in the golden dress appeared to him once more, holding in one hand two young laurel trees, a cherry laurel and a rose laurel, and in the other hand a little golden rake, a little golden bucket and a silken towel. She said:

'Plant these two laurels in two large pots, rake them over with the rake, water them with the bucket, and wipe them with the towel. When they have grown as tall as a girl of fifteen, say to each of them, "My beautiful laurel, with the golden rake I have raked you, with the golden bucket I have watered you, with the silken towel I have wiped you." Then, after that, ask anything you choose, and the laurels will give it to you.'

Michael thanked the lady in the golden dress, and when he woke he found the two laurel bushes beside him. So he carefully obeyed the orders given him by the lady.

The trees grew very fast and, when they were as tall as a girl of fifteen, he said to the cherry laurel, 'My lovely cherry laurel, with the golden rake I have raked you, with the golden bucket I have watered you, with the silken towel I have wiped you. Teach me how to become invisible.'

Instantly there appeared on the laurel a pretty white flower, which Michael gathered and stuck into his buttonhole.

THAT evening, when the princesses went upstairs to bed, he followed them barefoot, so he would make no noise, and hid himself under one of the twelve beds.

The princesses began at once to open their wardrobes and boxes. They took out of them the most magnificent dresses, which they put on before their mirrors, turning themselves all round to admire their appearance. Michael could see nothing from his hiding place, but he could hear everything, and he listened to the princesses laughing and talking with pleasure.

At last the eldest said, 'Be quick, my sisters, our partners will be impatient.'

When the Star Gazer peeped out, he saw the twelve sisters in splendid garments, with satin shoes on their feet, and in their hands the bouquets he had brought them.

'Are you ready?' asked the eldest.

'Yes,' replied the other eleven in chorus, and they took their places one by one behind her.

Then the eldest princess clapped her hands three times and a trap door opened. All the princesses disappeared down a secret staircase, and Michael hastily followed them. As he was following on the steps of the Princess Lina, he carelessly trod on her dress.

'There is somebody behind me,' cried the princess, 'holding my dress.'

'You foolish thing,' said her eldest sister, 'you are always afraid of something. It is only a nail which caught you.'

They went down, down, down, till at last they came to a passage with a door at one end, which was only fastened with a latch. The eldest princess opened it, and they found themselves immediately in a lovely little wood, where the leaves were spangled with drops of silver which shone in the brilliant light of the moon. Next they crossed another wood, where the leaves were sprinkled with gold, and after that still another where the leaves glittered with diamonds.

At last the Star Gazer perceived a large lake, and on the shore were twelve little boats with awnings, in which were seated twelve princes who, grasping their oars, awaited the princesses.

Each princess entered one of the boats, and Michael slipped in with the youngest. The boats glided along rapidly, but Lina's, being heavier, was always behind the rest.

'We never went so slowly before,' said the princess. 'What can be the reason?'

'I don't know,' answered the prince. 'I assure you I am rowing as hard as I can.'

On the other side of the lake the garden boy saw a beautiful castle, splendidly illuminated, whence came the lively music of fiddles and kettledrums and trumpets. In a moment they touched land, and the company jumped out of the boats. The princes, after having securely fastened their barques, gave their arms to the princesses and conducted them to the castle.

Michael followed and entered the ballroom in their train. Everywhere were mirrors, lights, flowers and damask hangings. The Star Gazer was quite bewildered at the magnificence of the sight.

He placed himself out of the way in a corner, admiring the grace and beauty of the princesses. Some were fair and some were dark; some had chestnut hair, or curls darker still, and some had golden locks. Never were so many beautiful princesses seen together at one time, but the one the garden boy thought the most beautiful and the most fascinating was the little princess with the velvet eyes.

With what eagerness she danced! Leaning on her partner's shoulder she swept by like a whirlwind. Her cheeks flushed, her eyes sparkled, and it was plain that she loved dancing better than anything else.

The poor garden boy envied those handsome young men with whom she danced so gracefully, but he did not know how little reason he had to be jealous of them.

The young men were really the princes who, to the number of fifty at least, had tried to steal the princesses' secret. The princesses had made them drink a philtre, which froze the heart and left nothing but the love of dancing.

They danced on till the shoes of the princesses were worn into holes. When the cock crowed the third time the fiddles stopped, and a delicious supper was served, of sugared orange flowers, crystallized rose leaves, powdered violets, cracknels and wafers, which are, as everyone knows, the favourite food of princesses.

After supper, the dancers all went back to their boats, and this time the Star Gazer entered that of the eldest princess. They crossed again the wood with the diamond-spangled leaves, the wood with the gold-sprinkled leaves, and the wood whose leaves glittered with drops of silver, and as a proof of what he had seen, the boy broke a small branch from a tree in the last wood. Lina turned as she heard the noise made by the breaking of the branch.

'What was that noise?' she asked.

'It was nothing,' replied her eldest sister. 'It was only the screech of the barn owl that roosts in one of the turrets of the castle.'

While she was speaking, Michael managed to slip ahead and, running up the staircase, he reached the princesses' room first. He flung open the window and sliding down the vine, which climbed up the wall, found himself in the garden just as the sun was beginning to rise and it was time for him to set to his work.

THAT day, when he made up the bouquets, Michael hid the branch with the silver drops in the nosegay intended for the youngest princess. When Lina discovered it she was much surprised. However, she said nothing to her sisters, but as she met the boy while she was walking under the shade of the elms, she suddenly stopped as if to speak to him. Then, changing her mind, she went on her way.

In the evening the twelve sisters went again to the ball, and the Star Gazer again followed them and crossed the lake in Lina's boat. This time it was the prince who complained that the boat seemed very heavy.

'It is the heat,' replied the princess. 'I, too, have been feeling very warm.'

During the ball she looked everywhere for the garden boy, but she never saw him.

As they came back, Michael gathered a branch from the

wood with the gold-spangled leaves, and now it was the eldest princess who heard the noise it made in breaking.

'It is nothing,' said Lina, 'only the cry of the owl which roosts in the turrets of the castle.'

THE next morning Lina found the branch in her bouquet. When the sisters went down she stayed a little behind and said to the garden boy, 'Where does this branch come from?'

'Your Royal Highness knows well enough,' answered Michael.

'So you have followed us?'

'Yes, Princess.'

'How did you manage it? We never saw you.'

'I hid myself,' replied the Star Gazer quietly.

The princess was silent a moment, and then said, 'You know our secret—keep it! Here is the reward for your discretion.' And she flung the boy a purse of gold.

'I do not sell my silence,' answered Michael, and he went away without picking up the purse.

For three nights Lina neither saw nor heard anything extraordinary. On the fourth she heard a rustling among the diamond-spangled leaves of the wood. The next day there was a branch of the trees in her bouquet.

She took the Star Gazer aside, and said to him in a harsh voice, 'You know what price my father has promised to pay for our secret?'

'I know, Princess,' answered Michael.

'Don't you mean to tell him?'

'That is not my intention.'

'Are you afraid?'

'No, Princess.'

'What makes you so discreet, then?'

But Michael was silent.

Lina's sisters had seen her talking to the garden boy, and jeered at her for it.

'What prevents your marrying him?' asked the eldest. 'You would become a gardener too; it is a charming profession. You could live in a cottage at the end of the park, and help your husband draw up water from the well, and you could bring us our bouquets.'

The Princess Lina was very angry, and when the Star Gazer presented her bouquet she received it in a disdainful manner. Michael behaved most respectfully. He never raised his eyes to her, but nearly all day she felt him at her side without ever seeing him.

One day she made up her mind to tell everything to her eldest sister. 'What!' said she. 'This rogue knows our secret and you never told me! I must lose no time in getting rid of him.'

'But how?'

'Why, by having him taken to the tower with the dungeons, of course.'

For this was the way in old times that beautiful princesses rid themselves of people who knew too much. But the astonishing part of it was that the youngest sister did not seem at all to relish this method of stopping the mouth of the garden boy who, after all, had said nothing to their father.

They agreed to ask the other ten sisters. All were on the side of the eldest. Then the youngest sister declared that, if they laid a finger on the garden boy, she would herself go and tell their father the secret of the holes in their shoes.

At last it was decided that Michael should be put to the test; they would take him to the ball, and at the end of supper would give him the philtre which was to enchant him like the rest. They sent for the Star Gazer and asked him how he had contrived to learn their secret, but still he remained silent.

Then, in commanding tones, the eldest sister gave him the order they had agreed upon. He only answered:

'I will obey.'

He had been present, invisible, at the council of princesses and had heard all. But he had made up his mind to drink of the philtre and sacrifice himself for the happiness of her he loved. Not wishing, however, to cut a poor figure at the ball by the side of the other dancers, he went at once to the laurels, and said:

'My lovely rose laurel, with the golden rake I have raked you, with the golden bucket I have watered you, with a silken towel I have dried you. Dress me like a prince.'

A beautiful pink flower appeared. Michael gathered it, and in a moment found himself clothed in velvet, which was as black as the eyes of the little princess, with a cap to match, a diamond aigrette, and a blossom of the rose laurel in his buttonhole.

Thus dressed, he presented himself that evening before the Duke of Belœil and obtained leave to try and discover his daughters' secret. He looked so distinguished that hardly anyone would have known who he was.

THE twelve princesses went upstairs to bed. Michael followed them and waited behind the open door till they gave the signal for departure. This time he did not cross in Lina's boat. He gave his arm to the eldest sister, danced with each in turn, and was so graceful that everyone was delighted with him. At last the time came for him to dance with the little princess. She found him the best partner in the world, but he did not dare speak a single word to her. When he was taking her back to her place she said to him in a mocking voice:

'Here you are at the summit of your wishes; you are being treated like a prince.'

'Don't be afraid,' replied the Star Gazer gently. 'You shall never be a gardener's wife.'

The little princess stared at him with a frightened face, and he left her without waiting for an answer.

When the satin slippers were worn through, the fiddles stopped, and they were at the banquet table, Michael was placed next to the eldest sister and opposite the youngest.

They gave him the most exquisite dishes to eat and the most delicate wines to drink; and in order to turn his head more completely, compliments and flattery were heaped on him from every side.

At last the eldest sister made a sign, and one of the pages brought in a large golden cup.

'The enchanted castle has no more secrets for you,' she said to the Star Gazer. 'Let us drink to your triumph.'

He cast a lingering glance at the little princess and without hesitation lifted the cup.

'Don't drink!' suddenly cried out the little princess. 'I would rather marry a gardener.' And she burst into tears. Michael flung the contents of the cup behind him, sprang over the table, and fell at Lina's feet. The rest of the princes fell likewise at the knees of the princesses, each of whom chose a husband and raised him to her side. The charm was broken.

The twelve couples embarked in the boats, which crossed back many times in order to carry over the other princes. Then they all went through the three woods, and when they had passed the door of the underground passage a great noise was heard as if the enchanted castle was crumbling to the earth.

They went straight to the room of the Duke of Belœil who had just awakened. Michael held in his hand the golden cup and he revealed the secret of the holes in the shoes.

'Choose, then,' said the duke, 'whichever one you prefer.'

'My choice is already made,' replied Michael, and he offered his hand to the youngest princess, who blushed and lowered her eyes.

The Princess Lina did not become a gardener's wife; on the contrary, it was the Star Gazer who became a prince. But before the marriage ceremony the princess insisted that Michael tell her how he came to discover the secret.

So he showed her the two laurels which had helped him, and she, being a prudent girl and thinking they gave him too much advantage over his wife, cut them off at the root and threw them into the fire.

And this is why the country girls go about singing:

Nous n'irons plus au bois,
Les lauriers sont coupés,

and dancing in summer by the light of the moon.

3

Princess Mayblossom

ONCE UPON A TIME
there lived a king and queen whose children had all died, first
one and then another, until at last only one little daughter remained. The queen was at her wits' end to know where to
find a really good nurse who would take care of her and bring
her up. A herald was sent, who blew a trumpet at every
street corner and commanded all the best nurses to appear
before the queen that she might choose one for the little princess. So on the appointed day the whole palace was crowded
with nurses, who came from the four corners of the world
to offer themselves, until the queen declared that if she
was ever to see the half of them, they must be brought out
to her, one by one, as she sat in a shady wood near the
palace.

This was accordingly done, and the nurses, after they had
made their curtsey to the king and queen, ranged themselves in
a line before her that she might choose. Most of them were fair
and fat and charming, but one was dark-skinned and ugly, and
spoke a strange language which nobody could understand. The
queen wondered how she dared offer herself and she was told
to go away. Upon which she muttered something and passed

on, but hid herself in a hollow tree, from which she could see all that happened.

The queen, without giving her another thought, chose a pretty rosy-faced nurse, but no sooner was her choice made than a snake bit that very nurse on her foot and she fell down as if dead. The queen was very much vexed by this accident, but she soon selected another nurse, who was just stepping forward when an eagle flew by and dropped a large tortoise upon her head. At this the queen was horrified; nevertheless, she chose a third time, but with no better fortune, for the nurse, moving quickly, ran into the branch of a tree and blinded herself with a thorn.

Then the queen in dismay cried out there must be some malignant influence at work and she would choose no more that day. She had just risen to return to the palace when she heard peals of malicious laughter behind her, and turning round saw the ugly stranger she had dismissed, making merry over the disasters and mocking everyone, but especially the queen. Suddenly, the witch, for she was a witch, with two blows from a wand, summoned a chariot of fire drawn by winged dragons, and was whirled off through the air uttering threats and cries. When the king saw this he cried:

'Alas! Now we are ruined indeed, for that was no other than the Fairy Carabosse, who has had a grudge against me ever since I was a boy and put sulphur into her porridge one day for fun.'

Then the queen began to cry. The king was sorry to have frightened her so much, and proposed they should hold a council and decide what had best be done to avert the misfortunes which Carabosse certainly meant to bring upon the little princess.

So all the counsellors were summoned to the palace, and

when they had shut every door and window and stuffed up every keyhole so they might not be overheard, they talked it over, and decided that every fairy for a thousand leagues round should be invited to the christening of the princess, and that the time of the ceremony should be kept a profound secret, in case the Fairy Carabosse should take it into her head to attend.

The queen and her ladies set to work to prepare presents for the fairies who were invited. For each one there was a blue-velvet cloak, a petticoat of apricot satin, a pair of high-heeled shoes, some sharp needles and a pair of golden scissors. Only five were able to come on the day appointed, but they began immediately to bestow gifts upon the princess. One promised that she should be perfectly beautiful, the second that she should understand anything, no matter what, the first time it was explained to her, the third that she should sing like a nightingale, the fourth that she should succeed in everything she undertook, and the fifth was opening her mouth to speak when a tremendous rumbling was heard in the chimney, and Carabosse, all covered with soot, came rolling down, crying:

'I say that she shall be the unluckiest of the unlucky until she is twenty years old.'

Then the queen and all the fairies begged her to think better of it, and not be so unkind to the poor little princess, who had never done her any harm. But the ugly old fairy only grunted and made no answer. So the last fairy, who had not yet given her gift, tried to mend matters by promising the princess a long and happy life after the fatal time was over. At this Carabosse laughed maliciously and climbed away up the chimney, leaving them all in great consternation, especially the queen. However, she entertained the fairies splendidly, and gave them beautiful ribbons, of which they are very fond, in addition to the other presents.

When they were going away the oldest fairy said that it would be best to shut the princess up with her waiting-women, until she was twenty years old. So the king had a tower built on purpose. It had no windows, so it was lighted with wax candles, and the only way into it was by an underground passage, which had iron doors only twenty feet apart, and guards were posted everywhere.

The princess had been named Mayblossom, because she was as fresh and blooming as spring itself, and she grew up tall and beautiful, and everything she did and said was charming. The king and queen came to see her and were more delighted with her than ever, but though she was weary of the tower, and often begged them to take her away, they always refused. The princess's nurse, who had never left her, sometimes told her about the world outside the tower, and though the princess had never seen anything for herself, she always understood exactly, thanks to the second fairy's gift. Often the king said to the queen:

'We were cleverer than Carabosse after all. Our Mayblossom will be happy in spite of her predictions.'

And the queen laughed until she was tired at the idea of having outwitted the old fairy. At last they had the princess's portrait painted and sent to all the neighbouring courts, for in four days she would have completed her twentieth year. All the town was rejoicing at the thought of the princess's approaching freedom, and when the news came that King Merlin was sending his ambassador to ask her in marriage for his son, they were still more delighted.

The nurse, who kept the princess informed of everything that went forward in the town, did not fail to repeat the news that so nearly concerned her, and gave such a description of the splendour in which the ambassador, Fanfaronade, would enter the town that the princess was wild to see the procession for herself.

'What an unhappy creature I am,' she cried. 'I have never seen the sun or the stars or a horse or a monkey or a lion, except in pictures, and though the king and queen tell me I am to be free when I am twenty, I believe they only say it to keep me amused. They never mean to let me out at all.' '

Then she began to cry, and her nurse and the nurse's daughter and the nursery maid, who all loved her dearly, cried too for company. When the princess saw that they all pitied her she made up her mind to have her own way. So she declared she would starve herself to death if they did not find some means of letting her see Fanfaronade's grand entry into the town.

'If you really love me,' she said, 'you will manage it, somehow or other, and the king and queen need never know anything about it.'

The nurse and all the others said everything they could think of to turn the princess from her idea. But the more they said the more determined she was, and at last they consented to make a tiny hole in the tower on the side that looked toward the city gates.

After scratching and scraping all day and all night, they presently made a hole through which they could, with great difficulty, push a very slender needle, and out of this the princess looked at the daylight for the first time. She was so dazzled and delighted by what she saw that she stayed there, never taking her eyes away from the peephole for a single minute, until presently the ambassador's procession appeared in sight.

At the head of it rode Fanfaronade himself upon a white horse which pranced and caracoled to the sound of the trumpets.

Nothing could have been more splendid than the ambassador's attire. His coat was nearly hidden under an embroidery of pearls and diamonds, his boots were solid gold, and from his helmet floated scarlet plumes. At the sight of him the princess lost her wits entirely and determined that Fanfaronade and nobody else would she marry.

'It is quite impossible,' she said, 'that his master should be half as handsome and delightful. I am not ambitious and, having spent all my life in this tedious tower, anything, even a house in the country, will seem a delightful change. I am sure that bread and water shared with Fanfaronade will please me

far better than roast chicken and sweetmeats with anybody else.'

And she went on talking, talking, talking, until her waiting-women wondered. When they tried to stop her, and represented that her high rank made it impossible that she should do any such thing, she would not listen and ordered them to be silent.

As soon as the ambassador arrived at the palace, the queen started to fetch her daughter. All the streets were spread with carpets, and the windows were crowded with ladies, who were waiting to see the princess and carried baskets of flowers and sweetmeats to shower upon her as she passed.

They had hardly begun to dress the princess when a dwarf arrived, mounted upon an elephant. He came from the five fairies and brought for the princess a crown, a sceptre and a robe of golden brocade, with a petticoat marvellously embroidered with butterflies' wings. They also sent a casket of jewels, so splendid that no one had ever seen anything like it before, and the queen was quite dazzled when she opened it. But the princess scarcely gave a glance at any of these treasures, for she thought of nothing but Fanfaronade. The dwarf was rewarded with a gold piece and decorated with so many ribbons that it was hardly possible to see him at all. The princess sent to each of the fairies a new spinning wheel with a distaff of cedar wood, and the queen said she must look through her treasures and find something very charming to send them also.

When the princess was arrayed in all the gorgeous things the dwarf had brought, she was more beautiful than ever, and as she walked along the streets the people cried:

'How pretty she is! How pretty she is!'

As they proceeded at a stately pace the sky began to grow dark, then suddenly the thunder growled, and rain and hail fell in torrents. The queen put her royal mantle over her head, and all the princesses did the same with their trains. Then a terrific croaking, as of an immense army of crows, rooks, ravens, screech-owls and all birds of ill-omen, was heard, and at the same instant a huge owl skimmed up to the princess and threw over her a scarf woven of spiders' webs and embroidered with bats' wings. Then peals of mocking laughter rang through the air, and they guessed that this was another of the Fairy Carabosse's unpleasant jokes.

The queen was terrified and tried to pull the black scarf from the princess's shoulders, but it really seemed as if it must be glued on, it clung so closely.

'Ah,' cried the queen, 'can nothing appease this enemy of ours? What good was it that I sent her more than fifty pounds of sweetmeats? She is as angry as ever.'

While she lamented, and everybody was as wet as if they had been dragged through a river, the princess still thought of nothing but the ambassador, and just at this moment he appeared before her, with the king. There was a great blowing of trumpets, and all the people shouted louder than ever.

Fanfaronade was not generally at a loss for something to say, but when he saw the princess, she was so much more beautiful and majestic than he had expected that he could only stammer out a few words and entirely forgot the harangue which he had been learning for months and knew well enough to have repeated in his sleep. To gain time to remember at least part of it, he made several low bows to the princess, who on her side dropped half a dozen curtseys without stopping to think. Then she said:

'Sir Ambassador, I am sure that everything you intend to say is charming, since it is you who mean to say it; but let us make haste into the palace. It is pouring cats and dogs, and the wicked Fairy Carabosse will be amused to see us all stand

dripping here. When we are once under shelter we can laugh
at her.'

Upon this the ambassador found his tongue and replied
gallantly. Then he offered his hand to conduct the princess, and
she said softly:

'As you could not possibly guess how much I like you, Sir
Fanfaronade, I am obliged to tell you plainly that, since I saw
you enter the town on your beautiful prancing horse, I have
been sorry you came to speak for another instead of for yourself.
So, if you think about it as I do, I will marry you instead of
your master. Of course I know you are not a prince, but I
shall be just as fond of you as if you were, and we can go and
live in some cosy little corner of the world and be as happy
as the days are long.'

The ambassador thought he must be dreaming and could
hardly believe what the lovely princess said, but he dared not
answer.

When they reached the palace the king kissed his daughter
on both cheeks. Then he and the queen led the way to the
banquet. Everybody feasted except Mayblossom and Fanfaronade, who looked at one another and forgot everything else.

After the banquet came a ball, and after that a ballet, and
at last they were all so tired that everyone fell asleep just where
he sat. Only the lovers were as wide-awake as mice, and the
princess, seeing there was nothing to fear, said to Fanfaronade:

'Let us be quick and run away, for we shall never have a
better chance.'

Then she took the king's dagger, which was in a diamond
sheath, and the queen's kerchief, and gave her hand to
Fanfaronade who carried a lantern, and they ran out together
into the muddy street and down to the seashore. Here they
got into a little boat in which the poor old boatman was sleep-

ing. When he woke up and saw the lovely princess, with all her diamonds and her spider-web scarf, he did not know what to think, and obeyed her instantly when she commanded him to set out.

They could see neither moon nor stars, but in the queen's kerchief there was a carbuncle which glowed like fifty torches. Fanfaronade asked the princess where she would like to go, but she only answered she did not care so long as he was with her.

'But, Princess,' said he, 'I dare not take you back to King Merlin's court. He would think hanging too good for me.'

'Oh, in that case,' she answered, 'we had better go to Squirrel Island. It is lonely enough and too far off for anyone to follow us there.' So she ordered the old boatman to steer for Squirrel Island.

Meanwhile the day was breaking, and the king and queen and all the courtiers began to wake up and rub their eyes and think it was time to finish the preparations for the wedding. The queen asked for her kerchief. Then there was a scurrying hither and thither and a hunting everywhere. They looked in every place, from the wardrobes to the stoves, and, the queen herself ran about from the garret to the cellar, but the kerchief was nowhere to be found.

By this time the king had missed his dagger, and the search began all over again. They opened boxes and chests of which the keys had been lost for a hundred years, and found numbers of curious things, but not the dagger, and the king tore his beard, and the queen tore her hair, for the kerchief and the dagger were the most valuable things in the kingdom.

When the king saw that the search was hopeless he said, 'Never mind, let us make haste and get the wedding over before anything else is lost.'

And then he asked where the princess was. Upon this her nurse came forward and said:

'Sire, I have been seeking her these two hours, but she is nowhere to be found.'

This was more than the queen could bear. She gave a shriek of alarm and fainted away, and they had to pour two barrels of eau de Cologne over her before she recovered. When she came to herself everybody was looking for the princess in the greatest terror and confusion, but as she did not appear, the king said to his page:

'Go and find Ambassador Fanfaronade, who is doubtless asleep in some corner, and tell him the sad news.'

So the page hunted hither and thither, but Fanfaronade was no more to be found than the princess, the dagger or the kerchief!

Then the king summoned his counsellors and his guards and, accompanied by the queen, went into his great hall. As he had not had time to prepare his speech beforehand, the king ordered that silence should be kept for three hours, and at the end of that time he spoke as follows:

'Listen, great and small! My dear daughter Mayblossom is lost; whether she has been stolen away or has simply disappeared I cannot tell. The queen's kerchief and my dagger, which are worth their weight in gold, are also missing, and what is worst of all, the Ambassador Fanfaronade is nowhere to be found. Advise me, my dear subjects, what I had better do to recover my daughter, Fanfaronade and the other things.'

This was the most eloquent speech the king had been known to make, and when everybody had done admiring it, the prime minister made answer:

'Sire, we are all very sorry to see you so sad. We would give everything we value in the world to take away the cause of

your sorrow, but this seems to be another of the tricks of the
Fairy Carabosse. The princess's twenty unlucky years were not
quite over, and really, if the truth must be told, I noticed that
Fanfaronade and the princess appeared to admire each other
greatly. Perhaps this may give some clue to the mystery of their
disappearance.'

Here the queen interrupted him, saying, 'Take care what
you say, sir. Believe me, the Princess Mayblossom was far too
well brought up to think of falling in love with an ambassador.'

At this the nurse came forward and, falling on her knees,
confessed how they had made the hole in the tower, and how
the princess had declared when she saw the ambassador that
she would marry him and nobody else. Then the queen was
very angry and gave the nurse and the nursery maid such a
scolding that they shook in their shoes.

But the Admiral Cocked Hat interrupted her, crying, 'Let
us be off after this good-for-nothing Fanfaronade, for without
a doubt he has run away with our princess.'

So while some embarked upon the sea, others ran from
kingdom to kingdom beating drums and blowing trumpets,
and wherever a crowd collected they cried:

'Whoever wants a beautiful doll, sweetmeats of all kinds,
a little pair of scissors, a golden robe and a satin cap has only to
say where Fanfaronade has hidden the Princess Mayblossom.'

But the answer everywhere was, 'You must go farther, we
have not seen them.'

However, those who went by sea were more fortunate, for
after sailing about for some time they noticed a light before
them which burned at night like a great fire. At first they dared
not go near it, not knowing what it might be, but by-and-by it
remained stationary over Squirrel Island. The light was the
glowing of the carbuncle. The princess and Fanfaronade on

landing upon the island had given the boatman a hundred gold pieces and made him promise solemnly to tell no one where he had taken them. But as he rowed away, he got into the midst of the fleet and, before he could escape, the admiral had seen him and sent a boat after him.

When he was searched they found the gold pieces in his pocket, and as they were new coins, struck in honour of the princess's wedding, the admiral felt certain the boatman must have been paid by the princess to aid her in her flight. But he would not answer any questions and pretended to be deaf and dumb.

Then the admiral said, 'Oh, deaf and dumb is he? Lash him to the mast and give him a taste of the cat-o'-nine-tails. I don't know anything better than that for curing the deaf and dumb!'

And when the old boatman saw that he was in earnest, he told all he knew about the cavalier and the lady he had landed upon Squirrel Island, and the admiral knew it must be the princess and Fanfaronade. So he gave the order for the fleet to surround the island.

Meanwhile Princess Mayblossom had found a grassy bank and throwing herself down had fallen into a profound slumber, when Fanfaronade, who happened to be hungry and not sleepy, came and woke her up, saying very crossly:

'Pray, madam, how long do you mean to stay here? I see nothing to eat, and though you may be very charming, the sight of you does not prevent me from famishing.'

'What? Fanfaronade,' said the princess, sitting up and rubbing her eyes, 'is it possible that, when I am here with you, you can want anything else? You ought to be thinking all the time how happy you are.'

'Happy,' cried he, 'say rather unhappy! I wish with all my heart that you were back in your dark tower again.'

'Darling, don't be cross,' said the princess. 'I will go and see if I can find some wild fruit for you.'

'I wish you might find a wolf to eat you up,' growled Fanfaronade.

The princess, in great dismay, ran hither and thither all about the wood, tearing her dress, and hurting her pretty white hands with the thorns and brambles, but she could find nothing good to eat, and at last she had to go back sorrowfully to Fanfaronade. When he saw that she came empty-handed he left her, grumbling to himself.

The next day they searched again, but with no better success.

'Alas,' said the princess, 'if only I could find something for you to eat, I should not mind being hungry myself.'

'No, I should not mind that either,' answered Fanfaronade.

'Is is possible,' said she, 'that you would not care if I died of hunger? Oh, Fanfaronade, you said you loved me!'

'That was when we were in quite another place and I was not hungry,' said he. 'It makes a great difference in one's ideas to be dying of hunger and thirst on a desert island.'

At this the princess was dreadfully vexed, and she sat down under a white-rose bush and began to cry bitterly.

'Happy roses,' she said to herself, 'they have only to blossom in the sunshine and be admired, and there is nobody to be unkind to them.'

The tears ran down her cheeks and splashed onto the rose-tree roots. Presently she was surprised to see the whole bush rustling and shaking, and a soft voice from the prettiest rosebud said:

'Poor Princess! Look in the trunk of that tree, and you will find a honeycomb, but don't be foolish enough to share it with Fanfaronade.'

Mayblossom ran to the tree, and sure enough there was the honey. Without losing a moment she ran with it to Fanfaronade, crying gaily:

'See, here is a honeycomb I have found. I might have eaten it all by myself, but I had rather share it with you.'

But without looking at her or thanking her Fanfaronade snatched the honeycomb out of her hands and ate it all—every bit, without offering her a morsel. Indeed, when she humbly asked for some, he said mockingly that it was too sweet for her and would spoil her teeth.

Mayblossom, more downcast than ever, went sadly away and sat down under an oak tree, and her tears and sighs were so piteous that the oak fanned her with his rustling leaves, and said:

'Take courage, pretty Princess, all is not lost yet. Take this pitcher of milk and drink it. Whatever you do, don't leave a drop for Fanfaronade.'

The princess, quite astonished, looked round and saw a big pitcher full of milk, but before she could raise it to her lips the thought of how thirsty Fanfaronade must be, after eating at least fifteen pounds of honey, made her run back to him and say:

'Here is a pitcher of milk. Drink some, for you must be thirsty, I am sure. But pray save a little for me, I am dying of hunger and thirst.'

But he seized the pitcher, drank all it contained at a single draught, and then broke it to atoms on the nearest stone, saying with a malicious smile, 'As you have not eaten anything you cannot be thirsty.'

'Ah,' cried the princess, 'I am well punished for disappointing

The princess sat down under a rose bush and began to cry bitterly

the king and queen, and running away with this ambassador about whom I knew nothing.'

And so saying she wandered away into the thickest part of the wood, and sat down under a thorn tree, where a nightingale was singing. Presently she heard him say:

'Search under the bush, Princess; you will find some sugar, almonds and some tarts there. But don't be silly enough to offer Fanfaronade any.'

And this time the princess, who was fainting with hunger, took the nightingale's advice and ate what she found all by herself. But Fanfaronade, seeing she had found something good and was not going to share it with him, ran after her in such a fury that she hastily drew out the queen's carbuncle, which had the property of rendering people invisible if they were in danger, and when she was safely hidden from him she reproached him gently for his unkindness.

Meanwhile Admiral Cocked Hat had despatched Jack the Chatterer of the Straw Boots, courier in ordinary to the prime minister, to tell the king that the princess and the ambassador had landed on Squirrel Island, but not knowing the country he had not pursued them, for fear of being captured by concealed enemies. Their majesties were overjoyed at the news, and the king sent for a great book, each leaf of which was eight ells long. It was the work of a very clever fairy and contained a description of the whole earth. He very soon found that Squirrel Island was uninhabited.

'Go,' said he to Jack the Chatterer, 'tell the admiral from me to land at once. I am surprised at his not having done so sooner.'

As soon as this message reached the fleet, every preparation was made for war, and the noise was so great that it reached the ears of the princess, who at once flew to protect Fanfaronade. As he was not very brave he accepted her aid gladly.

'You stand behind me,' said she, 'and I will hold the car-buncle which will make us invisible, and with the king's dagger I can protect you from the enemy.'

So when the soldiers landed they could see nothing, but the princess touched them one after another with the dagger, and they fell insensible upon the sand. At last the admiral, seeing there was some enchantment, hastily gave orders for a retreat to be sounded and got his men back into their boats in great confusion.

Fanfaronade, being once more left with the princess, began to think that if he could get rid of her, and possess himself of the carbuncle and the dagger, he would be able to make his escape. So as they walked back over the cliffs he gave the princess a great push, hoping she would fall into the sea. But she stepped aside quickly and over he went, sinking to the bottom of the sea like a lump of lead and was never heard of any more.

While the princess was still looking after him in horror, her attention was attracted by a rushing noise over her head. Looking up she saw two chariots approaching rapidly from opposite directions. One was bright and glittering, and drawn by swans and peacocks, while the fairy who sat in it was beautiful as a sunbeam. The other was drawn by bats and ravens and contained a frightful little dwarf who, dressed in a snake's skin, wore a great toad upon her head for a hood. The chariots met with a frightful crash in mid-air, and the princess looked on in breathless anxiety while a furious battle took place between the lovely fairy with her golden lance, and the hideous little dwarf and her rusty pike. Very soon it was evident that the beauty had the best of it, and the dwarf turned her bats' heads and flickered away in great confusion, while the fairy came down to where the princess stood, and said, smiling:

'You see, Princess, I have completely routed that malicious old Carabosse. Will you believe it? She actually wanted to claim you forever, because you came out of the tower four days before the twenty years were ended. However, I think I have settled her pretensions and I hope you will be very happy and enjoy the freedom I have won for you.'

The princess thanked her heartily, and then the fairy dispatched one of her peacocks to her palace to bring a gorgeous robe for Mayblossom, who certainly needed it, for her own was torn to shreds by the thorns and briars. Another peacock was sent to the admiral to tell him he could now land in safety, which he did, bringing all his men with him, even to Jack the Chatterer who, happening to pass the spit upon which the admiral's dinner was roasting, snatched it up and brought it with him.

Admiral Cocked Hat was greatly surprised when he came upon the golden chariot and saw two lovely ladies walking under the trees. When he reached them, he recognized the princess and went down on his knees and kissed her hand joyfully. Then she presented him to the fairy and told him how Carabosse had been finally routed, and he thanked and congratulated the fairy, who was most gracious to him.

While they were talking she cried suddenly, 'I declare I smell a savoury dinner.'

'Why yes, madam, here it is,' said Jack the Chatterer, holding up the spit, where all the pheasants and partridges were frizzling. 'Will Your Highness please to taste any of them?'

'By all means,' said the fairy, 'especially as the princess will certainly be glad of a good meal.'

So the admiral sent back to his ship for everything that was needful, and they feasted merrily under the trees. By the time they had finished, the peacock had come back with a robe for the princess, in which the fairy arrayed her. It was of green and gold brocade, embroidered with pearls and rubies, and her long golden hair was tied back with strings of diamonds and emeralds, and crowned with flowers.

The fairy made her mount beside her in the golden chariot and took her on board the admiral's ship, where she bade her farewell, sending many messages of friendship to the queen, and bidding the princess tell her that she was the fifth fairy who had attended the christening.

Then salutes were fired, the fleet weighed anchor, and very soon they reached the port. Here the king and queen were waiting, and they received the princess with such joy and kindness she could not get a word in edgewise to say how sorry she was for having run away with such a poor-spirited ambassador. But, after all, it must have been all Carabosse's fault.

Just at this lucky moment who should arrive but King Merlin's son, who had become uneasy at not receiving any news from his ambassador and had travelled with a magnificent escort of a thousand horsemen, and thirty bodyguards in gold and scarlet uniforms, to see what could have happened.

As he was a hundred times handsomer and braver than the ambassador, the princess found she could like him very much. So the wedding was held at once, with so much splendour and rejoicing that all the previous misfortunes were quite forgotten.

[*La Princesse Printanière,* par Madame d'Aulnoy]

Soria Moria Castle

THERE WAS ONCE UPON a time a couple who had a son called Halvor. Ever since he had been a little boy he had been unwilling to do any work, and just sat raking about among the ashes. His parents sent him away to learn several trades, but Halvor stayed nowhere, for when he had been gone two or three days he always ran away from his master, hurried off home, and sat down in the chimney corner to grub among the ashes again.

One day, however, a sea captain came and asked Halvor if he hadn't a fancy to come with him and go to sea and behold foreign lands. Halvor had a fancy for that, so he was not long in getting ready.

How long they sailed no one knows, but after a long, long time there was a terrible storm. When it was over and all had become calm again, they knew not where they were, for they had been driven away to a strange coast of which none of them had any knowledge.

As there was no wind at all they lay becalmed, and Halvor asked the skipper to give him leave to go on shore and look about him. He at last got leave, but he was to come back at once if the wind began to rise.

So he went on shore, and it was a delightful country; whithersoever he went there were wide plains with fields and meadows, but as for people, there were none to be seen. The wind began to rise, but Halvor thought he had not seen enough yet and would walk about a little longer, to try if he could not meet somebody. So after a while he came to a great highway, which was so smooth that an egg might have been rolled along it without breaking.

Halvor followed this, and when evening drew near he saw a castle far away in the distance, and there were lights in it. As he had now been walking the whole day and had not brought anything to eat with him, he was very hungry. Nevertheless, the nearer he came to the castle the more afraid he was.

A fire was burning in the castle, and Halvor went into the kitchen, which was more magnificent than any he had ever beheld. There were vessels of gold and silver, but not one human being was to be seen. When Halvor had stood there for some time, and no one had come out, he opened a door, and inside a princess was sitting at her wheel spinning.

'Nay!' she cried. 'Can Christian folk dare to come hither? The best thing you can do is to go away again, for if not the troll will devour you. A troll with three heads lives here.'

'I should have been just as well pleased if he had four heads more, for I should have enjoyed seeing the fellow,' said the youth, 'and I won't go away, for I have done no harm. But you must give me something to eat, for I am frightfully hungry.'

When Halvor had eaten his fill, the princess told him to try if he could wield the sword which was hanging on the wall. But he could not wield it, nor could he even lift it up.

'Well, then, you must take a drink out of that bottle which

At that very moment the troll came in, panting for breath, and Halvor
cut off all its heads

is hanging by its side, for that's what the troll does whenever he goes out and wants to use the sword,' said the princess.

Halvor took a draught, and in a moment he was able to swing the sword about with perfect ease. And now he thought it was high time for the troll to make his appearance, and at that very moment he came, panting for breath.

Halvor stood behind the door.

'Hutetu!' said the troll as he put his head in at the door. 'It smells just as if there were a Christian man's blood here!'

'Yes, you shall learn there is!' said Halvor, and cut off all the troll's heads.

The princess was so rejoiced to be free that she danced and sang, but then she remembered her sisters, and said, 'If my sisters were but free too!'

'Where are they?' asked Halvor.

So she told him where they were. One of them had been taken away by a troll to his castle, which was six miles off, and the other had been carried off to a castle which was nine miles farther off still.

'But now,' said she, 'you must first help me get this dead troll away from here.'

Halvor was so strong that he cleared everything away and made all clean and tidy very quickly. So then they ate and drank and were happy, and next morning he set off in the gray light of dawn. He gave himself no rest but walked or ran the livelong day. When he came in sight of the castle again he was just a little afraid. It was much more splendid than the other, but here too there was not a human being to be seen. Halvor went into the kitchen, and did not linger there either, but went straight on.

'Nay! Do Christian folk dare to come here?' cried the second princess. 'I know not how long it is since I myself came, but during all that time I have never seen a Christian man. It will be better for you to depart at once, for a troll lives here who has six heads.' .

'No, I shall not go,' said Halvor, 'even if he had six more I would not.'

'He will swallow you up alive,' said the princess.

But she spoke to no purpose, for Halvor would not go. He was not afraid of the troll, but he wanted some meat and drink, for he was hungry after his journey. So she gave him as much as he would eat, and then once more she tried to make him go away.

'No,' said Halvor, 'I will not go, for I have not done anything wrong and I have no reason to be afraid.'

'He won't ask any questions about that,' said the princess, 'for he will take you without leave or right. But as you will not go, try if you can wield that sword which the troll uses in battle.'

He could not brandish the sword, so the princess said that he was to take a draught from the flask which hung by its side, and when he had done that he could wield the sword.

Soon afterward the troll came, and he was so large and stout that he was forced to go sideways to get through the door. When the troll had his first head in he cried, 'Hutetu! It smells of a Christian man's blood here!'

With that Halvor cut off the first head, and so on with all the rest. The princess was now exceedingly delighted, but then she remembered her sisters, and wished they too were free. Halvor thought that might be managed, and wanted to set off immediately, but first he had to help the princess remove the troll's body, so it was not until morning that he set forth on his way.

It was a long way to the castle, and he both walked and ran

to get there in time. Late in the evening he caught sight of it, and it was much more magnificent than either of the others. And this time he was not in the least afraid, but went into the kitchen, and then straight on inside the castle. There a princess was sitting, who was so beautiful that never was anyone equal to her. She too said what the others had said, that no Christian folk had ever been there since she had come, and entreated him to go away again, else the troll would swallow him alive. The troll had nine heads, she told him.

'Yes, and if he had nine added to the nine, and then nine more still, I would not go away,' said Halvor and went and stood by the stove.

The princess begged him again to go lest the troll should devour him. But Halvor said, 'Let him come when he will.' So she gave him the troll's sword and bade him take a drink from the flask to enable him to wield it.

At that same moment the troll came, breathing hard, and he was ever so much bigger and stouter than either of the others, and he too was forced to go sideways to get in through the door.

'Hutetu! What a smell of Christian blood there is here!' said he.

Then Halvor cut off the first head, and after that the others, but the last was the toughest of them all, and it was the hardest work Halvor had ever done, but he knew he would have strength enough to do it.

And now all the princesses came to the castle and were together again, and they were happier than they had ever been in their lives. They were delighted with Halvor, and he with them, and he was to choose the one he liked best; but of the three sisters the youngest loved him best.

But Halvor went about and was so strange and so mournful

and quiet that the princesses asked what it was he longed for, and if he did not like to be with them. He said that he did like to be with them, for they had enough to live on, and he was very comfortable there; but he longed to go home, for his father and mother were alive and he had a great desire to see them again.

They thought that this might easily be done.

'You shall go and return in perfect safety if you will follow our advice,' said the princesses. So he said that he would do nothing they did not wish.

Then they dressed him so splendidly he was like a king's son, and they put a ring on his finger, and it was one which would enable him to go home and back again by wishing. But they told him he must not throw it away, or name their names, for if he did, all his magnificence would be at an end, and he would never see them more.

'If I were but at home again, or if home were but here!' said Halvor, and no sooner had he wished this than it was granted. Halvor was standing outside his father's and mother's cottage before he knew what he was about. The darkness of night was coming on, and when the father and mother saw a splendid and stately stranger walk in, they were so startled they both began to bow and curtsey.

Halvor then inquired if he could stay there and have lodging for the night. No, that he certainly could not. 'We can give you no such accommodation,' they said, 'for we have none of the things needful when a great lord like you is to be entertained. It will be better for you to go up to the farm. It is not far off, you can see the chimney pots from here, and there they have plenty of everything.'

Halvor would not hear of that, he was absolutely determined

to stay where he was. But the old folks stuck to what they had said, and told him he was to go to the farm, where he could get both meat and drink, whereas they themselves had not even a chair to offer him.

'No,' said Halvor, 'I will not go there till early tomorrow morning; let me stay here tonight. I can sit down on the hearth.'

They could say nothing against that, so Halvor sat down on the hearth and began to rake about among the ashes just as he had done before, when he lay there idling away his time.

They chatted about many things, and told Halvor of this and of that, and at last he asked them if they had never had any child.

'Yes,' they said, they had had a boy who was called Halvor, but they did not know where he had gone, and they could not even say whether he were dead or alive.

'Could I be he?' asked Halvor.

'I should know him well enough,' said the old woman, rising. 'Our Halvor was idle and slothful and he was so ragged that one hole ran into another all over his clothes. Such a fellow as he was could never turn into such a man as you are, sir.'

In a short time the old woman went to stir the fire, and when the blaze lit up Halvor, as it used to do when he was at home raking up the ashes, she knew him again.

'Good Heavens! It that you, Halvor?' said she, and such great gladness fell on the old parents there were no bounds to it. And now he had to relate everything that had befallen him, and the old woman was so delighted with him she would take him up to the farm at once to show him to the girls who had formerly looked down on him so. She went first and told them how Halvor had come home again, and now they should just see how magnificent he was. 'He looks like a prince,' she said.

'We shall see that he is just the same ragamuffin he was before,' said the girls, tossing their heads.

At that same moment Halvor entered, and the girls were so astonished they left their kirtles lying in the chimney corner and ran away in nothing but their petticoats. When they came in again they were so shamefaced they hardly dared to look at Halvor, toward whom they had always been so proud and haughty before.

'Ay, ay! you have always thought that you were so pretty and dainty no one was equal to you,' said Halvor. 'But you should just see the eldest princess whom I set free. You look like herdswomen compared with her, and the second princess is also much prettier than you; but the youngest, who is my sweetheart, is more beautiful than either sun or moon. I wish to Heaven they were here, and then you would see them.' And he named their names.

Scarcely had he said this before they were standing by his side, but then he was very sorrowful, for the words which they had said to him came to his mind.

At the farm a great feast was made ready for the princesses, and much respect paid to them, but they would not stay there.

'We want to go down to your parents,' they said to Halvor; 'we will go out and look about us.'

He followed them out, and they came to a large pond outside the farmhouse. Very near the water there was a pretty green bank, and there the princesses said they would sit down and while away an hour, for they thought it would be pleasant to sit and look out over the water.

There they sat down, and after a short time the youngest princess said, 'I may as well comb your hair a little, Halvor.'

So Halvor laid his head down on her lap, and she combed

it, and it was not long before he fell asleep. Then she took
her ring from him and put another in its place, and then she
said to her sisters:

'Hold me as I am holding you. I would that we were at
Soria Moria Castle.'

When Halvor awoke he knew that he had lost the princesses
and began to weep and lament and was so unhappy he could
not be comforted. In spite of all his father's and mother's entreaties he would not stay, but bade them farewell, saying that
he would never see them more, for if he did not find the
princess again he did not think it worth while to live.

He had some money which he put into his pocket and went
on his way. When he had walked some distance he met a man
with a tolerably good horse. Halvor longed to buy it, and
began to bargain with the man.

'Well, I have not exactly been thinking of selling him,' said
the man, 'but if we could agree, perhaps—'

Halvor inquired how much he wanted for the horse.

'I did not give much for him, and he is not worth much.
He is a capital horse to ride, but good for nothing at drawing;
but he will always be able to carry your bag of provisions and
you too, if you walk and ride by turns.'

At last they agreed about the price, and Halvor laid his bag
on the horse, and sometimes he walked and sometimes he rode.
In the evening he came to a green field, where stood a great
tree, under which he seated himself. Then he let the horse loose
and lay down to sleep, but before he did that he took his bag
off the horse. At daybreak he set off again, for he did not feel
he could take any rest.

So he walked and rode the whole day, through a great wood
where there were many green places which gleamed prettily
among the trees. Often he did not know where he was or

5

whither he was going, but he never lingered longer in any place than was enough to let his horse graze a little when they came to one of the green spots, while he himself took out his bag of provisions.

So he walked and he rode, and it seemed to him that the wood would never come to an end. But on the evening of the second day he saw a light shining through the trees. If only there were some people there I might warm myself and get something to eat, thought Halvor.

When he reached the place where the light had come from, he saw a wretched little cottage, and through a small pane of glass he saw a couple of old folks inside. They were very old, and as gray-headed as a pigeon, and the old woman had such a long nose that she sat in the chimney corner and used it to stir the fire.

'Good evening! Good evening!' said the old woman. 'What errand have you that can bring you here? No Christian folk have been here for more than a hundred years.'

So Halvor told her he wanted to go to Soria Moria Castle, and inquired if she knew the way thither.

'No,' said the old woman, 'that I do not, but the Moon will be here presently and I will ask her; she will know. She can easily see it, for she shines on all things.'

So when the Moon stood clear and bright above the treetops the old woman went out. 'Moon! Moon!' she cried. 'Canst tell me the way to Soria Moria Castle?'

'No,' said the Moon, 'that I can't, for when I shone there, a cloud was before me.'

'Wait a little longer,' said the old woman to Halvor, 'for the West Wind will presently be here, and he will know it, for he breathes gently or blows into every corner.'

'What! Have you a horse too?' she said when she came in again. 'Oh, let the poor creature loose in our bit of fenced-in pasture, and don't let it stand there starving at our very door. But won't you exchange him with me? We have a pair of old boots here with which you can go fifteen quarters of a mile at each step. You shall have them for the horse, and then you will be able to get sooner to Soria Moria Castle.'

Halvor consented to this at once, and the old woman was so delighted with the horse that she was ready to dance. 'For now I, too, shall be able to ride to church,' she said. Halvor could take no rest and wanted to set off immediately, but the old woman said there was no need to hasten. 'Lie down on the bench and sleep a little, for we have no bed to offer you,' said she, 'and I will watch for the coming of the West Wind.'

Ere long came the West Wind, roaring so loud that the walls creaked. The old woman went out and cried:

'West Wind! West Wind! Canst tell me the way to Soria Moria Castle? Here is one who would go thither.'

'Yes, I know it well,' said the West Wind. 'I am just on my

way there to dry the clothes for the wedding which is to take place. If he is fleet of foot he can go with me.'

Out ran Halvor.

'You will have to make haste if you mean to go with me,' said the West Wind. And away it went over hill and dale, and moor and morass, and Halvor had enough to do to keep up with it.

'Well, now I have no time to stay with you any longer,' said the West Wind, 'for I must first go and tear down a bit of spruce fir before I go to the bleaching ground to dry the clothes. Just go along the side of the hill and you will come to some girls who are standing there washing clothes, and then you will not have to walk far before you are at Soria Moria Castle.'

Shortly afterward Halvor came to the girls who were washing, and they asked him if he had seen anything of the West Wind, who was to come there to dry the clothes for the wedding.

'Yes,' said Halvor, 'he has only gone to break down a bit of spruce fir. It won't be long before he is here.' And then he asked them the way to Soria Moria Castle.

They put him on the right way, and when he came in front of the castle it was so full of horses and people that it swarmed with them. But Halvor was so ragged and torn with following the West Wind through bushes and bogs that he kept on one side and would not go among the crowd until the last day, when the feast was to be held at noon.

So when, as was the usage and custom, all were to drink to the bride and the young girls who were present, the cup-bearer filled the cup for each in turn, both bride and bridegroom, and knights and servants, and at last, after a very long time, he came to Halvor. He drank their health, and then slipped the ring, which the princess had put on his finger when they were sitting by the waterside, into the glass, and ordered the cupbearer to carry the glass to the bride from him and greet her.

Then the princess at once rose up from the table, and said, 'Who is most worthy to have one of us—he who has delivered us from the trolls or he who is sitting here as bridegroom?'

There could be but one opinion as to that, everyone thought, and when Halvor heard what they said he was not long in flinging off his beggar's rags and arraying himself as a bridegroom.

'Yes, he is the right one,' cried the youngest princess when she caught sight of him. So she held her wedding with Halvor.

[From P. C. Asbjornsen.]

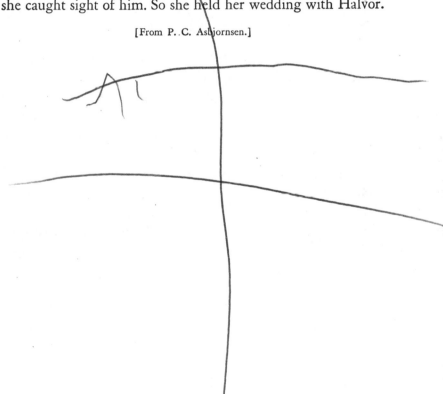

Black Thief and Knight of the Glen

IN TIMES OF YORE THERE were a king and a queen in the south of Ireland who had three sons, all beautiful children; but the queen, their mother, sickened unto death when they were yet very young, which caused great grief throughout the court, particularly to the king, her husband, who could in no wise be comforted. Seeing that death was drawing near her, she called the king to her and spoke as follows:

'I am now going to leave you, and as you are young and in your prime, after my death you will marry again. Now all I ask is that you build a tower on an island in the sea, wherein you will keep your three sons until they are come of age and that they may not be under the power of any other woman. Neglect not to give them the education suitable to their birth, and let them be trained up to every exercise and pastime requisite for kings' sons to learn. This is all I have to say, so farewell, noble husband.'

The king had scarce time, with tears in his eyes, to assure

her she should be obeyed in everything, when she turned away
with a last smile. Never was greater mourning seen than
throughout the court and the whole kingdom, for a better
woman than the queen to rich and poor was not to be found
in the world. She was interred with great pomp and magnificence, and the king, her husband, seemed inconsolable for her
loss. However, he caused the tower to be built and his sons
placed in it, under proper guardians, according to his promise.

In due time the lords and knights of the kingdom counselled
the king to live no longer as he had done, but to take a wife;
which counsel prevailing, they chose for him a rich and beautiful princess to be his consort—a neighbouring king's daughter,
of whom he was very fond. Not long after, the queen had a
fine son, which caused great feasting and rejoicing at the court,

insomuch that in a manner the late queen was entirely forgotten.

At length the queen, having some business with the henwife,
went to her and, after a long conference, was taking leave of
her, when the henwife prayed that if ever she should come back
to her again she might break her neck. The queen, greatly
incensed at such a daring insult from one of her meanest subjects, demanded immediately the reason, or she would have her
put to death.

'It were worth your while, madam,' said the henwife, 'to pay
me well for it, for the reason I prayed so concerns you much.'

'What must I pay you?' asked the queen.

'You must give me,' said the henwife, 'the full of a pack of
wool, and I have an ancient crock which you must fill with
butter, likewise a barrel which you must fill for me full of
wheat.'

'How much wool will it take to the pack?' asked the queen.

'It will take seven herds of sheep, and their increase for seven
years.'

'How much butter will it take to fill your crock?'

'Seven dairies,' said the henwife, 'and their increase for seven
years.'

'And how much will it take to fill the barrel you have?'
asked the queen.

'It will take the increase of seven barrels of wheat for seven
years.'

'That is a great quantity,' said the queen. 'But the reason must
be extraordinary, and before I want it, I will give you all you
demand.'

'Well,' said the henwife, 'it is because you are so stupid and
don't observe, or find out those affairs that are so dangerous
and hurtful to yourself and your child.'

'What is that?' asked the queen.

'Why, the king your husband has three fine sons he had by the late queen, whom he keeps shut up in a tower until they come of age, intending to divide the kingdom between them and let your son push his fortune. Now, if you don't find some means of destroying them, your child and perhaps yourself will be left desolate in the end.'

'And what would you advise me to do?' asked the queen.

'You must make known to the king,' said the henwife, 'that you have heard of his sons and wonder greatly that he concealed them all this time from you. Tell him you wish to see them, and that it is full time that he bring them to the court. Doubtless the king will then do so, and there will be a great feast prepared and also diversions of every sort to amuse the people. In these sports, ask the king's sons to play a game at cards with you, which they will not refuse.

'Now,' said the henwife, 'you must make a bargain, that if you win they must do whatever you command them, and if they win, that you must do whatever they command you to do; this bargain must be made before the assembly. Here is a pack of cards,' said she, 'that I am thinking you will not lose by.'

The queen immediately took the cards and thanking the henwife went back to the palace. She was quite uneasy until she could speak to the king about his three sons. At last she broke it to him in a very polite and engaging manner so he could see no mystery or design in it. He readily consented to her desire, and his sons were sent for. They gladly came to court, rejoicing that they were free. They were all very handsome and very expert in all arts and exercises, so they gained the love and esteem of all who saw them.

The queen, more jealous than ever, thought it an age until all the feasting and rejoicing was over, and she might make her proposal, depending greatly on the power of the henwife's cards. At length this royal assembly began to sport and play at all kinds of diversions, and the queen cunningly challenged the three princes to play at cards with her, as she had been instructed.

They accepted the challenge, and the eldest son and the queen played the first game which she won. Then the second son played and she won that game likewise. The third son and she then played the last game and he won it, which sorely grieved her, for she did not have him in her power as well as his brothers, and he was by far the handsomest and most beloved of the three.

Now everyone was anxious to hear the queen's commands to the two princes, not thinking that she had any ill design against them. Whether it was the henwife's instructions or whether it was from her own knowledge, she gave out they must go and bring her the Knight of the Glen's wild Steed of Bells, or they should lose their heads.

The young princes were not in the least concerned, not knowing what they had to do; but the whole court was amazed at her demand, believing that it was impossible for them ever to get the steed, as all who ever sought him perished in the attempt. However, they could not retract the bargain, and the youngest prince was desired to tell what demand he had on the queen, as he had won his game.

'My brothers,' said he, 'are now going to travel and, as I understand, on a perilous journey. They know not what road to take or what may happen to them. I am resolved, therefore, not to stay here, but to go with them, let what will betide. I command, according to my bargain, that the queen shall stand on the highest tower of the palace, until we come back or you find out that we are certainly dead, with nothing but sheaf corn for her food and cold water for her drink, even if it should be for seven years and longer.'

Then the three princes departed the court in search of the Knight of the Glen's palace, and travelling along the road they came up with a man who was a little lame and seemed somewhat advanced in years. They soon fell into discourse, and the youngest of the princes asked the stranger his name, and what was the reason he wore so remarkable a black cap.

'I am called,' said he, 'the Thief of Sloan, and sometimes the Black Thief from my cap.' And so, telling the prince some of his adventures, he asked him again where they were bound for and what they were about.

The prince, willing to gratify his request, told him their story from the beginning to the end. 'And now,' said he, 'we are travelling and do not know whether we are on the right road or not.'

'Ah, my brave fellows,' said the Black Thief, 'you little know the danger you run. I have been after that steed myself these seven years and can never steal him on account of a silk covering with sixty bells fixed to it, which he wears in the stable. Whenever you approach he quickly shakes himself and the sound of the bells alarms not only the prince and his guards, but the whole country round, so it is impossible ever to get him. Those so unfortunate as to be taken by the Knight of the Glen are boiled in a fiery furnace.'

'Bless me,' said the young prince, 'what will we do? If we return without the steed we will lose our heads, so you see we are ill fixed on both sides.'

'Well,' said the Thief of Sloan, 'if it were my case, I would rather die by the knight than by the wicked queen. Besides, I will go with you myself and show you the road and, whatever fortune you have, I will take my chance of the same.'

They returned him sincere thanks for his kindness, and in a short time he brought them within view of the knight's castle.

'Now,' said he, 'we must stay here till night comes, for I know all the ways of the place, and if there be any chance for success it is when they are all at rest, for the steed is all the watch the knight keeps there.'

Accordingly, in the dead hour of the night, the king's three sons and the Thief of Sloan attempted to reach the Steed of Bells. But before they could reach the stables the steed neighed terribly and shook himself so, and the bells rang with such noise, that the knight and all his men were up in a moment.

The Black Thief and the king's sons thought to make their escape, but they were suddenly surrounded by the knight's guards and taken prisoners. They were brought to that dismal part of the palace where the knight kept a furnace always boiling, in which he threw all offenders that came his way.

'Audacious villains,' said the Knight of the Glen, 'how dare you attempt so bold an action as to steal my steed? See, now, the reward of your folly! For your greater punishment I will not boil you all together, but one after the other, so the one who survives may witness the dire afflictions of his unfortunate companions.'

So saying he ordered his servants to stir up the fire. 'We will boil the eldest of these young men first,' said he, 'and so on to the last, which will be this old champion with the black cap. He seems to be the captain, and looks as if he had come through many toils.'

'I was as near death once as the prince is now,' said the Black Thief, 'and escaped; and so will he too.'

'No, you never were,' said the knight, 'for he is within two or three minutes of his end.'

'But,' said the Black Thief, 'I was within one moment of my death, and I am here yet.'

'How was that?' asked the knight. 'I would be glad to hear it, for it seems impossible.'

'If you think, sir knight,' said the Black Thief, 'that the danger I was in surpasses that of this young man, will you pardon him?'

'I will,' said the knight, 'so go on with your story.'

'I was, sir,' said he, 'a very wild boy in my youth; and once in particular, as I was on my rambling, I was benighted and could find no lodging. At length I came to an old kiln, and being much fatigued I went up and lay on the ribs. I had not been there long when I saw three witches come in, each with three bags of gold. They put their bags of gold under their heads, as if to sleep. I heard one of them say to the other that if the Black Thief came on them while they slept, he would not leave them a penny. I found by their talking that everybody had my name on their tongues, though I kept silent as death during their discourse. At length they fell fast asleep, and then I stole softly down, and seeing some turf convenient, I placed one under each of their heads, and off I went, with their gold, as fast as I could.

'I had not gone far,' continued the Thief of Sloan, 'when I saw a greyhound, a hare and a hawk in pursuit of me, and began to think it must be the witches who had taken the shapes in order that I might not escape them unseen either by land or water. Seeing they did not appear in any formidable shape, I more than once resolved to attack, thinking that with my broadsword I could easily destroy them. But considering again that it was perhaps still in their power to become alive again, I gave over the attempt and with difficulty climbed up a tree, bringing my sword in my hand and all the gold along with me. However, when they came to the tree, they found what I had done and, making further use of their black art, one of them changed into a smith's anvil and another into a piece of iron, of which the third soon made a hatchet. Having the hatchet made, she fell to cutting down the tree, and in the course of an hour it began to shake with me. At length it began to bend, and I found that one or two blows at the most would bring it down. I then began to think that my death was inevitable, but just as she drew back for the stroke that would send me crashing the cock crew, and the witches disappeared, resuming their natural shapes for fear of being known, and I went safely off with my bags of gold.

'Now, sir,' said he to the Knight of the Glen, 'if that be not as great an adventure as ever you heard, to be within one blow of a hatchet of my end, and that blow even drawn, and after all to escape, I leave it to yourself.'

'Well, I cannot but say it is very extraordinary,' said the Knight of the Glen, 'and on that account pardon this young man his crime. But stir up the fire, till I boil this second one.'

'Indeed,' said the Black Thief, 'I would fain think he would not die either.'

'How so?' said the knight. 'It is impossible for him to escape.'

'I escaped death more wonderfully myself,' said the Thief of Sloan, 'than if you had him ready to throw into the furnace, and I hope it will be the case with him likewise.'

'Why, have you been in another great danger?' asked the knight. 'I would be glad to hear the story too, and if it be as wonderful as the last, I will pardon this young man as I did the other.'

'My way of living, sir,' said the Black Thief, 'was not good, as I told you before, and being at a certain time fairly out of

'I observed a tall man standing in the entrance.'

cash, and meeting with no enterprise worthy of notice, I was reduced to great straits. At length a rich bishop died in the neighbourhood I was then in, and I heard he was interred with great jewels and rich robes upon him, all of which I intended in a short time to be master of. Accordingly, that very night I set about it. I understood he was placed at the farther end of a long dark vault, which I slowly entered. I had not gone in far before I heard someone coming toward me with a quick pace, and although naturally bold and daring, I lost courage, and ran toward the entrance of the vault.

'I had retreated but a few paces when I observed, between me and the light, the figure of a tall man standing in the entrance. Being in great fear and not knowing how to pass, I fired a pistol at him, and he immediately fell across the entrance. Perceiving he still retained the figure of a mortal man, I began to imagine that it could not be the bishop's ghost. Recovering myself therefore from the fear I was in, I ventured to the upper end of the vault, where I found a large bundle, and upon further examination I found that the corpse had already been rifled, and that which I had taken to be a ghost was no more than one of his own clergy. I was sorry that I had the misfortune to kill him, but it could not then be helped.

'I took up the bundle that contained everything valuable belonging to the corpse, intending to take my departure from this melancholy abode. But just as I came to the mouth of the entrance I saw the guards of the place coming toward me and distinctly heard them say that they would look in the vault, for the Black Thief would think little of robbing the corpse if he was anywhere in the place. I knew very well on their first sight of me I would be shot like a dog. However, I had no time to lose. I raised up the man I had killed, as if he was standing on his feet and, crouching behind him, I bore him up as well as I could so the guards readily saw him as they came up to the vault.

'Seeing the man in black, one of the guards cried that it was the Black Thief and, presenting his piece, fired at the man, at which I let him fall and crept into a little dark corner at the entrance of the place. When they saw the man fall, they all ran into the vault and never stopped until they were at the end of it, for fear, as I thought, there might be others along with him who was killed. But while they were busy inspecting the corpse and the vault to see what was missing, I slipped out and away, and they never had the Black Thief in their power since.'

'Well, my brave fellow,' said the Knight of the Glen, 'I see you have come through many dangers. You have freed these two princes by your stories, but I am sorry myself that this young prince must suffer for all. Now, if you could tell me something as wonderful as you have told already, I would pardon him likewise. I pity this youth and do not want to put him to death if I can help it.'

'That happens well,' said the Thief of Sloan, 'for I like him best myself, and have reserved the most curious adventure for the last on his account.'

'Well, then,' said the knight, 'let us hear it.'

'I was one day on my travels,' said the Black Thief, 'and came into a large forest, where I wandered a long time and could not get out of it. At length I came to a large castle, where I found a young woman with a child sitting on her knee, and she crying. I asked her what made her cry, and where the lord of the castle was, for I wondered greatly that I saw no stir of servants or any person about the place.

' "It is well for you," said the young woman, "that the lord of this castle is not at home at present, for he is a monstrous giant, with but one eye in his forehead, who lives on human flesh. He brought me this child, and ordered me to make it into a pie, and I cannot help crying at the command."

'I told her that if she knew of any place convenient that I could leave the child safely I would do it. She told me of a house a distance off where I would find a woman who would take care of it. "But what will I do for the pie?"

' "Cut his finger off," said I, "and I will bring you in a young wild pig out of the forest, which you may prepare for the pie, and put the finger in a certain place, so if the giant doubts anything about it you may know where to turn it over, and when he sees it he will be fully satisfied about the pie."

'She agreed to what I proposed and cut off the child's finger. I soon brought her the little pig in the place of the child, which I took to the house she told me of. She then made ready the pie, and after eating and drinking heartily myself, I was just taking leave of the young woman when we observed the giant coming through the castle gates.

' "Bless me," said she, "what will you do now? Run away and lie down among the dead (showing me the place) and strip off your clothes that he may not know you from the rest if he has occasion to go that way."

'I took her advice and laid myself down among the rest, as if dead, to see how he would behave. The first thing I heard was his calling for his pie. When she set it down before him he swore it smelled like swine's flesh, but knowing where to find the finger, she immediately turned it up, which fairly convinced him. The pie only served to sharpen his appetite, and I heard him sharpening his knife and saying he must have a collop or two, for he was not near satisfied. But what was my terror when I heard the giant groping among the bodies, fancying myself chosen. However, when he had eaten all he could, he began to drink hot liquors in great abundance. In a short time he could not hold up his head, but threw himself on a large creel and fell fast asleep. When I heard him snoring, I went to the giant's spit, reddened it in the fire, and ran it through his eye but was not able to kill him.

'However, I left the spit sticking in his head and took to my heels. But I soon found he was in pursuit of me, although blind, and having an enchanted ring he threw it at me, and it fell on my big toe and remained fastened to it.

'The giant then called to the ring, asking where it was, and to my great surprise it answered and he, guided by the same, made a leap at me which I had the good luck to observe and fortunately escaped. However, I found running was of no use in saving me, as long as I had the ring on my foot; so I took my sword and cut off the toe it was fastened on and threw both into a large fish-pond that was convenient. The giant called again to the ring which, by the power of enchantment, always made him answer. But he, not knowing what I had done, imagined it was still on some part of me and made a violent leap to seize me, when he went into the pond, over head and ears, and was drowned.

'Now, sir knight,' said the Thief of Sloan, 'you see what dangers I came through and always escaped; but, indeed, I am lame for the want of my toe ever since.'

'My lord and master,' said an old woman who was listening all the time, 'that story is but too true, as I well know, for I am the very woman who was in the giant's castle, and you, my lord, the child I was to make into a pie. This is the very man who saved your life, which you may know by the want of your finger that was taken off, as you have heard, to deceive the giant.'

The Knight of the Glen, greatly surprised at what he had heard the old woman tell, and knowing he had wanted his finger from his childhood, began to understand the story was true enough.

'And is this my deliverer?' said he. 'O brave fellow, I not only pardon you all, but will keep you with me while you live; you shall feast like princes and have every attendance that I have myself.'

They all returned thanks on their knees, and the Black Thief told him the reason for their attempt to steal the Steed of Bells, and the necessity they were under in going home.

'Well,' said the Knight of the Glen, 'if that's the case I bestow on you my steed rather than these brave fellows should die. You may go when you please, only remember to call and see me betimes, that we may know each other well.'

They promised they would, and with great joy they set off for their father's palace, and the Black Thief along with them.

The wicked queen was standing all this time on the tower and, hearing the bells ringing at a great distance off, knew very well it was the princes coming home, and the steed with them. And through spite and vexation she was shattered to pieces.

The three princes lived happy and well during their father's reign, always keeping the Black Thief along with them; but how they did after the old king's death is not known.

[The Hibernian Tales.]

Brother and Sister

BROTHER TOOK SISTER by the hand saying, 'Look here, we haven't had one single happy hour since our mother died. That stepmother of ours beats us every day, and if we dare go near her she kicks us away. We never get anything but hard dry crusts to eat—why, the dog under the table is better off than we are. She does throw him a good morsel or two now and then. Oh, dear, if our own dear mother only knew all about it! Come along, let us go forth into the wide world together.'

So off they started through fields and meadows, over hedges and ditches, and walked the whole day long, and when it rained sister said:

'Heaven and our hearts are weeping together.'

Toward evening they came to a large forest and, tired out with hunger and their long walk as well as all their trouble, crept into a hollow tree and soon fell fast asleep.

Next morning, when they woke up, the sun was already high in the heavens and was shining down bright and warm into the tree. Then said brother:

'I'm so thirsty, sister. Did I but know where to find a stream, I'd go and have a drink. I do believe I hear one.' He jumped up, took sister by the hand, and they set off to hunt for the brook.

Now their cruel stepmother was in reality a witch, and she knew perfectly well that the two children had run away. She had crept secretly after them and had cast her spells over all the streams in the forest.

Presently the children found a little brook dancing and glittering over the stones, and brother was eager to drink of it, but as it rushed past sister heard it murmuring:

'Who drinks of me will be a tiger! Who drinks of me will be a tiger!'

So she cried out, 'Oh, dear brother, pray don't drink, or you'll be turned into a wild beast and tear me to pieces.'

Brother was dreadfully thirsty, but he did not drink. 'Very well,' said he, 'I will wait until we come to the next spring.'

When they came to the second brook, sister heard it saying, 'Who drinks of me will be a wolf! Who drinks of me will be a wolf!'

And she cried, 'Oh, brother, pray don't drink here either, or you'll be turned into a wolf and eat me up.'

Again brother did not drink, but he said, 'Well, I'll wait a little longer till we reach the next stream, but then, whatever you may say, I really must drink, for I can bear this thirst no longer.'

When they reached the third brook, sister heard it say as it rushed past, 'Who drinks of me will be a roe! Who drinks of me will be a roe!'

And she begged, 'Ah, brother, don't drink yet, or you'll become a roe and run away from me.'

But her brother was already kneeling by the brook and bending over it to drink and, sure enough, no sooner had his lips touched the water than he fell on the grass transformed into a little roebuck.

Sister cried bitterly over her poor bewitched brother, and the little roe wept too, and sat sadly by her side. At last the girl said: 'Never mind, dear little fawn, I will never forsake you,' and she took off her golden garter and tied it round the roe's neck.

Then she plucked rushes and plaited a soft cord of them, which she fastened to the collar. When she had done this she led the roe farther and farther, right into the depths of the forest. After they had gone a long, long way they came to a little house, and when the girl looked into it she found it was empty, and she said, 'Perhaps we might stay and live here.'

So she hunted up leaves and moss to make a soft bed for the little roe, and every morning and evening she went out and gathered roots, nuts and berries for herself, and tender young grass for the fawn. And he fed from her hand, played round her, and seemed quite happy. In the evening, when sister was tired, she said her prayers and then laid her head on the fawn's back and fell sound asleep with it as a pillow. And if brother had but kept his natural form, really it would have been a most delightful kind of life.

They had been living for some time in the forest in this way, when it came to pass that the king of that country had a great hunt through the woods. Then the whole forest rang with such a blowing of horns, baying of dogs, and joyful cries of huntsmen, that the little roe heard it and longed to join in too.

'Ah,' said he to sister, 'do let me go off to the hunt! I can't keep still any longer.' And he begged and prayed till at last she consented.

'But,' said she, 'mind you come back in the evening. I shall lock my door fast for fear of those wild huntsmen. So to make

The little roe bounded to one side

sure of my knowing you, knock at the door and say, "My sister dear, open; I'm here." If you don't speak I shan't open the door.'

So off sprang the little roe, and he felt quite well and happy in the free open air.

The king and his huntsmen soon saw the beautiful creature and started in pursuit, but they could not come up with it, and whenever they thought they were sure to catch it, it bounded off to one side into the bushes and disappeared. When night came on it ran home and, knocking at the door of the little house, cried:

'My sister dear, open; I'm here.' The door opened, and he ran in and rested all night on his soft mossy bed.

Next morning the hunt began again, and as soon as the little roe heard the horns and the 'Ho! Ho!' of the huntsmen, he could not rest another moment, and said:

'Sister, open the door, I must get out.'

So sister opened the door and said, 'Now mind and get back by nightfall, and say your little rhyme.'

As soon as the king and his huntsmen saw the roe with the golden collar they all rode off after it, but it was far too quick and nimble for them. This went on all day, but as evening came on the huntsmen had gradually encircled the roe, and one of them wounded it slightly in the foot so that it limped and ran off slowly.

Then the huntsman stole after it as far as the little house, and heard it call out, 'My sister dear, open; I'm here,' and he saw the door open and close immediately the fawn had run in.

The huntsman remembered all this carefully, and went off straight to the king and told him all he had seen and heard.

'Tomorrow we will hunt again,' said the king.

Poor sister was terribly frightened when she saw how her

little fawn had been wounded. She washed off the blood, bound up the injured foot with herbs, and said:

'Now, dear, go lie down and rest so your wound may heal.'

The wound was really so slight that it was quite well next day, and the little roe did not feel it at all. No sooner did it hear the sounds of hunting in the forest than it cried:

'I can't stand this; I must be there too. I'll take care they don't catch me.'

Sister began to cry, and said, 'They are certain to kill you, and then I shall be left all alone in the forest and forsaken by everyone. I can't and won't let you out.'

'Then I shall die of grief,' replied the roe, 'for when I hear that horn I feel as if I must jump right out of my skin.'

So at last, when sister found there was nothing else to be done, with a heavy heart she opened the door, and the roe darted forth full of glee and health into the forest.

As soon as the king saw the roe, he said to his huntsman, 'Now then, give chase all day till evening, but mind and be careful not to hurt it.'

When the sun had set, the king said to his huntsman, 'Now come and show me the little house in the wood.' And when he reached the house he knocked at the door and said, 'My sister dear, open; I'm here.' Then the door opened and the king walked in, and there stood the loveliest maiden he had ever seen.

The girl was much startled when, instead of the little roe she expected, she saw a man with a golden crown on his head walk in. But the king looked kindly at her, held out his hand, and said, 'Will you come with me to my castle and be my dear wife?'

'Oh, yes,' replied the maiden, 'but you must let my roe come too. I could not possibly forsake it.'

'It shall stay with you as long as you live and shall want for nothing,' the king promised.

In the meantime the roe came bounding in, and sister tied the rush cord once more to its collar, took the end in her hand, and so they left the little house in the forest together. The king lifted the lovely maiden on to his horse, and led her to his castle, where the wedding was celebrated with the greatest splendour. The roe was petted and caressed, and ran about at will in the palace gardens.

Now all this time the wicked witch, who had been the cause of these poor children's misfortunes and trying adventures, was feeling sure that sister had been torn to pieces by wild beasts, and brother shot to death in the shape of a roe. When she heard how happy and prosperous they were, her heart was filled with envy and hatred, and she could think of nothing but how to bring some fresh misfortune on them. Her own daughter, who was as hideous as night and had only one eye, reproached her by saying, 'It is I who should have had this good luck and been queen.'

'Be quiet, will you?' said the old woman. 'When the time comes I shall be at hand.'

Now after some time, it happened one day, when the king was out hunting, that the queen gave birth to a beautiful little boy. The old witch thought here was a good chance for her, so she took the form of the lady-in-waiting and, hurrying into the room where the queen lay in her bed, called out, 'The bath is quite ready; it will help to make you strong again. Come, let us be quick, for fear the water should get cold.'

Her daughter was at hand, too, and between them they carried the queen, who was still very weak, into the bathroom and laid her in the bath. Then they locked the door and ran away.

The old witch tied a cap on her daughter's head and laid her in the queen's bed. She managed, too, to make her figure and general appearance look like the queen's, but even her power could not restore the eye she had lost; so she made her lie on the side of the missing eye, to prevent the king's noticing anything.

In the evening, when the king came home and heard the news of his son's birth, he was full of delight, and insisted on going at once to his dear wife's bedside to see how she was getting on. But the old witch cried out:

'Take care and keep the curtains drawn. Don't let the light get into the queen's eyes; she must be kept perfectly quiet.' So the king went away and never knew that it was a false queen who lay in the bed.

When midnight came and everyone in the palace was sound asleep, the nurse who alone watched by the baby's cradle in the nursery saw the door open gently, and who should come in but the real queen. She lifted the child from its cradle, laid it on her arm, and nursed it for some time. Then she carefully shook up the pillows of the little bed, laid the baby down, and tucked the coverlet in all round him. She did not forget the little roe either, but went to the corner where it lay and gently stroked its back. Then she silently left the room, and next morning when the nurse asked the sentries if they had seen anyone go into the castle that night, they all said, 'No, we saw no one at all.'

For many nights the queen came in the same way, but she never spoke a word, and the nurse was too frightened to say anything about her visits. After some little time had elapsed the queen spoke one night, and said:

'Is my child well? Is my roe well?
I'll come back twice, and then farewell.'

The nurse made no answer, but as soon as the queen had disappeared she went to the king and told him all.

The king exclaimed, 'Good heavens! What do you say? I will watch myself tonight by the child's bed.'

When the evening came he went to the nursery, and at midnight the queen appeared and said:

> *'Is my child well? Is my roe well?*
> *I'll come back once, and then farewell.'*

And she nursed and petted the child as usual before she disappeared. The king dared not trust himself to speak to her, but the following night he kept watch again.

That night when the queen came she said:

> *'Is my child well? Is my roe well?*
> *I've come this once, and now farewell.'*

Then the king could restrain himself no longer, but sprang to her side and cried, 'You can be no one but my dear wife!'

'Yes,' said she, 'I am your dear wife!' And in the same moment she was restored to life, as fresh and well and rosy as ever. Then she told the king all the cruel things the wicked witch and her daughter had done. The king had them both arrested at once and brought to trial, and they were condemned to death. The daughter was led into the forest, where the wild beasts tore her to pieces, and the old witch was burned at the stake.

Then the spell was taken off the little roe, and he was restored to his natural shape once more, and so brother and sister lived happily ever after.

[Jakob and Wilhelm Grimm.]

Princess Rosette

ONCE UPON A TIME
there lived a king and queen who had two beautiful sons and
one little daughter, who was so pretty that no one who saw
her could help loving her. When it was time for the christening
of the princess, the queen—as she always did—sent for all the
fairies to be present at the ceremony, and afterward invited
them to a splendid banquet.

When the festivities were over, and they were preparing
to go away, the queen said to them, 'Do not forget your
usual good custom. Tell me what is going to happen to
Rosette.'

For that was the name they had given the princess.

But the fairies said they had left their book of magic at home,
and they would come another day and tell her.

'Ah!' said the queen, 'I know very well what that means—
you have nothing good to say. But at least I beg that you will
not hide anything from me.'

So, after a great deal of persuasion, they said, 'Madam, we
fear that Rosette may be the cause of great misfortune to her
brothers; they may even meet with their death through her.
That is all we have been able to foresee about your dear little

daughter, and we are very sorry to have nothing better to tell you.'

Then they went away, leaving the queen very sad, so sad that the king noticed it, and asked her what was the matter.

The queen said she had been sitting too near the fire, and had burned all the flax that was upon her distaff.

'Oh, is that all?' said the king, and he went up into the garret and brought her down more flax than she could spin in a hundred years. But the queen still looked sad, and the king asked her again what was the matter. She answered that she had been walking by the river and had dropped one of her green satin slippers into the water.

'Oh, if that's all,' said the king, and he sent to all the shoe-makers in his kingdom, and they very soon made the queen ten thousand green satin slippers, but still she looked sad. So the king asked her again what was the matter, and this time she answered that in eating her porridge too hastily she had swallowed her wedding ring. But it so happened that the king knew better, for he had the ring himself, and he said:

'Oh, you are not telling me the truth, for I have your ring here in my purse.'

Then the queen was very much ashamed, and she saw that the king was vexed with her. So she told him all that the fairies had predicted about Rosette, and begged him to think how the misfortunes might be prevented.

Then it was the king's turn to look sad, and at last he said, 'I see no way of saving our sons except by having Rosette's head cut off while she is still little.'

But the queen cried that she would far rather have her own head cut off, and that he had better think of something else, for she would never consent to such a thing. So they thought and thought, but they could not tell what to do, until at last

7

the queen heard that in a great forest near the castle there was an old hermit, who lived in a hollow tree. People came from far and near to consult him, so she said:

'I had better go and ask his advice. Perhaps he will know what to do to prevent the misfortunes the fairies have foretold.'

She set out very early the next morning, mounted upon a pretty white mule, which was shod with solid gold, and two of her ladies rode behind her on beautiful horses. When they reached the forest they dismounted, for the trees grew so thickly

the horses could not pass, and made their way on foot to the
hollow tree where the hermit lived. At first when he saw them
coming he was vexed, but when he recognized the queen, he
said:

'You are welcome, Queen. What do you come to ask of me?'

Then the queen told him all the fairies had foreseen for
Rosette, and asked what she should do, and the hermit
answered that she must shut the princess up in a tower and
never let her come out of it again. The queen thanked and
rewarded him, and hastened back to the castle to tell the king.
When he heard the news he had a great tower built as quickly
as possible, and there the princess was shut up, and the king
and queen and her two brothers went to see her every day that
she might not be dull. The older brother was called 'the Great
Prince,' and the second 'the Little Prince.' They loved their
sister dearly, for she was the sweetest, prettiest princess ever
seen, and the least smile from her was worth more than a
hundred pieces of gold. When Rosette was fifteen years old
the elder prince went to the king and asked if it would not
soon be time for her to be married, and the little prince put the
same question to the queen.

Their majesties were amused at them for thinking of it but
did not make any reply. Soon after both the king and the queen
were taken ill and died on the same day. Everybody was sorry,
Rosette especially, and all the bells in the kingdom were tolled.

Then all the dukes and counsellors put the Great Prince upon
a golden throne and crowned him with a diamond crown,
and they all cried, 'Long live the king!' And after that there
was nothing but feasting and rejoicing.

The new king and his brother said to one another, 'Now that
we are the masters, let us take our sister out of that dull tower.'

They had only to go across the garden to reach the tower

which was very high and stood up in a corner. Rosette was busy at her embroidery, but when she saw her brothers she rose, and taking the king's hand, cried:

'Good morning, dear brother. Now that you are king, please take me out of this dull tower, for I am so tired of it.'

Then she began to cry, but the king kissed her and told her to dry her tears, as that was just what they had come for, to take her out of the tower and bring her to their beautiful castle. The prince showed her the pocketful of sugarplums he had brought for her, and said:

'Make haste, let us get away from this ugly tower, and very soon the king will arrange a grand marriage for you.'

When Rosette saw the beautiful garden, full of fruit and flowers, with green grass and sparkling fountains, she was so astonished that not a word could she say, for she had never in her life seen anything like it before. She looked about her, and ran hither and thither gathering fruit and flowers, and her little dog Frisk, who was bright green all over and had but one ear, danced before her, crying 'Bow-wow-wow,' and turning heels over head in the most enchanting way.

Everybody was amused at Frisk's antics, but all of a sudden he ran away into a little wood, and the princess was following him when, to her great delight, she saw a peacock spreading his tail in the sunshine. Rosette thought she had never seen anything so pretty. She could not take her eyes off him, and there she stood entranced until the king and the prince came up and asked what was amusing her so much. She showed them the peacock, and asked what it was, and they answered that it was a bird which people sometimes ate.

'What!' said the princess. 'Do they dare kill that beautiful creature and eat it? I declare I will never marry anyone but the King of the Peacocks, and when I am queen I will take very good care that nobody eats any of my subjects.'

At this the king was very much astonished. 'But, little sister,' said he, 'where shall we find the King of the Peacocks?'

'Oh, wherever you like, sire,' she answered, 'but I will never marry anyone else.'

After this they took Rosette to the beautiful castle, and the peacock was brought with her, and told to walk about on the terrace outside her windows, where she might always see him, and then the ladies of the court came to see the princess, and they brought her beautiful presents—dresses and ribbons and sweetmeats, diamonds and pearls and dolls and embroidered slippers, and she was so well brought up, and said, 'Thank you!' so prettily, and was so gracious, that everyone went away delighted with her.

Meanwhile the king and the prince were considering how they should find the King of the Peacocks, if there was such a person in the world. And first of all they had a portrait made of the princess, which was so like her that it almost seemed to speak. Then they said to her:

'Since you will not marry anyone but the King of the Peacocks, we are going out together into the wide world to search for him. If we find him for you we shall be very glad. In the meantime, mind you take good care of our kingdom.'

Rosette thanked them for all the trouble they were taking on her account, and promised to take great care of the kingdom, and only to amuse herself by looking at the peacock, and making Frisk dance while they were away.

So they set out, and asked everyone they met, 'Do you know the King of the Peacocks?'

But the answer was always, 'No, no.'

Then they went on and on, so far that no one has ever been farther, and at last they came to the kingdom of the cock-chafers.

They had never before seen such a number of cockchafers, and the buzzing was so loud that the king was afraid he should be deafened by it. He asked the most distinguished-looking cockchafer they met if he knew where they could find the King of the Peacocks.

'Sire,' replied the cockchafer, 'his kingdom is thirty thousand leagues from this; you have come the longest way.'

'And how do you know that?' said the king.

'Oh,' said the cockchafer, 'we all know you very well, since we spend two or three months in your garden every year.'

Thereupon the king and the prince made great friends with him, and they all walked arm-in-arm and dined together, and afterward the cockchafer showed them all the curiosities of his strange country, where the tiniest green leaf costs a gold piece and more. Then they set out again to finish their journey, and this time they were not long upon the road. It was easy to guess that they had come to the right place, for they saw peacocks in every tree, and their cries could be heard a long way off.

When they reached the city they found it full of men and women dressed entirely in peacocks' feathers, which were evidently thought prettier than anything else.

They soon met the king, who was driving about in a beautiful golden carriage, glittering with diamonds, and drawn at full speed by twelve peacocks. The king and the prince were delighted to see that the King of the Peacocks was as handsome as possible. He had curly golden hair and was very pale, and he wore a crown of peacocks' feathers.

When he saw Rosette's brothers he knew at once they were

strangers, and stopping his carriage, he sent for them. When they had greeted him, they said:

'Sire, we have come from very far away to show you a beautiful portrait.' So saying they drew from their travelling bag the picture of Rosette.

The king looked at it in silence a long time, but at last he said, 'I would not have believed there was such a beautiful princess in the world!'

'Indeed, she is really a hundred times prettier than that,' said her brothers.

'I think you must be making fun of me,' replied the King of the Peacocks.

'Sire,' said the prince, 'my brother is a king like yourself. That is the portrait of our sister, Princess Rosette. We have come to ask if you would like to marry her. She is as good as she is beautiful, and we will give her a bushel of gold pieces for her dowry.'

'Oh, with all my heart,' replied the king, 'and I will make her very happy. She shall have whatever she likes, and I shall love her dearly; only I warn you that if she is not as pretty as you have told me, I will have your heads cut off.'

'Oh, certainly, we quite agree to that,' said the brothers in one breath.

'Very well. Off with you into prison, and stay there until the princess arrives,' said the King of the Peacocks.

And the princes were so sure that Rosette was far prettier than her portrait that they went without a murmur. They were kindly treated, and that they might not feel dull the king came often to see them. As for Rosette's portrait, that was taken up to the palace and the king did nothing but gaze at it day and night.

As the king and the prince had to stay in prison, they sent

a letter to the princess telling her to pack up all her treasures as quickly as possible and come to them, for the King of the Peacocks was waiting to marry her, but they did not say they were in prison, for fear of making her uneasy.

When Rosette received the letter she was so delighted that she ran about telling everyone that the King of the Peacocks was found and she was going to marry him.

Guns were fired, and fireworks set off. Everyone had as many cakes and sweetmeats as he wanted. And for three days everybody who came to see the princess was presented with a slice of bread and jam, a nightingale's egg and some hippocras. After having thus entertained her friends, she distributed her dolls among them and left her brother's kingdom to the care of the wisest old men of the city, telling them to take charge of everything, not to spend any money but save it all up until the king should return, and above all, not to forget to feed her peacock. Then she set out, only taking with her her nurse, and the nurse's daughter, and the little green dog Frisk.

They took a boat and put out to sea, carrying with them the bushel of gold pieces and enough dresses to last the princess ten years if she wore two every day, and they did nothing but laugh and sing. The nurse asked the boatman:

'Can you take us, can you take us to the kingdom of the Peacocks?'

But he answered, 'Oh, no! Oh, no!'

Then she said, 'You must take us, you must take us.'

And he answered, 'Very soon, very soon.'

Then the nurse said, 'Will you take us? Will you take us?'

And the boatman answered, 'Yes, yes.'

Then she whispered in his ear, 'Do you want to make your fortune?'

And he said, 'Certainly I do.'

'I can tell you how to get a bag of gold,' said she.

'I ask nothing better,' said the boatman.

'Well,' said the nurse, 'tonight, when the princess is asleep, you must help me throw her into the sea, and when she is drowned I will put her beautiful clothes upon my daughter and we will take her to the King of the Peacocks, who will be only too glad to marry her, and for your reward you shall have your boat full of diamonds.'

The boatman was very much surprised at this proposal, and said, 'But what a pity to drown such a pretty princess!'

However, at last the nurse persuaded him to help her, and when the night came and the princess was fast asleep as usual, with Frisk curled up on his own cushion at the foot of her bed, the wicked nurse fetched the boatman and her daughter, and between them they picked up the princess, feather bed, mattress, pillows, blankets and all, and threw her into the sea, without even waking her.

Now, luckily, the princess's bed was entirely stuffed with phœnix feathers, which are very rare, and have the property of always floating upon water, so Rosette was sailing about as if she had been in a boat. After a little while she began to feel very cold, and turned round so often that she woke Frisk, who started up and began to bark. He barked so long and so loud that he woke all the fish, who came swimming up round the princess's bed, poking at it with their great heads. As for her, she said to herself:

'How our boat does rock upon the water! I am really glad I am not often as uncomfortable as I have been tonight.'

The wicked nurse and the boatman, who were by this time quite a long way off, heard Frisk barking, and said to each other:

'That horrid little animal and his mistress are drinking our health in sea water now. Let us make haste to land, for we must be quite near the city of the King of the Peacocks.'

The king had sent a hundred carriages to meet them, drawn by every kind of strange animal. There were lions, bears, wolves, stags, horses, buffaloes, eagles and peacocks. The carriage intended for the Princess Rosette had six blue monkeys, which could turn somersaults and dance on a tightrope and do many other charming tricks. Their harness was all of crimson velvet with gold buckles, and behind the carriage walked sixty beautiful ladies chosen by the king to wait upon Rosette and amuse her.

The nurse had taken all the pains imaginable to deck out her daughter. She dressed her in Rosette's prettiest frock, and covered her with diamonds from head to foot. But she was so ugly nothing could make her look better, and what was worse, she was sulky and ill-tempered and did nothing but grumble all the time.

When she stepped from the boat and the escort sent by the King of the Peacocks caught sight of her, they were so surprised that they could not say a single word.

'Now then, look alive!' cried the false princess. 'If you don't bring me something to eat I will have all your heads cut off.'

Then they whispered one to another, 'Here's a pretty state of things! She is as wicked as she is ugly. What a bride for our poor king! She certainly was not worth bringing from the other end of the world.'

But she went on ordering them all about, and for no fault at all would give slaps and pinches to everyone she could reach.

As the procession was so long it advanced but slowly, and the nurse's daughter sat up in her carriage trying to look like a queen. But the peacocks, who were sitting upon every tree waiting to salute her, and who had made up their minds to

Rosette was sailing as if she was in a boat

cry, 'Long live our beautiful queen!' when they caught sight of the false bride could not help crying instead:

'Oh, how ugly she is!'

This offended her so much that she said to the guards, 'Make haste and kill all these insolent peacocks who have dared to insult me.'

But the peacocks only flew away, laughing at her.

The rogue of a boatman, who noticed all this, said softly to the nurse, 'This is a bad business for us, gossip. Your daughter ought to have been prettier.'

But she answered, 'Be quiet, stupid, or you will spoil everything.'

Now they told the king that the princess was approaching.

'Well,' said he, 'did her brothers tell me truly? Is she prettier than her portrait?'

'Sire,' they answered, 'if she were as pretty that would do very well.'

'That's true,' said the king. 'I for one shall be quite satisfied if she is. Let us go and meet her.' For they knew by the uproar that she had arrived, but they could not tell what all the shouting was about. The king thought he could hear the words:

'How ugly she is! How ugly she is!' and he fancied they must refer to some dwarf the princess was bringing with her. It never occurred to him that they could apply to the bride herself.

The Princess Rosette's portrait was carried at the head of the procession, and after it walked the king surrounded by his courtiers. He was all impatience to see the lovely princess, but when he caught sight of the nurse's daughter he was furiously angry and would not advance another step. For she was really ugly enough to have frightened anybody.

'What!' he cried. 'Have the two rascals who are my prisoners dared to play me such a trick as this? Do they propose that I shall marry this hideous creature? Let her be shut up in my great tower with her nurse and those who brought her here. As for her brothers, I will have their heads.'

Meanwhile the king and the prince, who knew their sister must have arrived, had made themselves smart and sat expecting every minute to be summoned to greet her. So when the gaoler came with soldiers and carried them down into a black dungeon which swarmed with toads and bats, and where they were up to their necks in water, nobody could have been more surprised and dismayed than they were.

'This is a dismal kind of wedding,' they said. 'What can have happened that we should be treated like this? They must mean to kill us.'

And this idea annoyed them very much. Three days passed before they heard any news, and then the King of the Peacocks came and berated them through a hole in the wall.

'You have called yourselves king and prince,' he cried, 'to try and make me marry your sister, but you are nothing but beggars, not worth the water you drink. I mean to make short work with you, and the sword is being sharpened that will cut off your heads!'

'King of the Peacocks,' answered the king angrily, 'you had better take care what you are about. I am as good a king as yourself, and have a splendid kingdom and robes and crowns, and plenty of good red gold to do with what I like. You are pleased to jest about having our heads cut off. Perhaps you think we have stolen something from you?'

At first the King of the Peacocks was taken aback by this bold speech and had half a mind to send them all away together, but his prime minister declared it would never do to let such a trick pass unpunished; everybody would laugh at him. So the accusation was drawn up against them, that they were impostors because they had promised the king a beautiful princess in marriage who, when she arrived, proved to be an ugly peasant girl.

This accusation was read to the prisoners, who cried out they had spoken the truth, their sister was indeed a princess more beautiful than the day, and there was some mystery about all this which they could not fathom. Therefore they demanded seven days in which to prove their innocence. The King of the Peacocks was so angry that he would hardly even grant them this favour, but at last he was persuaded to do so.

While all this was going on at court, what had been happening to the real princess? When the day broke she and Frisk were equally astonished at finding themselves alone upon the sea, with no boat and no one to help them. The princess cried and cried, until even the fishes were sorry for her.

'Alas,' she said, 'the King of the Peacocks must have ordered me to be thrown into the sea because he had changed his mind and did not want to marry me. But how strange of him, when I should have loved him and we should have been happy together!'

And she cried harder than ever, for she could not help still loving him. So for two days they floated up and down the sea, wet and shivering with the cold, and so hungry that when the princess saw some oysters she caught them, and she and Frisk both ate some, though they didn't like them at all. When night came the princess was so frightened that she said to Frisk:

'Oh, do please keep on barking, for fear the soles should come and eat us up!'

Now it happened that they floated close in to the shore,

where a poor old man lived all alone in a little cottage. When he heard Frisk's barking, he thought there must have been a shipwreck, and he went out to see if he could be of any use. He soon saw the princess and Frisk floating up and down, and Rosette, stretching out her hands to him, cried:

'Oh, good old man, do save me, or I shall die of cold and hunger!'

When he heard her cry out so piteously he ran back into his house to fetch a long boat hook. Then he waded into the water up to his chin, and after being nearly drowned once or twice, he at last succeeded in getting hold of the princess's bed and dragging it on shore.

Rosette and Frisk were joyful enough to find themselves once more on dry land, and the princess thanked the old man heartily. Wrapping herself up in her blankets, she daintily picked her way up to the cottage on her little bare feet. There the old man lighted a fire of straw, and then drew from an old box his wife's dress and shoes, which the princess put on, and thus roughly clad looked as charming as possible, and Frisk danced his very best to amuse her.

The old man saw that Rosette must be some great lady, for her bed coverings were all of satin and gold. He begged her to tell him all her history as she might safely trust him. The princess told him everything, weeping bitterly again at the thought that it was by the king's orders she had been thrown overboard.

'And now, my daughter, what is to be done?' asked the old man. 'You are a great princess, accustomed to fare daintily, and I have nothing to offer you but black bread and radishes, which will not suit you at all. Shall I go and tell the King of the Peacocks that you are here? If he sees you he will certainly wish to marry you.'

'Oh, no!' cried Rosette. 'He must be wicked, since he tried to drown me. Don't let us tell him, but if you have a little basket give it to me.'

The old man gave her a basket, and tying it round Frisk's neck, she said to him, 'Go and find out the best cooking pot in the town and bring the contents to me.'

Away went Frisk, and as there was no better dinner cooking in all the town than the king's, he adroitly took the cover off the pot and brought all it contained to the princess, who said:

'Now go back to the pantry and bring the best of everything you find there.'

So Frisk went back and filled his basket with white bread and red wine and every kind of sweetmeat, until it was almost too heavy for him to carry.

When the King of the Peacocks wanted his dinner there was nothing in the pot and nothing in the pantry. All the courtiers looked at one another in dismay, and the king was terribly cross.

'Oh, well,' he said, 'if there is no dinner I cannot dine! But take care that plenty of things are roasted for supper.'

When evening came, the princess said to Frisk, 'Go into the town and find out the best kitchen, and bring me all the nicest morsels that are being roasted upon the spit.'

Frisk did as he was told, and as he knew of no better kitchen than the king's, he went in softly and, when the cook's back was turned, took everything that was upon the spit. As it happened it was all done to a turn and looked so good that it made him hungry only to see it. He carried his basket to the princess, who at once sent him back to the pantry to bring all the tarts and sugarplums that had been prepared for the king's supper.

The king, as he had had no dinner, was very hungry and wanted his supper early, but when he asked for it, lo and behold! It was all gone and he had to go to bed half starved and in a terrible temper. The next day the same thing happened, and the next, and for three days the king got nothing at all to eat, because just when the dinner or the supper was ready to be served it mysteriously disappeared.

At last the prime minister began to be afraid the king would be starved to death, so he resolved to hide himself in some dark corner of the kitchen and never take his eyes off the cooking pot. His surprise was great when he presently saw a little green dog slip softly into the kitchen, uncover the pot, transfer all its contents to his basket, and run off. The prime minister followed hastily, and tracked him all through the town to the cottage of the good old man. Then he ran back to the king and told him he had found out where all his dinners and suppers went. The king, who was very much astonished, said he should like to go and see for himself. So he set out, accompanied by the prime minister and a guard of archers, and arrived just in time to find the old man and the princess finishing the king's dinner.

The king ordered them to be seized and bound with ropes, and Frisk also. When they were brought back to the palace, the king said:

'Today is the last day of the respite granted to those impostors. They shall have their heads cut off at the same time as these stealers of my dinner.'

Then the old man went down on his knees and begged for time to tell him everything. While he spoke the king for the first time looked attentively at the princess, and when he heard the old man saying that her name was Rosette and that she had been treacherously thrown into the sea, he turned heels over head three times without stopping, in spite of being quite weak from hunger, and ran to embrace her. He untied the ropes which bound her with his own hands, declaring that he loved her with all his heart.

Messengers were sent to bring the princes out of prison, and they came very sadly, believing they were to be executed at once; the nurse and her daughter and the boatman were brought also. As soon as they came in Rosette ran to embrace her brothers, while the traitors threw themselves down before her and begged for mercy. The king and the princes were so happy that they freely forgave them, and the good old man was splendidly rewarded and spent the rest of his days in the palace. The King of the Peacocks made ample amends to the king and the prince for the way in which they had been treated and did everything in his power to show how sorry he was.

The nurse restored to Rosette all her dresses and jewels and the bushel of gold pieces. The wedding was held at once, and they all lived happily ever after—even to Frisk, who enjoyed the greatest luxury, and never had anything worse than the wing of a partridge for dinner all the rest of his life.

[Madame d'Aulnoy.]

The Enchanted Pig

ONCE UPON A TIME
there lived a king who had three daughters. Now it happened
that he had to go out to battle, so he called his daughters and
said to them:

'My dear children, I am obliged to go to the wars. The enemy
is approaching us with a large army. It is a great grief to me
to leave you all. During my absence take care of yourselves and
be good girls; behave well and look after everything in the
house. You may walk in the garden, and you may go into all
the rooms in the palace, except the room at the back in the
right-hand corner. Into that you must not enter, for harm
would befall you.'

'You may keep your mind easy, Father,' they replied. 'We
have never been disobedient to you. Go in peace, and may
Heaven give you a glorious victory!'

When everything was ready for his departure, the king gave
them the keys of all the rooms and reminded them once more
of what he had said. His daughters kissed his hands, with tears
in their eyes, and wished him prosperity, and he gave the
eldest the keys.

Now when the girls found themselves alone they felt so sad

and dull they did not know what to do. So to pass the time, they decided to work for part of the day, to read for part of the day, and to enjoy themselves in the garden for part of the day. As long as they did this all went well with them. But this happy state of things did not last long. Every day they grew more and more curious.

'Sisters,' said the eldest princess, 'all day long we sew, spin and read. We have been several days quite alone, and there is no corner of the garden that we have not explored. We have been in all the rooms in our father's palace and have admired the rich and beautiful furniture. Why should we not go into the room our father forbade us to enter?'

'Sister,' said the youngest, 'I cannot think how you can tempt us to break our father's command. When he told us not to go into that room he must have had a good reason for saying it.'

'Surely the sky won't fall about our heads if we do go in,' said the second princess. 'Dragons and such monsters will not be hidden in the room. And how will our father ever find out that we have gone in?'

While they were speaking thus, encouraging each other, they reached the room. The eldest fitted the key into the lock, and snap! The door stood open.

The three girls entered and they saw that the room was quite empty and without any ornament. But in the middle stood a large table, with a gorgeous cloth, and on it lay a big open book.

Now the princesses were curious to know what was written in the book, especially the eldest, and this is what she read:

The eldest daughter of this king will marry a prince from the East.

Then the second girl stepped forward, and turning over the page she read:

The second daughter of this king will marry a prince from the West.

The girls were delighted, and laughed and teased each other.

But the youngest princess did not want to go near the table nor to open the book. Her elder sisters however left her no peace, and will she, nill she, they dragged her up to the table. In fear and trembling she turned over the page, and read:

The youngest daughter of this king will be married to a pig from the North.

Now if a thunderbolt had fallen upon her from Heaven it would not have frightened her more. She almost died of misery, and if her sisters had not held her up, she would have sunk to the ground. When she came out of the fainting fit into

which she had fallen in her terror, her sisters tried to comfort her, saying:

'How can you believe such nonsense? When did it ever happen that a king's daughter married a pig?'

'What a baby you are!' said the other sister. 'Has not our father enough soldiers to protect you, even if the disgusting creature did come to woo you?'

The youngest princess would fain have been convinced by her sisters' words, and have believed what they said, but her heart was heavy. Her thoughts kept turning to the book, in which was written that great happiness awaited her sisters, but that a fate was in store for her such as had never before been known in the world.

Besides, the thought weighed on her heart that she had been guilty of disobeying her father. She fell ill, and in a few days she was so changed it was difficult to recognize her; formerly she had been rosy and merry, now she was pale and nothing gave her any pleasure. She gave up playing with her sisters in the garden, ceased to gather flowers to put in her hair, and never sang when they sat together at their spinning and sewing.

In the meantime the king won a great victory, and having completely defeated and driven off the enemy, he hurried home to his daughters, to whom his thoughts had constantly turned. Everyone went out to meet him with cymbals and fifes and drums, and there was great rejoicing over his victorious return. The king's first act on reaching home was to thank Heaven for the victory. He then entered his palace, and the three princesses stepped forward to meet him. His joy was great when he saw that they were all well, for the youngest did her best not to appear sad.

In spite of this, however, it was not long before the king noticed that his third daughter was very thin and sad-looking.

He felt as if a hot iron were entering his heart, for it flashed through his mind she had disobeyed his word. He felt sure he was right; but to be quite certain he called his daughters to him, questioned them, and ordered them to speak the truth. They confessed everything, but took good care not to say which had led the other two into temptation.

The king was so distressed he was almost overcome by grief. But he took heart and tried to comfort his daughters, who looked frightened to death. He saw that what had happened had happened and a thousand words would not alter matters by a hair's breadth.

Well, these events had almost been forgotten when one fine day a prince from the East appeared at the court and asked the king for the hand of his eldest daughter. The king gladly gave his consent. A great wedding banquet was prepared, and after three days of feasting the happy pair were accompanied to the frontier with much ceremony and rejoicing.

After some time the same thing befell the second daughter, who was wooed and won by a prince from the West.

Now when the young princess saw that everything fell out exactly as had been written in the book, she grew very sad. She refused to eat and would not put on her fine clothes nor go out walking, but the king comforted her in all possible ways.

So the time passed, till lo and behold! One fine day an enormous pig from the North walked into the palace, and going straight up to the king said, 'Hail, O King! May your life be as prosperous and bright as sunrise on a clear day!'

'I am glad to see you well, friend,' answered the king, 'but what has brought you hither?'

'I come a-wooing,' replied the pig.

Now the king was astonished to hear so fine a speech from a pig, and at once it occurred to him that here was something

Then he told her to kiss him. What was the poor girl to do?

strange. He would gladly have turned the pig's thoughts in another direction, as he did not wish to give him the princess for a wife. But when he heard that the court and the whole street were full of all the pigs in the world he saw there was no escape and he must give his consent. The pig was not satisfied with mere promises, but insisted that the wedding should take place within a week and would not go away till the king had sworn a royal oath upon it.

The king then sent for his daughter and advised her to submit to fate as there was nothing else to be done. And he added:

'My child, the words and whole behaviour of this pig are quite unlike those of other pigs. I do not myself believe that he always was a pig. Depend upon it, some magic or witchcraft has been at work. Obey him, and do everything he wishes, and I feel sure that Heaven will shortly send you release.'

'If you wish me to do this, dear Father, I will do it,' replied the girl.

In the meantime the wedding day drew near. After the marriage, the pig and his bride set out for his home in one of the royal carriages. On the way they passed a great bog, and the pig ordered the carriage to stop and got out and rolled about in the mire till he was covered with mud from head to foot. Then he got back into the carriage and told his wife to kiss him. What was the poor girl to do? She bethought herself of her father's words and, pulling out her pocket handkerchief, she gently wiped the pig's snout and kissed it.

By the time they reached the pig's dwelling, which stood in a thick wood, it was quite dark. They sat down quietly for a while, for they were tired after their drive. Then they had supper together and lay down to rest. During the night the princess noticed that the pig had changed into a man. She was not a little surprised but, remembering her father's words, she took courage and determined to wait and see what would happen.

And now she noticed that every night the pig became a man, and every morning he was changed into a pig before she awoke. This happened several nights running, and the princess could not understand it at all. Clearly her husband must be bewitched. In time she grew quite fond of him, he was so kind and gentle.

One fine day as she was sitting alone she saw an old witch go past. It was long since she had seen a human being, and she called out to the old woman to come and talk to her. Among other things the witch told her that she understood all magic arts, could foretell the future, and knew the healing powers of herbs and plants.

'I shall be grateful to you all my life, old dame,' said the princess, 'if you will tell me what is the matter with my husband. Why is he a pig by day and a human being by night?'

'I was just going to tell you that, my dear, to show you what a good fortuneteller I am. If you like, I will give you an herb to break the spell.'

'If you will only give it to me,' said the princess, 'I will give you anything you choose to ask for, for I cannot bear to see him in this state.'

'Here, then, my dear child,' said the witch, 'take this thread, but do not let him know about it, for if he did it would lose its healing power. At night, when he is asleep you must get up very quietly and fasten the thread round his left foot as firmly as possible. You will see in the morning that he will not have changed back into a pig, but will still be a man. I do not want any reward. I shall be sufficiently repaid by knowing you are happy. It almost breaks my heart to think of all you have suffered, and I only wish I had known it sooner, for I should have come to your rescue at once.'

When the old witch had gone away the princess hid the thread carefully, and at night she rose quietly and, with a beating heart, bound the thread round her husband's foot. Just as she was pulling the knot tight there was a crack and the thread broke, for it was rotten.

Her husband awoke with a start, and said to her, 'Unhappy woman, what have you done? Three days more and this unholy spell would have fallen from me, and now, who knows how long I may have to go about in this disgusting shape? I must leave you at once, and we shall not meet again until you have worn out three pairs of iron shoes and blunted a steel staff in your search for me.' So saying he disappeared.

Now, when the princess was left alone she began to weep in a way that was pitiful to hear. But when she saw that her tears and groans did her no good, she determined to go wherever fate should lead her.

On reaching a town, the first thing she did was to order three pairs of iron sandals and a steel staff, and having made these preparations, she set out in search of her husband. On and on she wandered, over nine seas and across nine continents; through forests with trees whose stems were as thick as barrels; stumbling and knocking herself against the fallen branches, then picking herself up and going on. The boughs of the trees scratched her face, and the shrubs tore her hands, but on she went and never looked back. At last, wearied with her long journey and worn out with sorrow, but still with hope at her heart, she reached a house.

Now who do you think lived there? The Moon.

The princess knocked at the door and begged that she might rest a little. The mother of the Moon, when she saw her sad plight, felt a great pity for her, and took her in and nursed and tended her. And while she was there the princess had a little baby.

One day the mother of the Moon asked her, 'How was it possible for you, a mortal, to come hither to the house of the Moon?'

Then the poor princess told her all that happened to her, and added, 'I shall always be thankful to Heaven for leading me hither, and grateful to you that you took pity on me and on my baby. Now I beg one last favour of you. Can your daughter, the Moon, tell me where my husband is?'

'She cannot tell you that, my child,' replied the mother, 'but, if you will travel toward the east until you reach the dwelling of the Sun, he may be able to tell you something.'

Then she gave the princess a roast chicken to eat, and warned her to be very careful not to lose any of the bones, because they might be of great use to her.

When the princess had thanked her once more for her hospitality and for her good advice, and had thrown away one pair of shoes that were worn out, and had put on a second pair, she tied up the chicken bones in a bundle, and taking her baby in her arms and her staff in her hand, she set out once more on her wanderings.

On and on, and on she went across bare sandy deserts, where the roads were so heavy that for every two steps she took forward she fell back one; but she struggled on till she had passed these dreary plains. Next she crossed high rocky mountains, jumping from crag to crag and from peak to peak. Sometimes she would rest for a little on a mountain, and then start afresh, always farther and farther on. She had to cross swamps and scale mountain peaks covered with flints; her feet and knees and elbows were torn and bleeding, and sometimes she

came to a precipice across which she could not jump, and she
had to crawl round on hands and knees, helping herself along
with her staff. At length, wearied to death, she reached the
palace in which the Sun lived. She knocked and begged for
admission.

The mother of the Sun opened the door, and was astonished
at beholding a mortal from the distant earthly shores and wept
with pity when she heard of all she had suffered. Then, having
promised to ask her son about the princess's husband, she hid
her in the cellar that the Sun might notice nothing on his
return home, for he was always in a bad temper when he came
in at night.

The next day the princess feared things would not go well
with her, for the Sun had noticed that someone from the other
world had been in the palace. But his mother had soothed him
with soft words. So the princess took heart when she saw how
kindly she was treated, and asked:

'But how in the world is it possible for the Sun to be angry?
He is so beautiful and so good to mortals.'

'This is how it happens,' replied the Sun's mother. 'In the
morning when he stands at the gates of paradise he is happy
and smiles on the whole world, but during the day he gets
cross, because he sees all the evil deeds of men, and that is why
his heat becomes so scorching. But in the evening he is both
sad and angry, for he stands at the gates of death; that is his
usual course. From there he comes back here.'

She then told the princess that she had asked about her
husband, but her son had replied that he knew nothing about
him, and that her only hope was to go and inquire of the
Wind.

Before the princess left, the mother of the Sun gave her a
roast chicken to eat, and advised her to take great care of the

bones, which she did, wrapping them up in a bundle. She then threw away her second pair of shoes, which were quite worn out, and with her child on her arm and her staff in her hand, she set forth on her way to the Wind.

In these wanderings she met with even greater difficulties than before, for she came upon one mountain of flints after another, out of which tongues of fire would flame up. She passed through woods which had never been trodden by human foot and had to cross fields of ice and avalanches of snow. The poor woman nearly died of these hardships, but she kept a brave heart and at length she reached an enormous cave in the side of a mountain. This was where the Wind lived.

There was a little door in the railing in front of the cave, and here the princess knocked and begged for admission. The mother of the Wind had pity on her and took her in that she might rest a little. Here too she was hidden away so the Wind might not notice her.

The next morning the mother of the Wind told her that her husband was living in a thick wood, so thick that no axe had been able to cut a way through it. Here he had built himself a sort of house by placing trunks of trees together and fastening them with withes and here he lived alone, shunning human kind.

After the mother of the Wind had given the princess a chicken to eat and had warned her to take care of the bones, she advised her to go by the Milky Way, which at night lies across the sky, and to wander on till she reached her goal.

Having thanked the old woman with tears in her eyes for her hospitality, and for the good news she had given her, the princess set out on her journey and rested neither night nor day, so great was her longing to see her husband again. On and on she walked until her last pair of shoes fell to pieces.

So she threw them away and went on with bare feet, not heeding the bogs nor the thorns that wounded her, nor the stones that bruised her.

At last she reached a beautiful green meadow on the edge of a wood. Her heart was cheered by the sight of the flowers and the soft cool grass, and she sat down and rested for a while. But hearing the birds chirping to their mates among the trees made her think with longing of her husband, and she wept bitterly and, taking her child in her arms and her bundle of chicken bones on her shoulder, she entered the wood.

For three days and three nights she struggled through it, but could find nothing. She was worn out with weariness and hunger, and even her staff was no further help to her, for in her many wanderings it had become quite blunted. She almost gave up in despair, but made one last great effort, and suddenly in a thicket she came upon the house that the mother of the Wind had described. It had no windows and the door was up in the roof. Round the house she went in search of steps, but could find none. What was she to do? How was she to get in? She thought and thought and tried in vain to climb up to the door. Then suddenly she bethought her of the chicken bones she had dragged all that weary way, and she said to herself:

'They would not all have told me to take such good care of these bones if there had not been some good reason for doing so. Perhaps now, in my hour of need, they may be of use to me.'

So she took the bones out of her bundle and, having thought for a moment, she placed the two ends together. To her surprise they stuck tight; then she added the other bones, till she had two long poles the height of the house; these she placed against the wall, at a distance of a yard from one another. Across them she placed the other bones, piece by piece, like the steps of a ladder. As soon as one step was finished she stood upon it and made the next one, and then the next, till she was close to the door. But just as she neared the top she noticed there were no bones left for the last rung of the ladder.

What was she to do? Without that last step the whole ladder was useless. She must have lost one of the bones. Then suddenly an idea came to her. Taking a knife, she chopped off her little finger and placed it on the last step where it stuck as the bones had done. The ladder was complete, and with her child on her arm she entered the door of the house. Here she found everything in perfect order. Having taken some food, she laid the child down to sleep in a trough that was on the floor and sat down herself to rest.

When her husband, the pig, came back to his house, he was startled by what he saw. At first he could not believe his eyes and stared at the ladder of bones and at the little finger on the top of it. He felt that some fresh magic must be at work, and in his terror he almost turned away from the house. But then a better idea came to him, and he changed himself into a dove, so no witchcraft could have power over him, and flew into the room without touching the ladder.

Here he found a woman rocking a child. At the sight of her, looking so changed by all she had suffered for his sake, his heart was moved by such love and longing and by so great a pity that he suddenly became a man.

The princess stood up when she saw him and her heart beat with fear, for she did not know him. But when he had told her who he was, in her great joy she forgot all her sufferings, and they seemed as nothing to her. He was a very handsome man, as straight as a fir tree. They sat down together, and she told him all her adventures, and he wept with pity at the tale. And then he told her his own history.

'I am a king's son. Once when my father was fighting against some dragons, who were the scourge of our country, I slew the youngest dragon. His mother, who was a witch, cast a spell over me and changed me into a pig. It was she who in the disguise of an old woman gave you the thread to bind round my foot, so that instead of the three days that had to run before the spell was broken, I was forced to remain a pig for three more years. Now that we have suffered for each other, and have found each other again, let us forget the past.'

And in their joy they kissed each other.

Next morning they set out early to return to his father's kingdom. Great was the rejoicing of all the people when they saw him and his wife. His father and his mother embraced them both, and there was feasting in the palace for three days and three nights.

Then they set out to see her father. The old king nearly went out of his mind with joy at beholding his daughter again. When she had told him all her adventures, he said to her:

'Did not I tell you that I was quite sure the creature who wooed and won you as his wife had not been born a pig? You see, my child, how wise you were in doing what I told you.'

As the king was old and had no heir, he put them on the throne in his place, and they ruled as only kings rule who have suffered many things. And if they are not dead they are still living and ruling happily.

[*Rumänische Märchen* übersetzt von Nite Kremnitz.]

The Wonderful Birch

ONCE UPON A TIME there were a man and a woman, who had an only daughter. Now it happened that one of their sheep went astray, and they set out to look for it, and searched and searched, each in a different part of the wood. Then the good wife met a witch, who said to her:

'You miserable creature, I shall change you into a black sheep.' Then she made herself look exactly like the woman, and called out to the good man:

'Ho, old man, halloa! I have found the sheep already!'

The man thought she was really his wife, and he did not know that his wife was the sheep; so he went home with the witch, glad at heart because his sheep was found. When they were safe at home the witch said to the man:

'Look here, old man, we must really kill that sheep lest it run away to the wood again.'

The man, who was a peaceable, quiet fellow, made no objections, but simply said, 'Good, let us do so.'

The daughter, however, had overheard their talk, and she ran to the flock and lamented aloud, 'Oh, dear little Mother, they are going to slaughter you!'

'Well, then, if they do slaughter me,' was the black sheep's answer, 'eat you neither the meat nor the broth, but gather all my bones and bury them by the edge of the field.'

Shortly after this they took the black sheep from the flock and slaughtered it. The witch made pease soup of it and set it before the daughter. But the girl remembered her mother's warning. She did not touch the soup, but she carried the bones to the edge of the field and buried them; and there sprang up on the spot a birch tree—a very lovely birch tree.

Some time had passed away when the witch, to whom a child had been born in the meantime, began to take an ill-will to the man's daughter, and to torment her in all sorts of ways.

Now it happened that a great festival was to be held at the palace, and the king had commanded that all the people should be invited, and that this proclamation should be made:

Come, people all!
Poor and wretched, one and all!
Blind and crippled though ye be,
Mount your steeds or come by sea.

And so they drove to the king's feast all the outcasts and the maimed and the halt and the blind. In the good man's house, too, preparations were made to go to the palace. The witch said to the man:

'Go you on in front, old man, with our youngest; I will give the elder girl work to keep her from being dull in our absence.'

So the man took the child and set out. But the witch kindled a fire on the hearth, threw a potful of barleycorns among the cinders, and said to the girl:

'If you have not picked the barley out of the ashes, and put it all back in the pot before nightfall, I shall eat you up!'

Then she hastened after the others, and the poor girl stayed at home and wept. She tried, to be sure, to pick up the grains of barley, but she soon saw how useless her labour was; and so she went in her sore trouble to the birch tree on her mother's grave, and cried and cried, because her mother lay dead beneath the sod and could help her no longer. In the midst of her grief she suddenly heard her mother's voice say to her:

'Why do you weep, little daughter?'

'The witch has scattered barleycorns on the hearth and bade me pick them out of the ashes,' said the girl. 'That is why I weep, dear little Mother.'

'Do not weep,' said her mother consolingly. 'Break off one of my branches, strike the hearth with it crosswise, and all will be put right.'

The girl did so. She struck the hearth with the birchen branch, and lo! The barleycorns flew into the pot and the hearth was clean. Then she went back to the birch tree and laid the branch upon the grave. Then her mother bade her bathe on one side of the trunk, dry herself on another, and dress on the third.

When the girl had done all that, she had grown so lovely that no one on earth could rival her. Splendid clothing was given to her, and a horse, with hair partly of gold, partly of silver, and partly of something more precious still. The girl sprang into the saddle and rode as swift as an arrow to the palace. As she turned into the courtyard of the castle the king's son came out to meet her, tied her steed to a pillar, and led her in. He never left her side as they passed through the castle rooms; and all the people gazed at her, and wondered who the lovely maiden was, and from what castle she came; but no one knew her—no one knew anything about her.

At the banquet the prince invited her to sit next him in the

The witch's daughter gnawed bones under the table

place of honour; but the witch's daughter gnawed the bones
under the table. The prince did not see her, and thinking it
was a dog, he gave her such a push with his foot that her arm
was broken. Are you not sorry for the witch's daughter? It was
not her fault that her mother was a witch.

Toward evening the good man's daughter thought it was
time to go home; but as she went, her ring caught on the latch
of the door, for the king's son had ordered it smeared with tar.
She did not take time to pull it off, but hastily unfastening her
horse from the pillar, she rode away beyond the castle walls as
swift as an arrow. Arrived at home, she took off her clothes by
the birch tree, left her horse standing there, and hastened to
her place behind the stove. In a short time the man and the
woman came home again too, and the witch said to the girl:

'Ah, you poor thing, there you are to be sure. You don't
know what fine times we have had at the palace. The king's
son carried my daughter about, but the poor thing fell and
broke her arm.'

The girl knew well how matters really stood, but she pretended to know nothing about it and sat dumb behind the
stove.

The next day they were invited again to the king's banquet.

'Hey, old man,' said the witch, 'get on your clothes as quick
as you can; we are bidden to the feast. Take you the child; I
will give the other one work, lest she weary.'

She kindled the fire, threw a potful of hemp seed among
the ashes, and said to the girl:

'If you do not get this sorted, and all the seed back into the
pot, I shall kill you!'

The girl wept bitterly; but then she went to the birch tree,
washed herself on one side of it and dried herself on the other;
and this time still finer clothes were given to her, and a very

beautiful steed. She broke off a branch of the birch tree and struck the hearth with it so that the seeds flew into the pot and then hastened to the castle.

Again the king's son came out to meet her, tied her horse to a pillar, and led her into the banqueting hall. At the feast the girl sat next him in the place of honour, as she had done the day before. But the witch's daughter gnawed bones under the table, and the prince gave her a push by mistake, which broke her foot—he had never noticed her crawling about among the people's feet. She was very unlucky!

The good man's daughter hastened home again betimes, but the king's son had smeared the doorposts with tar, and the girl's golden circlet stuck to it. She had not time to look for it, but sprang to the saddle and rode like an arrow to the birch tree. There she left her horse and her fine clothes, and said to her mother:

'I have lost my circlet at the castle; the doorpost was tarred, and it stuck fast.'

'And even had you lost two of them,' answered her mother, 'I would give you finer ones.'

Then the girl hurried into the house and, when her father came home from the feast with the witch, she was in her usual place behind the stove. Then the witch said to her:

'You poor thing! What is there to see here compared with what we have seen at the palace? The king's son carried my daughter from one room to another; he let her fall, 'tis true, and my child's foot was broken.'

The man's daughter held her peace and busied herself about the hearth.

The night passed, and when the day began to dawn, the witch awakened her husband, crying:

'Hi, get up, old man! We are bidden to the royal banquet.'

So the old man got up. Then the witch gave him the child, saying, 'Take you the little one; I will give the other girl work to do, else she will weary at home alone.'

She did as usual. This time it was a dish of milk she poured upon the ashes, saying:

'If you do not get all the milk into the dish again before I come home, you will suffer for it.'

How frightened the girl was this time! She ran to the birch tree, and by its magic power her task was accomplished; and then she rode away to the palace as before. In the courtyard she found the prince waiting for her. He led her into the hall, where she was highly honoured. But the witch's daughter gnawed the bones under the table, and crouching at the people's feet she had an eye knocked out, poor thing! Now no one knew any more than before about the good man's daughter, no one knew whence she came; but the prince had ordered the threshold smeared with tar, and as she fled her gold slippers stuck to it. She reached the birch tree, and laying aside her finery, she said:

'Alas, dear little Mother, I have lost my gold slippers!'

'Let them be,' was her mother's reply; 'if you need them I shall give you finer ones.'

Scarcely was she in her usual place behind the stove when her father came home with the witch. Immediately the witch began to mock her, saying:

'Ah, you poor thing, there is nothing for you to see here, and we—ah, what great things we have seen at the palace! My little girl was carried about again, but had the ill-luck to fall and get her eye knocked out. You stupid thing, you, what do you know about anything?'

'Yes, indeed, what can I know?' replied the girl. 'I had enough to do to get the hearth clean.'

Now the prince had kept all the things the girl had lost, and he soon set about finding the owner of them. A great banquet was given on the fourth day, and all the people were invited to the palace. The witch got ready to go too. She tied a wooden beetle on where her child's foot should have been, a log of wood instead of an arm, and stuck a bit of stone in the empty socket for an eye, and took the child with her to the castle. When all the people were gathered together, the king's son stepped in among the crowd and cried:

'The maiden whose finger this ring slips over, whose head this golden hoop encircles, and whose foot this shoe fits, shall be my bride.'

What a great trying on there was now among them all! The things would fit no one, however.

'The cinder wench is not here,' said the prince at last. 'Go and fetch her, and let her try on the things.'

So the girl was fetched, and the prince was just going to hand the ornaments to her, when the witch held him back, saying:

'Don't give them to her; she soils everything with cinders. Give them to my daughter rather.'

Well, then the prince gave the witch's daughter the ring, and the woman filed and pared away till the ring fitted. It was the same with the circlet and the shoes of gold. The witch would not allow them to be handed to the cinder wench; she worked at her own daughter's head and feet till she forced the things on. What was to be done now? The prince had to take the witch's daughter for his bride whether he would or no.

Some days passed, and at last he had to take his bride home to the palace and made ready to do so. Just as they were taking leave, the cinder wench sprang down from her place by the stove, on the pretext of fetching something from the cowhouse, and in going by she whispered in the prince's ear as he stood in the yard:

'Alas, dear Prince, do not rob me of my silver and my gold.'

Thereupon the king's son recognized the cinder wench; so he took both the girls with him and set out. After they had gone some little way they came to the bank of a river, and the prince threw the witch's daughter across to serve as a bridge, and so walked over with the cinder wench. There lay the witch's daughter then, like a bridge over the river, and could not stir, though her heart was consumed with grief. No help was near, so she cried at last in her anguish:

'May there grow a golden hemlock out of my body! Perhaps my mother will know me by that token.'

Scarcely had she spoken when a golden hemlock sprang up from her and stood upon the bridge.

Now, as soon as the prince had got rid of the witch's daughter, he greeted the cinder wench as his bride, and they wandered together to the birch tree which grew upon the mother's grave. There they received all sorts of treasures and riches, three sacks full of gold and as much silver, and a splendid steed which bore them home to the palace. There they lived a long time together, and the young wife bore a son to the prince. Immediately word was brought to the witch that her daughter had borne a son—for they all believed the young prince's wife to be the witch's daughter.

'So, so,' said the witch to herself, 'I had better away with my gift for the infant, then.'

And so saying she set out. Thus it happened that she came to the bank of the river and there she saw the beautiful golden hemlock growing in the middle of the bridge. And when she

began to cut it down to take to her grandchild, she heard a
voice moaning:

'Alas, dear Mother, do not cut me so!'

'Are you here?' demanded the witch.

'Indeed I am, dear little Mother,' answered the daughter.
'They threw me across the river to make a bridge of me.'

In a moment the witch had the bridge shivered to atoms,
and then she hastened away to the palace. Stepping up to the
young queen's bed, she began to try her magic arts upon her,
saying:

'You wretch, I shall change you into a reindeer of the forest.'

'Are you there again to bring trouble upon me?' asked the
young woman.

The witch changed her into a reindeer, and smuggled her
own daughter into her place as the prince's wife. But now the
child grew restless and cried, because it missed its mother's
care. They took it to the court, and tried to pacify it in every
conceivable way, but its crying never ceased.

'What makes the child so restless?' asked the prince, and he
went to a wise widow woman to ask her advice.

'Ay, ay, your own wife is not at home,' said the widow
woman. 'She is living like a reindeer in the wood. You have
the witch's daughter for a wife now, and the witch herself for
a mother-in-law.'

'Is there any way of getting my own wife back from the
wood again?' asked the prince.

'Give me the child,' answered the widow woman. 'I'll take
it with me tomorrow when I go to drive the cows to the wood.
I'll make a rustling among the birch leaves and a trembling
among the aspens—perhaps the boy will grow quiet when he
hears it.'

'Yes, take the child away, take it to the wood with you to

quiet it,' said the prince, and he led the widow woman into the castle.

'How now? You are going to send the child away to the wood?' said the witch in a suspicious tone, and tried to inter-fere. But the king's son stood firm by what he had com-manded, and said:

'Carry the child about the wood; perhaps that will pacify it.'

So the widow woman took the child to the wood. She came to the edge of a marsh and, seeing a herd of reindeer there, she began all at once to sing:

> '*Little Bright-eyes, little Redskin,*
> *Come nurse the child you bore!*
>   *That bloodthirsty monster,*
>   *That man-eater grim,*
> *Shall nurse him, shall tend him no more.*
>   *They may threaten and force as they will,*
>   *He turns from her, shrinks from her still,'*

and immediately the reindeer drew near and tended the child the whole day long. But at nightfall it had to follow the herd, and said to the widow woman:

'Bring me the child tomorrow, and again the following day; after that I must wander with the herd far away to other lands.'

The following morning the widow woman went back to the castle to fetch the child. The witch interfered, of course, but the prince said:

'Take it, and carry it about in the open air; the boy is quieter at night, to be sure, when he has been in the wood all day.'

So the widow took the child in her arms, and carried it to the marsh in the forest. There she sang as on the preceding day:

'Little Bright-eyes, little Redskin,
Come nurse the child you bore!
That bloodthirsty monster,
That man-eater grim,
Shall nurse him, shall tend him no more.
They may threaten and force as they will,
He turns from her, shrinks from her still,'

and immediately the reindeer left the herd and came to the child, and tended it as on the day before. And so it was that the child throve, till not a finer boy was to be seen anywhere. But the king's son had been pondering over all these things, and he said to the widow woman:

'Is there no way of changing the reindeer into a human being again?'

'I don't rightly know,' was her answer. 'Come to the wood with me, however. When the woman puts off her reindeer skin I shall comb her hair for her, while I am doing so you must burn the skin.'

Thereupon they both went to the wood with the child. Scarcely were they there when the reindeer appeared and nursed the child as before. Then the widow woman said to the reindeer:

'Since you are going far away tomorrow, and I shall not see you again, let me comb your hair as a remembrance of you.'

'Good.' The young woman stripped off the reindeer skin, and let the widow woman do as she wished. In the meantime the king's son threw the reindeer skin into the fire unobserved.

'What smells of singeing here?' asked the young woman, and looking round she saw her own husband. 'Woe is me! You have burned my skin. Why did you do that?'

'To give you back your human form again.'

'Alack-a-day! I have nothing to cover me now, poor creature that I am!' cried the young woman, and transformed herself first into a distaff, then into a wooden beetle, then into a spindle, and into all imaginable shapes. But all these shapes the king's son went on destroying till she stood before him in human form again.

'Alas, wherefore take me home with you again?' cried the young woman. 'The witch is sure to eat me up.'

'She will not eat you up,' answered her husband. And they started for home with the child.

But when the witch saw them she ran away with her daughter, and if she has not stopped she is running still, though at a great age. And the prince, and his wife, and the baby lived happily ever afterward.

[From the Russo-Karelian.]

Jack and the Beanstalk

NCE UPON A TIME there was a poor widow who lived in a little cottage with her only son Jack, who was a giddy, thoughtless boy, but very kind-hearted and affectionate. There had been a hard winter, and after it the poor woman had suffered from fever and ague. Jack did no work as yet, and by degrees they grew dreadfully poor. The widow saw there was no means of keeping Jack and herself from starvation but by selling her cow; so one morning she said to her son:

'I am too weak to go myself, Jack, so you must take the cow to market for me and sell her.'

Jack liked going to market to sell the cow very much; but, as he was on the way, he met a butcher who had some beautiful beans in his hand. Jack stopped to look at them, and the butcher told the boy that they were of great value, and persuaded the silly lad to sell the cow for these beans.

When he brought them home to his mother instead of the money she expected for her nice cow, she was vexed and shed many tears, scolding Jack for his folly. He was very sorry, but when mother and son went to bed sadly that night their last hope seemed gone.

At daybreak Jack rose and went out into the garden. At least, he thought, I will sow the wonderful beans. Mother says that they are just common scarlet-runners and nothing else, but I may as well sow them.

So he took a piece of stick, and made some holes in the ground, and put in the beans.

That day they had very little dinner and went sadly to bed, knowing that next day there would be none. Jack, unable to sleep from grief and vexation, got up at daydawn and went out into the garden.

What was his amazement to find that the beans had grown up in the night, and climbed up and up till they covered the high cliff that sheltered the cottage, and disappeared above it! The stalks had twined and twisted themselves together till they formed quite a ladder.

It would be easy to climb it, thought Jack. And, having thought of it, he at once resolved to carry it out, for Jack was a good climber. However, after his late mistake about the cow, he thought he had better consult his mother first.

So Jack called his mother, and they both gazed in silent wonder at the beanstalk, which was not only of great height, but was thick enough to bear Jack's weight.

'I wonder where it ends,' said Jack to his mother. 'I think I will climb up and see.'

His mother did not wish him to venture up this strange ladder, but Jack coaxed her to give her consent to the attempt, for he was certain there must be something wonderful in the beanstalk. So at last she yielded to his wishes.

Jack instantly began to climb, and went up and up on the ladder-like beanstalk till everything he had left behind him— the cottage, the village, and even the tall church tower—

looked quite small, and still he could not see the top of the beanstalk.

Jack felt tired and thought for a moment that he would go back again; but he was a very persevering boy and he knew that the way to succeed in anything is not to give up. So after resting for a moment he went on.

After climbing higher and higher, till he grew afraid to look down for fear he should be giddy, Jack at last reached the top of the beanstalk and found himself in a beautiful country, finely wooded, with beautiful meadows covered with sheep. A crystal stream ran through the pastures, and not far from the place where he had got off the beanstalk stood a fine, strong castle.

Jack wondered that he had never heard of or seen this castle before. But when he reflected on the subject, he saw that it was as much separated from the village by the perpendicular rock on which it stood as if it were in another land.

While Jack was standing looking at the castle, a very strange-looking woman came out of the wood, and advanced toward him. She wore a pointed cap of quilted red satin turned up with ermine, her hair streamed loose over her shoulders, and she walked with a staff. Jack took off his cap and made her a bow.

'If you please, ma'am,' said he, 'is this your house?'

'No,' said the old woman. 'Listen, and I will tell you the story of that castle.

'Once upon a time there was a noble knight who lived in this castle, which is on the borders of Fairyland. He had a fair and beloved wife and several lovely children. And as his neighbours, the little people, were very friendly toward him, they bestowed on him many excellent and precious gifts.

'Rumour whispered of these treasures; and a monstrous giant, who lived at no great distance, and who was a very wicked being, resolved to take possession of them.

'So he bribed a false servant to let him inside the castle, when the knight was in bed and asleep, and he killed him as he lay. Then he went to the part of the castle which was the nursery and also killed all the poor little ones he found there.

'Happily for her, the lady was not to be found. She had gone with her infant son, who was only two or three months old, to visit her old nurse who lived in the valley; and she had been detained all night there by a storm.

'The next morning, as soon as it was light, one of the servants at the castle, who had managed to escape, came to tell the poor lady of the sad fate of her husband and her pretty babes. She could scarcely believe him at first, and was eager at once to go back and share the fate of her dear ones. But the old nurse, with many tears, besought her to remember that she had still a child, and that it was her duty to live for his sake.

'The lady yielded to this reasoning and consented to remain in concealment at her nurse's house, for the servant told her that the giant had vowed, if he could find her, he would kill both her and her baby. Years rolled on. The old nurse died, leaving her cottage and its few articles of furniture to her poor lady, who dwelt in it, working as a peasant for her daily bread. Her spinning wheel and the milk of a cow, which she had purchased with the little money she had with her, sufficed for the scanty subsistence of herself and her little son. There was a nice little garden attached to the cottage, in which they cultivated peas, beans and cabbages, and the lady was not ashamed to go out at harvest time and glean in the fields to supply her little son's wants.

'Jack, that poor lady is your mother. This castle was once your father's and must again be yours.'

Jack uttered a cry of surprise.

'My mother! Oh, madam, what ought I to do? My poor father! My dear mother!'

'Your duty requires you to win it back for your mother. But the task is a very difficult one and full of peril, Jack. Have you courage to undertake it?'

'I fear nothing when I am doing right,' said Jack.

'Then,' said the lady in the red cap, 'you are one of those who slay giants. You must get into the castle, and if possible possess yourself of a hen that lays golden eggs and a harp that talks. Remember, all the giant possesses is really yours.'

As she ceased speaking, the lady of the red hat suddenly disappeared, and of course Jack knew she was a fairy.

Jack determined at once to attempt the adventure; so he advanced and blew the horn which hung at the castle portal. The door was opened in a moment or two by a frightful giantess, with one great eye in the middle of her forehead.

As soon as Jack saw her he turned to run away, but she caught him and dragged him into the castle.

'Ho, ho!' she laughed terribly. 'You didn't expect to see me here, that is clear! No, I shan't let you go again. I am overworked, and I don't see why I should not have a page as well as other ladies. And you shall clean the knives and black the boots and make the fires, and help me generally when the giant is out. When he is at home I must hide you, for he has eaten up all my pages hitherto, and you would be a dainty morsel, my little lad.'

While she spoke she dragged Jack right into the castle. The poor boy was very much frightened, but he remembered that fear disgraces a man; so he struggled to be brave and make the best of things.

'I am quite ready to help you and do all I can to serve you,

madam,' he said, 'only I beg you will be good enough to hide
me from your husband, for I should not like to be eaten at all.'

'That's a good boy,' said the giantess, nodding her head.
'It is lucky for you that you did not scream out when you saw
me, as the other boys did, for if you had done so my husband
would have awakened and eaten you for breakfast. Come here,
child; go into my wardrobe: he never ventures to open that.
You will be safe there.'

She opened a huge wardrobe which stood in the great hall
and shut him into it. The keyhole was so large that it admitted
plenty of air, and Jack could see everything that took place
through it. By-and-by he heard a heavy tramp on the stairs, like
the lumbering along of a great cannon, and then a voice like
thunder cried out:

> *'Fe, fa, fi-fo-fum,*
> *I smell the blood of an Englishman.*
> *Be he alive or be he dead,*
> *I'll grind his bones to make my bread.'*

'Wife,' cried the giant, 'there is an Englishman in the castle.
Let me have him for breakfast.'

'You have grown old and stupid,' cried the giantess in her
loud tones. 'It is only a nice fresh steak off an elephant that I
have cooked for you, which you smell. There, sit down and
make a good breakfast.'

And she placed a huge dish before him of savoury steaming
meat, which greatly pleased him, and made him forget his
idea of an Englishman being in the castle. When he had
breakfasted he went out for a walk; and then the giantess
made Jack come out to help her. He helped her all day. She fed
him well and, when evening came, put him back in the
wardrobe.

The giant came in to supper. Jack watched him through the keyhole and was amazed to see him pick a wolf's bone, and put half a fowl at a time into his capacious mouth. When the supper was ended he bade his wife bring him his hen that laid the golden eggs.

'It lays as well as it did when it belonged to that paltry knight,' he said. 'Indeed I think the eggs are heavier than ever.'

The giantess went away, and soon returned with a little brown hen, which she placed on the table before her husband.

'And now, my dear,' she said, 'I am going for a walk, if you don't want me any longer.'

'Go,' said the giant, 'I shall be glad to have a nap by-and-by.'

Then he took up the brown hen and said to her:

'Lay!' And she instantly laid a golden egg.

'Lay!' said the giant again. And she laid another.

'Lay!' he repeated the third time. And again a golden egg lay on the table.

Now Jack was sure this hen was the one of which the fairy had spoken. By-and-by the giant put the hen down on the floor, and soon after went fast asleep, snoring so loud that it sounded like thunder.

Directly Jack perceived that the giant was fast asleep, he pushed open the door of the wardrobe and crept out. Very softly he stole across the room and, picking up the hen, hurried away. He knew the way to the kitchen, the door of which he found ajar. He opened it, shut and locked it after him, and flew back to the beanstalk, which he descended as fast as his feet would move.

When his mother saw him she wept for joy, for she had feared the fairies had carried him away, or that the giant had found him. But Jack put the brown hen down before her, and told her he had been in the giant's castle, and all his adventures.

Softly Jack stole across the room

She was very glad to see the hen, which would make them rich once more.

Jack made another journey up the beanstalk to the giant's castle one day while his mother had gone to market; but first he dyed his hair and disguised himself. The old woman did not know him again and dragged him in as she had done before to help do the work; but she heard her husband coming and hid him in the wardrobe, not thinking that it was the same boy who had stolen the hen. She bade him stay quite still there, or the giant would eat him.

Then the giant came in saying:

'Fe, fa, fi-fo-fum,
I smell the blood of an Englishman.
Be he alive or be he dead,
I'll grind his bones to make my bread.'

'Nonsense!' said the wife. 'It is only a roasted bullock that I thought would be a titbit for your supper. Sit down and I will bring it at once.'

The giant sat down, and soon his wife brought up a roasted bullock on a large dish, and they began their supper. Jack was amazed to see them pick the bones of the bullock as if it had been a lark. As soon as they had finished their meal, the giantess rose and said:

'Now, my dear, with your leave I am going up to my room to finish the story I am reading. If you want me, call for me.'

'First,' answered the giant, 'bring me my money bags, that I may count my gold pieces before I sleep.'

The giantess obeyed. She soon brought two large bags over her shoulders, which she put down by her husband.

'There,' she said, 'that is all that is left of the knight's money.

When you have spent it you must go and take another baron's castle.'

'That he shan't, if I can help it,' said Jack to himself.

The giant, when his wife was gone, took out heaps and heaps of gold pieces, counted them, and put them in piles, till he was tired of the amusement. Then he swept them all back into their bags, and leaning back in his chair fell fast asleep, snoring so loud that no other sound was audible.

Jack stole softly out of the wardrobe, and taking up the bags of money, which were his very own, because the giant had stolen them from his father, he ran off, and with great difficulty descending the beanstalk, laid the bags of gold on his mother's table. She had just returned from town and was crying at not finding Jack.

'There, Mother, I have brought you the gold that my father lost.'

'Oh, Jack, you are a very good boy, but I wish you would not risk your precious life in the giant's castle! Tell me how you came to go there again.'

And Jack told her all about it. Jack's mother was very glad to have the money, but she did not like him to run any risk for her. But after a time Jack made up his mind to go again to the giant's castle.

So he climbed the beanstalk once more and blew the horn at the giant's gate. The giantess soon opened the door. She was very stupid and did not know him again, but she stopped a moment before she took him in. She feared another robbery, but Jack's fresh face looked so innocent she bade him come in, and again she hid him away in the wardrobe.

By-and-by the giant came home, and as soon as he had crossed the threshold, he roared out:

'Fe, fa, fi-fo-fum,
I smell the blood of an Englishman.
Be he alive or be he dead,
I'll grind his bones to make my bread.'

'You stupid old giant,' said his wife, 'you only smell a nice sheep, which I have grilled for your dinner.'

The giant sat down, and his wife brought up a whole sheep for his dinner. When he had eaten it all, he said:

'Now bring me my harp, and I will have a little music while you take your walk.'

The giantess obeyed and returned with a beautiful harp. The framework was all sparkling with diamonds and rubies, and the strings were all of gold.

'This is one of the nicest things I took from the knight,' said

the giant. 'I am very fond of music, and my harp is a faithful
servant.'

So he drew the harp toward him, and said, 'Play!'

And the harp played a very soft sad air.

'Play something merrier!' said the giant.

And the harp played a gay tune.

'Now play me a lullaby,' roared the giant. And the harp
played a sweet lullaby, to the sound of which its master fell
asleep.

Then Jack stole softly out of the wardrobe and went into
the huge kitchen to see if the giantess had gone out. He found
no one there, so he went to the door and opened it softly.
Then he entered the giant's room, seized the harp and ran
away with it; but as he jumped over the threshold the harp
called out:

'Master! Master!'

The giant woke up. With a tremendous roar he sprang from
his seat and in two strides reached the door. But Jack was very
nimble. He fled like lightning with the harp, talking to it as
he went, for he saw it was a fairy, and telling it he was the
son of its old master, the knight.

Still the giant came on so fast that he was quite close to poor
Jack and stretched out his great hand to catch him. But,
luckily, just at that moment he stepped upon a loose stone,
stumbled, and fell flat on the ground, where he lay at his full
length.

Jack had just time to get on the beanstalk and hasten down
it; but as he reached their own garden he beheld the giant
descending after him.

'Mother! Mother!' cried Jack. 'Make haste and give me
the axe.'

His mother ran to him with the axe in her hand, and Jack

with one tremendous blow cut through all the beanstalks except one.

'Now, mother, stand out of the way!' said he.

Jack's mother shrank back, and it was well she did, for just as the giant took hold of the last branch of the beanstalk, Jack cut the stem quite through and darted away. Down came the giant with a terrible crash, and that was the end of him. Before Jack and his mother had recovered from their alarm, a beautiful lady stood before them.

'Jack,' said she, 'you have acted like a brave knight's son and deserve to have your inheritance restored to you. Dig a grave and bury the giant, and then go and kill the giantess.'

'But,' said Jack, 'I could not kill anyone unless I were fighting with him, and I could not draw my sword upon a woman. Moreover, the giantess was very kind to me.'

The fairy smiled on Jack. 'I am much pleased with your generous feeling,' she said. 'Nevertheless, return to the castle, and act as you will find needful.'

Jack asked the fairy to show him the way to the castle, as the beanstalk was now down. She told him she would drive him there in her chariot, which was drawn by two peacocks. Jack thanked her and sat down in the chariot with her.

The fairy drove him a long distance round, till they reached a village which lay at the bottom of the hill. Here they found a number of miserable-looking men assembled. The fairy stopped her carriage and addressed them:

'My friends,' said she, 'the cruel giant who oppressed you and ate up all your flocks and herds is dead, thanks to this young gentleman. He is the son of your kind old master, the knight.'

The men gave a loud cheer at these words and pressed forward to say that they would serve Jack as faithfully as they had served his father. The fairy bade them follow her to the castle, and they marched thither in a body, and Jack blew the horn and demanded admittance.

The old giantess saw them coming from the turret loophole. She was very much frightened, for she guessed that something had happened to her husband; and as she came downstairs very fast she caught her foot in her dress and fell from the top to the bottom.

When the people outside found that the door was not opened to them, they took crowbars and forced the portal. Nobody was to be seen, but on leaving the hall they found the body of the giantess at the foot of the stairs.

Thus Jack took possession of the castle. The fairy brought his mother to him, with the hen and the harp. He had the giantess buried and endeavoured to help those whom the giant had robbed. Before her departure for Fairyland, the fairy explained to Jack that she had sent the butcher to meet him with the beans, to try what sort of lad he was.

'If you had looked at the gigantic beanstalk and only stupidly wondered about it,' she said, 'I should have left you where misfortune had placed you, only restoring her cow to your mother. But you showed an inquiring mind and great courage and enterprise, therefore you deserve to rise; and when you mounted the beanstalk you climbed the ladder of fortune.'

She then took her leave of Jack and his mother.

The Little Good Mouse

ONCE UPON A TIME
there lived a king and queen who loved each other so much
they were never happy unless they were together. Day after
day they went out hunting or fishing; night after night they
went to balls or to the opera. They sang and danced and ate
sugarplums, and were the gayest of the gay, and all their subjects followed their example so that the kingdom was called
the Joyous Land.

Now in the next kingdom everything was as different as it
could possibly be. The king was sulky and savage, and never
enjoyed himself at all. He looked so ugly and cross that all his
subjects feared him. He hated the very sight of a cheerful face;
and if he ever caught anyone smiling he had his head cut off
that very minute. This kingdom was very appropriately called
the Land of Tears.

Now when this Wicked King heard of the happiness of the
Jolly King, he was so jealous that he collected a great army
and set out to fight him, and the news of his approach was
soon brought to the king and queen. The queen, when she
heard of it, was frightened out of her wits and began to cry
bitterly.

'Sire,' she said, 'let us collect all our riches and run away as far as ever we can, to the other side of the world.'

But the king answered, 'Fie, madam! I am far too brave for that. It is better to die than to be a coward.'

Then he assembled all his armed men and, after bidding the queen a tender farewell, he mounted his splendid horse and rode away. When he was lost to sight the queen could do nothing but weep and wring her hands and cry.

'Alas! If the king is killed, what will become of me and of my little daughter?' And she was so sorrowful she could neither eat nor sleep.

The king sent her a letter every day, but at last, one morning

as she looked out of the palace window, she saw a messenger
approaching in hot haste.

'What news, courier? What news?' cried the queen, and he
answered:

'The battle is lost and the king is dead, and in another
moment the enemy will be here.'

The poor queen fell back insensible. Her ladies carried her
to bed and stood round her weeping and wailing. There was
a tremendous noise and confusion, and they knew that the

enemy had arrived, and very soon they heard the Wicked King himself stamping about the palace seeking the queen. Then her ladies put the little princess into her arms and covered her up, head and all, in the bedclothes, and ran for their lives, and the poor queen lay there shaking and hoping she would not be found.

Very soon the Wicked King clattered into the room, and in a fury because the queen would not answer when he called to her, he tore back her silken coverings and tweaked off her lace cap, and when all her lovely hair came tumbling down over her shoulders, he wound it three times round his hand and threw her over his shoulder, where he carried her like a sack of flour.

The poor queen held her little daughter safe in her arms and shrieked for mercy, but the king only mocked her and begged her to go on shrieking, as it amused him, and so he mounted his great black horse and rode back to his own country. There he declared he would hang the queen and the little princess on the nearest tree; but his courtiers said that seemed a pity, for when the baby grew up she would be a very nice wife for the king's only son.

The king was rather pleased with this idea. He shut the queen up in the highest room of a tall tower, which was very tiny and miserably furnished. Then he sent for a fairy who lived near his kingdom, and after receiving her with more politeness than he generally showed, and entertaining her at a sumptuous feast, he took her up to see the queen. The fairy was so touched by the sight of her misery that when she kissed her hand she whispered:

'Courage, madam! I think I see a way to help you.'

The queen, a little comforted by these words, received her graciously and begged her to take pity upon the poor little princess. But the king, when he saw them whispering together, cried harshly:

'Make an end of these fine speeches, madam. I brought you here to tell me if the child will grow up pretty and fortunate.'

Then the fairy answered that the princess would be as pretty and clever and sweet-natured as possible, and the old king growled to the queen that it was lucky for her. Then he stamped off, taking the fairy with him and leaving the poor queen in tears.

'How can I wish my little daughter to grow up pretty if she is to be married to that horrid little dwarf, the king's son,' she said to herself, 'and yet, if she is ugly we shall both be killed. If I could only hide her away somewhere so the cruel king could never find her.'

As the days went on, the queen and the little princess grew thinner and thinner, for their hard-hearted gaoler gave them every day only three boiled peas and a tiny morsel of black bread. They were always terribly hungry. At last, one evening, as the queen sat at her spinning wheel—for the king was so avaricious she was made to work day and night—she saw a pretty little mouse creep out of a hole, and said to it:

'Alas, little creature! What are you coming to look for here? I only have three peas for my day's provision, so unless you wish to fast you must go elsewhere.'

But the mouse ran hither and thither and danced and capered so prettily that at last the queen gave it her last pea, which she was keeping for her supper, saying:

'Here, little one, eat it. I have nothing better to offer, but I give this willingly in return for the amusement I have had from you.'

She had hardly spoken when she saw upon the table a delicious roast partridge and two dishes of preserved fruit.

'Truly,' said she, 'a kind action never goes unrewarded,' and she and the little princess ate their supper with great satisfaction, and then the queen gave what was left to the little mouse, who danced better than ever afterward. The next morning the gaoler brought the queen's allowance of three peas in a large dish to make them look smaller, but as soon as he set it down the little mouse came and ate all three. When the queen wanted her dinner there was nothing left for her, and she was quite provoked.

'What a bad little beast that mouse must be! If this goes on I shall be starved.'

But when she glanced at the dish again it was covered with all sorts of nice things to eat, and the queen made a very good dinner and was gayer than usual over it. But afterward as she sat at her spinning wheel she said to herself:

'Oh, if I could only think of some way of escaping!'

As she spoke she saw the little mouse playing in a corner with some long straws. The queen took them and began to plait them, saying:

'If only I had straws enough I would make a basket with them and let my baby down in it from the window to any kind passer-by who would take care of her.'

By the time the straws were all plaited, the little mouse had dragged in more and more, until the queen had plenty to make her basket, and she worked at it day and night, while the little mouse danced for her amusement. At dinner and supper time the queen gave it the three peas and the bit of black bread, and always found something good in their place. She really could not imagine where all the nice things came from. At last, one day, when the basket was finished, the queen was looking out of the window to see how long a cord she must make to lower it to the bottom of the tower, when she noticed a little old

woman leaning upon her stick and looking up at her. Presently
she said:

'I know your trouble, madam. If you like I will help you.'

'Oh, my dear friend,' said the queen, 'if you really wish to
be of use to me I will let down my poor little baby in a basket.
If you will take her and bring her up for me, when I am rich
I will reward you splendidly.'

'I don't care about the reward,' said the old woman, 'but
there is one thing I should like. You must know that I am
very particular about what I eat, and if there is one thing I
fancy above all others, it is a plump, tender little mouse. If
there is such a thing in your garret just throw it down to me,
and in return I will promise that your little daughter shall be
well taken care of.'

When the queen heard this she began to cry, but made no
answer, and the old woman after waiting a few minutes asked
her what was the matter.

'Why,' said the queen, 'there is only one mouse in this garret,
and it is such a dear, pretty little thing, I cannot bear to think
of its being killed.'

'What!' cried the old woman, in a rage. 'Do you care more
for a miserable mouse than for your own baby? Good-bye,
madam! I leave you to enjoy its company, and for my own part
I thank my stars I can get plenty of mice without troubling
you to give them to me.'

And she hobbled off grumbling and growling. The queen
was so disappointed that, in spite of finding a better dinner
than usual and seeing the little mouse dancing in its merriest
mood, she could do nothing but cry. That night when her baby
was fast asleep she packed it in the basket and wrote on a slip
of paper, *This unhappy little girl is called Delicia.* This she
pinned to its robe, and then very sadly she was shutting the

basket, when in sprang the little mouse and sat on the baby's pillow.

'Ah, little one,' said the queen, 'it cost me dear to save your life. How shall I know now whether my Delicia is being taken care of or no? Anyone else would have let the greedy old woman have you to eat, but I could not bear to do it.'

Whereupon the mouse answered, 'Believe me, madam, you will never repent of your kindness.'

The queen was astonished when the mouse spoke and more so when she saw its little sharp nose turn to a beautiful face, and its paws to hands and feet. It suddenly grew tall, and the queen recognized the fairy who had come with the Wicked King to visit her. The fairy smiled at her astonished look, and said:

'I wanted to see if you were faithful and capable of a real friendship for me, for you see we fairies are rich in everything but friends, and those are hard to find.'

'It is not possible that you should want for friends, you charming creature,' said the queen, kissing her.

'Indeed it is so,' the fairy said. 'For those who are only friendly with me for their own advantage, I do not count at all. But when you cared for the poor little mouse you could not know there was anything to be gained, and to try you further I took the form of the old woman you talked to from the window, and then I was convinced you really loved me.'

Then, turning to the little princess, she kissed her rosy cheek three times, saying:

'Dear little one, I promise that you shall be richer than your father and shall live a hundred years, always pretty and happy, without fear of old age and wrinkles.'

The queen, quite delighted, thanked the fairy gratefully, and begged her to take charge of Delicia and bring her up as her own daughter. This the fairy agreed to do, and they shut the basket and lowered it carefully, baby and all, to the ground at the foot of the tower. The fairy then changed herself back into a mouse, and this delayed her a few seconds, after which she ran nimbly down the straw rope, only to find when she reached the bottom that the baby had disappeared.

In the greatest terror she ran up again to the queen, crying, 'All is lost! My enemy Cancaline has stolen the princess away. You must know that she is a cruel fairy who hates me, and as she is older than I am and has more power, I can do nothing against her. I know no way of rescuing Delicia from her clutches.'

When the queen heard this terrible news she was heartbroken and begged the fairy to do all she could to find the poor little princess. At this moment in came the gaoler, and when he missed the little princess he at once told the king, who came in a great fury asking what the queen had done with her. She answered that a fairy, whose name she did not know, had come and carried her off by force. Upon this the king stamped upon the ground and cried in a terrible voice:

'You shall be hanged! I always told you you should.' And without another word he dragged the unlucky queen out into the nearest wood and climbed up into a tree to look for a branch to which he could hang her. But when he was quite high up, the fairy, who had made herself invisible and followed them, gave him a sudden push, which made him lose his footing and fall to the ground with a crash and break four of his teeth. While he was trying to mend them the fairy carried the queen off in her flying chariot to a beautiful castle, where but for the loss of Delicia, the queen would have been perfectly happy. But though the good little mouse did her utmost, they could not find out where Cancaline had hidden the princess.

Thus fifteen years went by, and the queen had somewhat recovered from her grief, when the news reached her that the son of the Wicked King wished to marry the little maiden who kept the turkeys, and that she had refused him. The wedding dresses had been made, nevertheless, and the festivities were to be so splendid that people for leagues round were flocking in to be present. The queen felt quite curious about a little turkey maiden who did not wish to be a queen, so the little mouse went to the poultry yard to find out what she was like.

She found the turkey maiden sitting upon a big stone, barefooted and miserably dressed in an old, coarse linen gown and cap. The ground at her feet was all strewn with robes of gold and silver, ribbons and laces, diamonds and pearls, over which the turkeys were stalking to and fro, while the king's ugly, disagreeable son stood opposite her, declaring angrily that if she would not marry him she should die.

The turkey maiden answered proudly, 'I never will marry you! You are too much like your cruel father. Leave me in peace with my turkeys, which I like far better than all your fine gifts.'

The little mouse watched her with the greatest admiration, for she was as beautiful as the spring. As soon as the wicked prince was gone, she took the form of an old peasant woman and said to her:

'Good day, my pretty one! You have a fine flock of turkeys there.'

The young turkey maiden turned her gentle eyes upon the old woman, and answered, 'Yet they wish me to leave them to become a miserable queen!'

'My child,' said the fairy, 'a crown is a very pretty thing, but you know neither the price nor the weight of it.'

'I know so well that I have refused to wear one,' said the

little maiden, 'though I don't know who was my father, or who was my mother, and I have not a friend in the world.'

'You have goodness and beauty, which are of more value than ten kingdoms,' said the wise fairy. 'But tell me, child, how came you here and how is it you have neither father, nor mother, nor friend?'

'A fairy called Cancaline is the cause of my being here,' answered the girl. 'While I lived with her I got nothing but blows and harsh words, until at last I could bear it no longer and ran away from her without knowing where I was going; and as I came through a wood the wicked prince met me and offered to give me charge of the poultry yard. I accepted gladly, not knowing I should have to see him day by day. Now he wants to marry me, but to that I will never consent.'

Upon hearing this the fairy became convinced that the little turkey maiden was none other than Princess Delicia.

'What is your name, my little one?' said she.

'I am called Delicia, if it please you,' she answered.

Then the fairy threw her arms round the princess's neck, and nearly smothered her with kisses, saying, 'Ah, Delicia! I am a very old friend of yours and I am truly glad to find you at last. But you might look nicer than you do in that old gown, take this pretty dress and let us see the difference it will make.'

So Delicia took off the ugly cap and shook out her fair shining hair, and bathed her hands and face in clear water from the nearest spring till her cheeks were like roses. When she was adorned with the diamonds and the splendid robe the fairy had given her, she looked the most beautiful princess in the world, and the fairy with great delight cried:

'Now you look as you should look, Delicia! What do you think about it yourself?'

And Delicia answered, 'I feel as if I were the daughter of some great king.'

'And would you be glad if you were?' asked the fairy.

'Indeed I should,' answered she.

'Ah, well,' said the fairy, 'tomorrow I may have some pleasant news for you.'

So she hurried back to her castle, where the queen sat busy with her embroidery, and cried, 'Well, madam, will you wager your thimble and your golden needle that I am bringing you the best news you could possibly hear?'

'Alas,' sighed the queen, 'since the death of the Jolly King and the loss of my Delicia, all the news in the world is not worth a pin to me.'

'There, there, don't be melancholy,' said the fairy. 'I assure you the princess is quite well, and I have never seen her equal for beauty. She might be a queen tomorrow if she chose,' and then she told all that had happened. The queen first rejoiced over the thought of Delicia's beauty and then wept at the idea of her being a turkey maiden.

'I will not hear of her being made to marry the Wicked King's son,' she said. 'Let us go at once and bring her here.'

In the meantime the wicked prince, who was very angry with Delicia, had sat himself down under a tree and cried and howled with rage and spite until the king heard him, and cried out from the window:

'What is the matter with you that you are making all this disturbance?'

The prince replied, 'It is all because our turkey maiden will not love me!'

'Won't love you, eh!' said the king. 'We'll very soon see about that!' So he called his guards and told them to fetch

Delicia. 'See if I don't make her change her mind pretty soon,' said the Wicked King with a chuckle.

Then the guards began to search the poultry yard and could find nobody there but Delicia who, with her splendid dress and her crown of diamonds, looked such a lovely princess they hardly dared to speak to her. But she said to them politely:

'Pray tell me what you are looking for here?'

'Madam,' they answered, 'we are sent for an insignificant little person called Delicia.'

'Alas,' said she, 'that is my name. What can you want with me?'

So the guards tied her hands and feet with thick ropes, for fear she might run away, and brought her to the king, who was waiting with his son.

When he saw her he was very much astonished at her beauty, which would have made anyone less hard-hearted sorry for her. But the Wicked King only laughed and mocked at her, and cried:

'Well, little fright, little toad! Why don't you love my son, who is far too handsome and too good for you? Make haste and begin to love him this instant, or you shall be tarred and feathered.'

Then the poor little princess, shaking with terror, went down on her knees, crying, 'Oh, don't tar and feather me, please! It would be so uncomfortable. Let me have two or three days to make up my mind, and then you shall do as you like with me.'

The wicked prince would have liked very much to see her tarred and feathered, but the king ordered that she should be shut up in a dark dungeon. It was just at this moment that the queen and the fairy arrived in the flying chariot. The queen was distressed at the turn affairs had taken, and said miserably that she was destined to be unfortunate all her days. But the fairy bade her take courage.

'I'll pay them out yet,' said she, nodding her head with an air of great determination.

That very same night, as soon as the Wicked King had gone to bed, the fairy changed herself into the little mouse and, creeping up on to his pillow, nibbled his ear. The king squealed loudly and turned over on his other side, but that was no good, for the little mouse only gnawed away at the second ear until it hurt more than the first one.

Then the king cried 'Murder!' and 'Thieves!' and all his guards ran to see what was the matter, but they could find nothing and nobody, for the little mouse had run off to the prince's room and was serving him in exactly the same way. All night long she ran from one to the other, until at last, driven frantic by terror and want of sleep, the king rushed out of the palace crying:

'Help! Help! I am pursued by rats.'

The prince, when he heard this, got up also and ran after the king, and they had not gone far when they both fell into the river and were never heard of again.

Then the good fairy ran to tell the queen, and they went together to the black dungeon where Delicia was imprisoned. The fairy touched each door with her wand, and it sprang open instantly, but they had to go through forty before they came to the princess. The queen rushed in and kissed her twenty times in a minute and laughed and cried and told Delicia all her history. The princess was wild with delight. Then the fairy showed her all the wonderful dresses and jewels she had brought for her, and said:

'Don't let us waste time; we must go and speak to the people.'

So she walked first, looking very serious and dignified, and wearing a dress with a train at least ten ells long. Behind her came the queen wearing a blue-velvet robe embroidered with gold and a diamond crown that was brighter than the sun itself.

Last of all walked Delicia, who was so beautiful it was nothing short of marvellous. They proceeded through the streets, returning the salutations of all they met, great or small, and all the people turned and followed them, wondering who these noble ladies could be.

When the audience hall was quite full, the fairy said to the subjects of the Wicked King that if they would accept Delicia, who was the daughter of the Jolly King, as their queen, she would undertake to find a suitable husband for her and would promise that during their reign there should be nothing but rejoicing and merry-making, and all dismal things should be entirely banished. Upon this the people cried with one accord:

'We will, we will! We have been gloomy and miserable too long already.' And they all took hands and danced round the queen and Delicia and the good fairy, singing, 'Yes, yes; we will, we will!'

Then there were feasts and fireworks in every street in the town, and early the next morning the fairy, who had been all over the world in the night, brought back with her in her flying chariot the most handsome and good-tempered prince she could find anywhere. He was so charming that Delicia loved him from the moment their eyes met, and as for him of course he could not help thinking himself the luckiest prince in the world. And they all lived happily ever after.

[*La bonne petite Souris*, par Madame d'Aulnoy.]

Graciosa and Percinet

ONCE UPON A TIME
there lived a king and queen who had one charming daughter.
She was so graceful and pretty and clever that she was called
Graciosa, and the queen was so fond of her she could think of
nothing else. Every day she gave the princess a lovely new
frock of gold brocade, or satin, or velvet, and when she was
hungry she had bowls full of sugarplums, and at least twenty
pots of jam. Everybody said she was the happiest princess in
the world.

Now there lived at this same court a very rich old duchess
whose name was Grumbly. She was more frightful than tongue
can tell; her hair was red as fire, and she had but one eye, and
that not a pretty one! Her face was as broad as a full moon, and
and her mouth was so large that anybody who met her would
have been afraid of being eaten, only she had no teeth. As she
was as cross as she was ugly, she could not bear to hear everyone saying how pretty and charming Graciosa was. She presently went away from the court to her own castle, which was
not far off. But if anybody happened to mention the charming
princess, she would cry angrily:

'It's not true that she is lovely. I have more beauty in my little finger than she has in her whole body.'

Soon after this, to the great grief of the princess, the queen was taken ill and died, and the king became so melancholy that for a whole year he shut himself up in his palace. At last his physicians, fearing he would fall ill, ordered that he should go out and amuse himself. A hunting party was arranged, but as it was very hot weather the king was soon tired and said he would dismount and rest at the castle they were passing.

This happened to be the Duchess Grumbly's castle. When she heard the king was coming she went out to meet him and said that the cellar was the coolest place in the castle if he would condescend to come down into it. So down they went together, and the king, seeing about two hundred great casks ranged side by side, asked if it was only for herself that she had this immense store of wine.

'Yes, sire,' answered she, 'but I shall be most happy to have

12

you taste some of it. Which do you like, canary, St. Julien, champagne, hermitage sack, raisin or cider?'

'Well,' said the king, 'since you are so kind as to ask me, I prefer champagne to anything else.'

Then Duchess Grumbly took up a little hammer and tapped upon the cask twice, and out came at least a thousand crowns.

'What is the meaning of this?' said she smiling.

Then she tapped the next cask, and out came a bushel of gold pieces.

'I don't understand this at all,' said the duchess, smiling more than before.

Then she went on to the third cask, tap, tap, and out came such a stream of diamonds and pearls that the ground was covered with them.

'Ah,' she cried, 'this is altogether beyond my comprehension, sire. Someone must have stolen my good wine and put all this rubbish in its place.'

'Rubbish, do you call it, Madam Grumbly?' cried the king. 'Rubbish! Why there is enough there to buy ten kingdoms.'

'Well,' said she, 'you must know that all those casks are full of gold and jewels, and if you will marry me it shall all be yours.'

Now the king loved money more than anything else in the world, so he cried joyfully, 'Marry you? Why, with all my heart! Tomorrow if you like.'

'But I make one condition,' said the duchess; 'I must have your daughter to do with as I please.'

'Oh, certainly, you shall have your own way. Let us shake hands upon the bargain,' said the king.

So they shook hands and went up out of the cellar of treasure together, and the duchess locked the door and gave the key to the king.

When he was back in his own palace Graciosa ran out to meet him, and asked if he had had good sport.

'I have caught a dove,' answered he.

'Oh, do give it to me,' said the princess. 'I will keep it and take care of it.'

'I can hardly do that,' said he, 'for, to speak more plainly, I mean that I met the Duchess Grumbly and have promised to marry her.'

'And you call her a dove?' cried the princess. 'I should have called her a screech owl.'

'Hold your tongue,' said the king crossly. 'I intend you to behave prettily to her. So now go and make yourself fit, for I am going to take you to visit her.'

So the princess went sorrowfully to her own room, and her nurse, seeing her tears, asked what was vexing her.

'Alas! Who would not be vexed?' answered she. 'The king intends to marry again, and has chosen for his new bride my enemy, the hideous Duchess Grumbly.'

'Oh, well,' said the nurse, 'you must remember that you are a princess and are expected to set a good example. Make the best of whatever happens. You must promise me not to let the duchess see how much you dislike her.'

At first the princess would not promise, but the nurse showed her so many good reasons for it that, in the end, she agreed to be amiable to her stepmother.

Then the nurse dressed her in a robe of pale green and gold brocade and combed out her long fair hair till it floated round her like a golden mantle and put on her head a crown of roses and jasmine with emerald leaves. When she was ready nobody could have been prettier, but the princess still could not help looking sad.

Meanwhile the Duchess Grumbly was also occupied in

attiring herself. She had one of her shoe heels made an inch or so higher than the other that she might not limp so much, and put in a cunningly made glass eye in the place of the one she had lost. She dyed her red hair black and painted her face. Then she put on a gorgeous robe of lilac satin lined with blue and a yellow petticoat trimmed with violet ribbons, and because queens always rode into their new dominions, she ordered a horse to be made ready for her to ride.

While Graciosa was waiting for the king to set out, she went all alone through the garden into a little wood, where she sat down upon a mossy bank. Her thoughts were so doleful that very soon she began to cry, and she cried and cried and forgot all about going back to the palace, until she suddenly saw a handsome page standing before her. He was dressed in green, and the cap which he held in his hand was adorned with white plumes. When Graciosa looked at him he went down on one knee, and said to her:

'Princess, the king awaits you.'

The princess was surprised and, if the truth must be told, very much delighted at the appearance of this charming page. She could not remember having seen him before. Thinking he might belong to the household of the duchess, she said:

'How long have you been one of the king's pages?'

'I am not in the service of the king, madam,' answered he, 'but in yours.'

'In mine?' said the princess with great surprise. 'Then how is it I have never seen you before?'

'Ah, Princess!' said he, 'I have never before dared to present myself to you, but now the king's marriage threatens you with so many dangers that I must tell you at once how much I love you, and I trust that in time I may win your regard. I am Prince Percinet, of whose riches you may have heard, and whose fairy gift will, I hope, be of use to you in all your difficulties, if you will permit me to accompany you under this disguise.'

'Ah, Percinet,' cried the princess, 'is it really you? I have so often heard of you and wished to see you. If you will indeed be my friend, I shall not be afraid of that wicked old duchess any more.'

So they went back to the palace together, and there Graciosa found a beautiful horse which Percinet had brought for her to ride. As it was very spirited he led it by the bridle, and this enabled him to turn and look at the princess often, which he did not fail to do. Indeed, she was so pretty that it was a real pleasure to look at her.

Beside Graciosa's, the horse the duchess was to ride appeared no better than a cart horse, and as to their trappings, there was simply no comparison between them. The princess's saddle and bridle were one glittering mass of diamonds. The king had so many other things to think of that he did not notice, but all his courtiers were entirely taken up with admiring the princess and her charming page in green, and agreeing he was more handsome and distinguished-looking than all the rest of the court put together.

When they met the Duchess Grumbly she was seated in an open carriage trying in vain to look dignified. The king and the princess saluted her, and her horse was brought forward for her to mount. But when she saw Graciosa's she cried angrily:

'If that child is to have a better horse than mine, I will go back to my own castle this very minute. What is the good of being a queen if one is to be slighted like this?'

Upon this the king commanded Graciosa to dismount and beg the duchess to honour her by mounting her horse. The princess obeyed in silence, and the duchess, without even looking at her or thanking her, scrambled up upon the beautiful horse. There she sat looking like a bundle of clothes, and eight officers had to hold her up for fear she should fall off.

Even then she was not satisfied and was still grumbling and muttering, so they asked her what was the matter.

'I wish that page in green to come and lead the horse, as he did when Graciosa rode it,' said she very sharply.

And the king ordered the page to come and lead the queen's horse. Percinet and the princess looked at one another but said never a word, and then he did as the king commanded, and the procession started in great pomp. The duchess was greatly elated and, as she sat there in state, would not have wished to change places even with Graciosa. But at the least expected moment the beautiful horse began to plunge and rear and kick, and finally to run away at such a pace it was impossible to stop him.

At first the duchess clung to the saddle, but very soon she was thrown off and fell in a heap among the stones and thorns, and there they collected what was left of her as if she had been a broken glass. Her bonnet was here and her shoes there, her face was scratched and her fine clothes were covered with mud. Never was a bride seen in such a dismal plight. They carried her back to the palace and put her to bed, but as soon as she was able to speak, she scolded and raged and declared that the whole affair was Graciosa's fault, that she had contrived it on purpose to try and get rid of her and that if the king would not have her punished, she would go back to her castle and enjoy her riches by herself.

The king did not want to lose all those barrels of gold and jewels, so he hastened to appease the duchess and told her she might punish Graciosa in any way she pleased.

Thereupon she sent for Graciosa, who trembled at the summons, for she guessed that it promised nothing agreeable for her. She looked all about for Percinet, but he was nowhere to be seen; so she had no choice but to go to the Duchess Grumbly's room. There she was seized by four waiting women, so tall and strong and cruel that the princess shuddered at the sight of them, and still more when she saw the great bundles of rods, and heard the duchess call out to them from her bed to beat the princess without mercy.

Poor Graciosa wished miserably that Percinet could only know what was happening and come to rescue her. But no sooner did they begin to beat her than she found, to her great relief, that the rods had changed to bundles of peacock's feathers, and though the duchess's women went on till they were so tired they could no longer raise their arms, yet she was not hurt in the least.

However, the duchess thought she must be black and blue so Graciosa pretended to feel very bad. She went away into her own room, where she told her nurse all that had happened, and then the nurse left her. When the princess turned round there stood Percinet beside her. She thanked him gratefully for helping her so cleverly, and they laughed and were very merry over the way they had taken in the duchess and her waiting maids. Percinet advised her to pretend to be ill for a few days, and after promising to come to her aid whenever she needed him, he disappeared as suddenly as he had come.

The duchess, delighted at the idea that Graciosa was really ill, recovered twice as fast as she would have otherwise, and the wedding was held with great magnificence. Now as the king knew that, above all things, the queen loved to be told she was beautiful, he ordered her portrait to be painted, and a tournament to be held, at which all the bravest knights of his court should maintain against all comers that Grumbly was the most beautiful queen in the world.

Numbers of knights came from far and wide to accept the challenge, and the hideous queen sat in great state in a balcony hung with cloth of gold to watch the contests, and Graciosa had to stand up behind her, where her loveliness was so marked the combatants could not keep their eyes off her. But the queen was so vain that she thought all their admiring glances were for herself, especially as, in spite of their worthless cause, the king's knights were so brave they were the victors in every combat.

However, when nearly all the challengers had been defeated, a young unknown knight presented himself. He carried a portrait, enclosed in a box encrusted with diamonds and declared himself willing to maintain against them all that the queen was the ugliest creature in the world and the princess, whose portrait he carried, was the most beautiful.

So one by one the knights came out against him, and one by one he vanquished them all. Then he opened the box and said that, to console them, he would show them the portrait of his Queen of Beauty, and when he did so everyone recognized the Princess Graciosa. The unknown knight then saluted her gracefully and retired, without telling his name to anybody. But Graciosa had no difficulty in guessing that it was Percinet.

As for the queen, she was so furiously angry she could hardly speak. But she soon recovered her voice and overwhelmed Graciosa with reproaches.

'What,' she said, 'do you dare dispute with me for the prize of beauty and expect me to endure this insult to my knights? But I will not bear it, proud Princess. I will have my revenge.'

'I assure you, madam,' said the princess, 'that I had nothing to do with it and am quite willing that you shall be declared Queen of Beauty.'

'Ah, you are pleased to jest, popinjay!' said the queen. 'But it will be my turn soon!'

The king was speedily told what had happened, and how the princess was in terror of the angry queen, but he only said, 'The queen must do as she pleases. Graciosa belongs to her!'

The wicked queen waited impatiently until night fell, and then she ordered her carriage. Graciosa was forced into it, and away they drove, and never stopped until they reached a great forest, a hundred leagues from the palace. This forest was so gloomy, and so full of lions, tigers, bears and wolves, that nobody dared pass through it even by daylight, and here they set down the unhappy princess in the middle of the black night and left her in spite of all her tears and entreaties.

The princess stood quite still at first from sheer bewilderment, but when the last sound of the retreating carriage died away in the distance, she ran aimlessly hither and thither, sometimes knocking herself against a tree, sometimes tripping over a stone, fearing every moment that she would be eaten up by the lions. Presently, too tired to advance another step, she threw herself down upon the ground and cried miserably:

'Oh, Percinet! Where are you? Have you forgotten me altogether?'

She had hardly spoken when all the forest was lighted up with a sudden glow. Every tree seemed to be sending out a soft radiance, clearer than moonlight and softer than daylight, and at the end of a long avenue of trees, the princess saw a palace of clear crystal which blazed like the sun. At that moment a slight sound behind her made her turn round, and there stood Percinet himself.

'Did I frighten you, my Princess?' said he. 'I come to bid you welcome to our fairy palace, in the name of the queen, my mother, who is prepared to love you as much as I do.'

The princess joyfully mounted with him into a little sledge, drawn by two stags, which bounded off and drew them swiftly to the wonderful palace, where the queen received her with the greatest kindness and a splendid banquet was served at once. Graciosa was so happy to have found Percinet and to have escaped from the gloomy forest and its terrors, that she was very hungry and merry, and they were a gay party. After supper they went into another lovely room, where the crystal walls were covered with pictures, and the princess saw with great surprise that her own history was represented, even down to the moment when Percinet found her in the forest.

'Your painters must indeed be diligent,' she said, pointing out the last picture to the prince.

'They are obliged to be, for I will not have anything forgotten that happens to you,' he answered.

When the princess grew sleepy, twenty-four charming maidens put her to bed in the prettiest room she had ever seen and then sang to her so sweetly that Graciosa's dreams were all of mermaids and cool sea waves and caverns, in which she wandered with Percinet. But when she woke her first thought was that, delightful as this fairy palace seemed to her, yet she must go back to her father.

When she had been dressed by the four-and-twenty maidens in a charming robe the queen had sent, and in which she looked prettier than ever, Prince Percinet came to see her. He was bitterly disappointed when she told him what she had been thinking. He begged her to consider again how unhappy the wicked queen would make her, and how, if she would but marry him, all the fairy palace would be hers and his one thought to please her.

But, in spite of everything he could say, the princess was determined to go back, though he persuaded her to stay eight days, which were so full of pleasure and amusement that they passed like a few hours. On the last day, Graciosa, who had felt anxious to know what was going on in her father's palace, asked Percinet what reason the queen had given her father for her sudden disappearance.

Percinet said, 'You shall see for yourself.'

So up they went together to the top of a very high tower which, like the rest of the castle, was built entirely of rock-crystal. There the prince held Graciosa's hand in his and made her put the tip of her little finger into her mouth and look toward the town, and immediately she saw the wicked queen go to the king and heard her say to him:

'That miserable princess is dead, and no great loss either. I have ordered that she shall be buried at once.'

And then the princess saw how she dressed up a log of wood and had it buried, and how the old king cried, and all the people murmured that the queen had killed Graciosa with her cruelties, and that she ought to have her head cut off. When the princess saw that the king was so sorry for her pretended death that he could neither eat nor drink, she cried:

'Ah, Percinet, take me back quickly if you love me.'

'You may not regret me, Princess,' he said sadly, 'I fear you do not love me. But I foresee that you will more than once regret that you left this fairy palace where we have been so happy.'

But, in spite of all he could say, she bade farewell to the queen, his mother, and prepared to set out. Percinet brought the little sledge with the stags and she mounted beside him. But they had hardly gone twenty yards when a tremendous noise behind her made Graciosa look back, and she saw the palace of crystal fly into a million splinters, like the spray of a fountain, and vanish.

'Oh, Percinet!' she cried. 'What has happened? The palace is gone.'

'Yes,' he answered, 'my palace is a thing of the past. You will see it again, but not until after you have been buried.'

'Now you are angry with me,' said Graciosa in her most coaxing voice, 'though after all I am more to be pitied than you are.'

When they came near the palace the prince made the sledge and themselves invisible, so the princess went in unobserved, and ran up to the great hall where the king was sitting by himself. At first he was startled by Graciosa's sudden appearance, but she told him how the queen had left her out in the forest, and how she had caused a log of wood to be buried. The king, who did not know what to think, sent quickly and had it dug up, and sure enough it was as the princess had said. Then he caressed Graciosa and made her sit down to supper with him, and they were as happy as possible.

But by this time someone had told the wicked queen that Graciosa had come back and was at supper with the king, and in she flew in a terrible fury. The poor old king trembled before her, and when she declared that Graciosa was not the princess at all, but a wicked impostor, and that if the king did not give her up at once she would go back to her own castle and never see him again, he had not a word to say. So the queen in great triumph sent for her waiting women, who dragged the unhappy princess away and shut her up in a garret. They took away all her jewels and her pretty dress and gave her a rough cotton frock, wooden shoes and a little cloth cap.

There was some straw in a corner, which was all she had for a bed, and they gave her a little black bread to eat. In this

The broken threads joined together and the skein wound itself
smoothly off

miserable plight Graciosa did indeed regret the fairy palace, and she would have called Percinet, only she felt sure he was still vexed with her for leaving him and thought that she could not expect him to come to her aid.

Meanwhile the queen had sent for an old fairy, as malicious as herself, and said to her, 'You must find me some task for this fine princess which she cannot possibly do, for I mean to punish her, and if she does not do what I order, she will not be able to say that I am unjust.'

So the old fairy brought a skein of thread, three times as big as herself. It was so fine that a breath of air would break it and so tangled that it was impossible to see the beginning or the end of it.

The queen sent for Graciosa and said to her, 'Do you see this skein? Set your clumsy fingers to work, for I must have it disentangled by sunset, and if you break a single thread it will be the worse for you.' So saying she left, locking the door behind her with three keys.

The princess stood dismayed at the sight of the terrible skein. If she did but turn it over to see where to begin, she broke a thousand threads, and not one could she disentangle. At last she threw it onto the floor, crying:

'Oh, Percinet! This fatal skein will be the death of me if you will not forgive me and help once more.'

And immediately in came Percinet as easily as if he had all the keys.

'Here I am, Princess, as much as ever at your service,' said he. 'Though really you are not very kind to me.'

Then he stroked the skein with his wand, and all the broken threads joined themselves together, and the whole skein wound itself smoothly off in the most surprising manner. Then the prince asked Graciosa if there was anything else she wished, and if the time would ever come when she wished for him for his own sake.

'Don't be vexed with me, Percinet,' she said. 'I am unhappy enough without that.'

'But why should you be unhappy, my Princess?' cried he. 'Only come with me and we shall be as happy as the day is long.'

'But suppose you grow tired of me?' said Graciosa.

The prince was so grieved at this want of confidence that he left her without another word.

The wicked queen was in such a hurry to punish Graciosa that she thought the sun would never set. And indeed it was before the appointed time that she came with her four waiting women. As she fitted the three keys into the locks she said:

'I'll venture to say that idle minx has not done anything at all—she prefers to sit with her hands before her to keep them white.'

But, as soon as she entered, Graciosa presented her with the ball of thread in perfect order, so she had no fault to find and could only pretend to discover that it was soiled, for which imaginary fault she gave Graciosa a blow on each cheek, that made her white and pink skin turn green and yellow. And then she locked her in the garret once more.

Then the queen sent for the fairy again and scolded her furiously. 'Don't make such a mistake again. Find me something that it will be quite impossible for her to do,' she said.

So the next day the fairy appeared with a huge barrel full of the feathers of all sorts of birds: nightingales, canaries, goldfinches, linnets, tomtits, parrots, owls, sparrows, doves, ostriches, bustards, peacocks, larks, partridges, and every bird that one can think of. These feathers were all so mixed up the birds themselves could not have chosen their own.

'Here,' said the fairy, 'is a little task which it will take all your prisoner's skill and patience to accomplish. Tell her to pick out and lay in a separate heap the feathers of each bird. She would need to be a fairy to do it.'

The queen was more than delighted at the despair this task would cause the princess. She sent for her, and with the same threats as before locked her up with the three keys, ordering that all the feathers should be sorted by sunset. Graciosa set to work at once, but before she had taken out a dozen feathers she found that it was impossible to know one from another.

'Ah, well,' she sighed, 'the queen wishes to kill me, and if I must die I must. I cannot ask Percinet to help me again, for if he really loved me he would not wait till I called him.'

'I am here, my Graciosa,' cried Percinet, springing out of the barrel where he had been hiding. 'How can you still doubt that I love you with all my heart?'

Then he gave three strokes of his wand upon the barrel, and all the feathers flew out in a cloud and settled down in neat little separate heaps all round the room.

'What should I do without you, Percinet?' said Graciosa gratefully. But still she could not quite make up her mind to go with him and leave her father's kingdom forever. So she begged him to give her more time to think of it, and he had to go away disappointed once more.

When the wicked queen came at sunset she was amazed and infuriated to find the task done. However, she complained that the heaps of feathers were badly arranged, and for that the princess was beaten and locked in her garret. Then the queen sent for the fairy once more and scolded her until she promised to go home and think of another task for Graciosa, worse than either of the others.

At the end of three days she came again, bringing with her

13

a box. 'Tell your slave,' said she, 'to carry this wherever you please, but on no account to open it. She will not be able to help doing so, and then you will be quite satisfied with the result.'

So the queen came to Graciosa, and said, 'Carry this box to my castle and place it upon the table in my own room. But I forbid you on pain of death to look at what it contains.'

Graciosa set out, wearing her little cap and wooden shoes and the old cotton frock, but even in this disguise she was so beautiful that all the passers-by wondered who she could be. She had not gone far before the heat of the sun and the weight of the box tired her so much that she sat down to rest in the shade of a little wood which lay on one side of a green meadow. She was carefully holding the box upon her lap when she suddenly felt the greatest desire to open it.

'What could possibly happen if I did?' she asked herself. 'I should not take anything out. I should only just see what was there.'

And without further hesitation she lifted the cover.

Instantly out came swarms of little men and women, no taller than her finger, and scattered themselves all over the meadow, singing and dancing and playing the merriest games. At first Graciosa was delighted and watched them with much amusement. But presently, when she was rested and wished to go on her way, she found that, do what she would, she could not get them back into their box. If she chased them in the meadow they fled into the wood, and if she pursued them into the wood they dodged round trees and behind sprigs of moss, and with peals of elfin laughter scampered back again into the meadow.

At last, weary and terrified, Graciosa sat down and cried. 'It is my own fault,' she said sadly. 'Percinet, if you can still care for such an imprudent princess, do come and help me once more.'

Immediately Percinet stood before her. 'Ah, Princess,' he said, 'but for the wicked queen you would never think of me at all.'

'Indeed I should,' said Graciosa. 'I am not so ungrateful as you think. Only wait a little and I believe I shall love you quite dearly.'

Percinet was pleased at this, and with one stroke of his wand compelled all the wilful little people to come back to their places in the box, and then took her in his chariot to the castle.

When the princess presented herself at the door and said the queen had ordered her to place the box in her own room, the governor laughed heartily at the idea.

'No, no, my little shepherdess,' said he, 'that is not the place for you. No wooden shoes have ever been over that floor yet.'

Then Graciosa begged him to give her a written message telling the queen that he had refused to admit her. This he did, and she went back to Percinet, who was waiting for her, and they set out together for the palace. They did not go the shortest way, but the princess did not find it too long, and before they parted she had promised that, if the queen was still cruel to her, she would leave home and come to Percinet forever.

When the queen saw her returning she fell upon the fairy, whom she had kept with her, and pulled her hair and scratched her face and would really have killed her if a fairy could be killed. And when the princess presented the letter and the box she threw them both upon the fire without opening them and looked very much as if she would like to throw the princess after them. However, what she really did do was to have a

great hole as deep as a well dug in her garden and the top of
it covered with a flat stone. Then she went and walked near it,
and said to Graciosa and all her ladies who were with her:

'I am told that a great treasure lies under that stone. Let us
see if we can lift it.'

So they all began to push and pull at it, Graciosa among the
others, which was just what the queen wanted, for as soon as
the stone was lifted high enough, she gave the princess a push
which sent her down to the bottom of the well, and then the
stone was let fall again, and there she was a prisoner. Graciosa
felt that now indeed she was hopelessly lost, surely not even
Percinet could find her in the heart of the earth.

'This is like being buried alive,' she said with a shudder. 'Oh,
Percinet! If you only knew how I am suffering for my want
of trust in you! But how could I be sure you would not tire
of me from the moment you were sure I loved you?'

As she spoke she suddenly saw a little door open, and the
sunshine blazed into the dismal well. Graciosa did not hesitate
an instant but passed through into a charming garden. Flowers
and fruit grew on every side, fountains plashed, and birds sang
in the branches overhead, and when she reached a great avenue
of trees and looked up to see where it would lead her, she
found herself close to the palace of crystal. Yes! There was no
mistaking it, and the queen and Percinet were coming to
meet her.

'Ah, Princess,' said the queen, 'don't keep poor Percinet in
suspense any longer. You little guess the anxiety he has suffered
while you were in the power of that miserable Grumbly.'

The princess kissed her gratefully and promised to do as she
wished in everything, and holding out her hand to Percinet
with a smile, she said:

'Do you remember telling me that I should not see your

palace again until I had been buried? I wonder if you guessed, that when that happened, I should tell you that I love you with all my heart and will marry you whenever you like?'

Prince Percinet joyfully took the hand that was given him and, for fear the princess should change her mind, the wedding was held at once with the greatest splendour, and Graciosa and Percinet lived happily ever after.

[*Gracieuse et Percinet,* par Madame d'Aulnoy.]

Three Princesses of Whiteland

HERE WAS ONCE UPON
a time a fisherman, who lived hard by a palace and fished for
the king's table. One day he was out fishing but do what he
might with rod and line, there was never even so much as a
sprat on his hook. When the day was well-nigh over, a head
rose up out of the water, and said:

'If you will give me what your wife shows you when you
go home, you shall catch fish enough.'

So the man said 'Yes' in a moment, and then he caught fish
in plenty. But when he arrived home that night, and his wife
showed him a baby which had just been born and fell a-weeping and wailing when he told her of the promise he had given,
he was very unhappy.

All this was soon told to the king at the palace, and when he
heard what sorrow the woman was in, and the reason for it, he
said that he himself would take the child and see if he could
not save it. The baby was a boy, and the king brought him up as
his own son.

Then one day, the boy begged to have leave to go out with

his father to fish; he had a strong desire to do this, he said. The king was very unwilling to permit it, but at last the lad had leave. He stayed with his father, and all went well with them the whole day, until they came back to land in the evening. Then the lad found he had lost his pocket handker- chief and would go out in the boat after it. But no sooner was he in the boat than it began to move off with him so quickly that the water foamed all round about, and all that the lad did to keep the boat back with the oars was done to no purpose, for it went on and on the whole night through, and at last he came to a white strand that lay far, far away. There he landed, and when he had walked on for some distance he met an old man with a long white beard.

'What is the name of this country?' said the youth.

'Whiteland,' answered the man, and then he begged the youth to tell him whence he came and what he was going to do, and the youth did so.

'Well, then,' said the man, 'if you walk along the seashore here, you will come to three princesses who are standing in the earth so that their heads alone are out of it. Then the first of them will call you—she is the eldest—and will beg you very prettily to come to her and help her, and the second will do the same, but you must not go near either of them. Hurry past, as if you neither saw nor heard them, but you shall go to the third and do what she bids. It will bring you good fortune.'

When the youth came to the first princess, she called to him and begged him to come to her very prettily, but he walked on as if he did not even see her, and he passed by the second in the same way, but he went up to the third.

'If you will do what I say, you shall choose among us three,' said the princess.

So the lad said he was most willing, and she told him that

three trolls had planted them in the earth, but that formerly
they had dwelt in the castle which he could see at some distance
in the wood.

'Now,' she said, 'go into the castle, and let the trolls beat
you one night for each of us, and if you can but endure that,
you will set us free.'

'Yes,' answered the lad, 'I will certainly try to do so.'

'When you go in,' continued the princess, 'two lions will
stand by the doorway, but you go straight between them and
they will do you no harm. Go straight forward into a small dark
chamber; there lie down. Then the troll will come and beat

you, but you shall take the flask which is hanging on the wall, and anoint yourself wheresoever he has wounded you, after which you will be as well as before. Then lay hold of the sword which is hanging by the side of the flask and smite the troll dead.'

So he did what the princess told him. He walked straight in between the lions just as if he did not see them, and then into the small chamber and lay down on the bed.

The first night a troll came with three heads and three rods and beat the lad most unmercifully; but he held out until the troll was done with him, and then he took the flask and rubbed himself. Having done this, he grasped the sword and smote the troll dead.

In the morning when he went to the seashore, the princesses were out of the earth as far as their waists.

The next night everything happened in the same way, but the troll who came then had six heads and six rods, and he beat him much more severely than the first had done, but when the lad went out of doors next morning, the princesses were out of the earth as far as their knees.

On the third night a troll came who had nine heads and nine rods, and he flogged the lad so long that at last he swooned away; so the troll took him up and flung him against the wall. This made the flask of ointment fall down, and it splashed all over him, and he became as strong as ever again.

Then, without loss of time, he grasped the sword and struck the troll dead, and in the morning when he went out of the castle the princesses were standing there entirely out of the earth. So he took the youngest for his queen, and lived with her very happily for a long time.

At last, however, he took a fancy to go home for a short

time to see his parents. His queen did not like this, but when his longing grew so great that he told her he must and would go, she said to him:

'One thing shall you promise me, and that is, to do what your father bids you, but not what your mother bids.'

And this he promised. So she gave him a ring, which enabled him who wore it to obtain two wishes.

He wished himself at home, and instantly found himself there, but his parents were so amazed at the splendour of his apparel their wonder never ceased. When he had been at home for some days his mother wanted him to go to the palace, to show the king what a great man he had become.

The father said, 'No, he must not do that, for if he does we shall have no more delight in him this time.' But he spoke in vain, for the mother begged and prayed until at last he went. When he arrived at the palace he was more splendid, both in raiment and in all else, than the other king, who did not like it, and said:

'Well, you can see what kind of queen mine is, but I can't see yours. I do not believe you have such a pretty queen as I have.'

'Would to Heaven she were standing here, and then you would be able to see!' said the young king, and in an instant she was standing there.

But she was sorrowful, and said to him, 'Why did you not remember my words and listen only to what your father said? Now must I go home again at once, and you have wasted both your wishes."

Then she tied a ring in his hair, which had her name upon it, and wished herself at home again. And now the young king was deeply afflicted, and day out and day in went about thinking of naught else but how to get back again to his queen.

I will try to see if there is any place where I can learn how to find Whiteland, he thought, and journeyed forth into the world.

When he had gone some distance he came to a mountain, where he met a man who was lord over all the beasts in the forest—for they all came to him when he blew a horn which he had. So the king asked where Whiteland was.

'I do not know that,' he answered, 'but I will ask my beasts.' Then he blew his horn and inquired whether any of them knew where Whiteland lay, but there was not one who knew. So the man gave him a pair of snowshoes.

'When you have these on,' he said, 'you will come to my brother, who lives hundreds of miles from here. He is lord over all the birds in the air—ask him. When you are there, just turn the shoes so the toes point this way; then they will come home again of their own accord.'

When the king arrived there he turned the shoes as the lord of the beasts had bidden him, and they went back. And now he once more asked about Whiteland, and the man summoned all the birds together and inquired if any of them knew where Whiteland lay. No, none knew this. Long after the others there came an old eagle. He had been absent ten whole years, but he too knew no more than the rest.

'Well, well,' said the man, 'then you shall have the loan of a pair of snowshoes of mine. If you wear them they will take you to my brother, who lives hundreds of miles from here. He is lord of all the fish in the sea—you can ask him. But do not forget to turn the shoes round.'

The king thanked him and put on the shoes. When he had come to him who was lord of all the fish in the sea, he turned the snowshoes round, and back they went just as the others had gone, and he asked once more where Whiteland was.

The man called the fish together with his horn, but none of them knew anything about it. At last came an old, old pike, which he had great difficulty in bringing home to him. When he asked the pike, it said:

'Yes, Whiteland is well known to me, for I have been cook there these ten years. Tomorrow morning I have to go back there, for now the queen, whose king is staying away, is to marry someone else.'

'If that be the case I will give you a piece of advice,' said the man. 'Not far from here on a moor stand three brothers, who have stood there a hundred years fighting for a hat, a cloak and a pair of boots. If anyone has these three things he can make himself invisible, and if he desires to go to any place, he has but to wish and he is there. You may tell them that you have a desire to try these things, and then you will be able to decide which of the men is to have them.'

So the king thanked him and did what he had been told.

'What is this you are standing fighting about forever and ever?' said he to the brothers. 'Let me make a trial of these things, and then I will judge between you.'

They willingly consented to this, but when he had the hat, the cloak and the boots, he said, 'Next time we meet you shall have my decision.' And thereupon he wished himself away.

While he was going quickly through the air he fell in with the North Wind.

'And where may you be going?' said the North Wind.

'To Whiteland,' said the king, and then he related what had happened to him.

'Well,' said the North Wind, 'you can easily go a little quicker, than I can, for I have to puff and blow into every corner; but when you get there, place yourself on the stairs by the side of the door, and then I will come blustering in as if I wanted

to blow down the whole castle, and when the prince who is to
have your queen comes out to see what is astir, just take him
by the throat and fling him out, and then I will try to carry him
away from court.'

As the North Wind had said, so did the king. He stood on
the stairs, and when the North Wind came howling and roaring and caught the roof and walls of the castle till they shook
again, the prince went out to see what was the matter. But
as soon as he came the king took him by the neck and flung
him out, and then the North Wind laid hold of him and
carried him off. And when he was rid of him the king went
into the castle.

At first the queen did not know him, because he had grown
so thin and pale from having travelled so long and so sorrowfully. But when she saw her ring she was heartily glad, and
then the rightful celebration was held, and held in such a way
that it was talked about far and wide.

[From J. E. Moe.]

The Six Sillies

ONCE UPON A TIME there was a girl who reached the age of thirty-seven without ever having had a suitor, for she was so foolish that no one wanted to marry her.

One day, however, a young man arrived to pay his addresses to her, and her mother, beaming with joy, sent her daughter down to the cellar to draw a jug of beer.

As the girl did not come back the mother went down to see what had become of her and found her sitting on the stairs, her head in her hands, while by her side the beer was running all over the floor, for she had forgotten to close the tap.

'What are you doing?' asked the mother.

'I was thinking what I shall call my first child, after I am married to that young man. All the names in the calendar are taken already.'

The mother sat down on the staircase beside her daughter and said, 'I will think about it with you, my dear.'

The father who had stayed upstairs with the young man was surprised that neither his wife nor his daughter came back, and in his turn went down to look for them. He found them both sitting on the stairs, while beside them the beer was running all over the ground from the tap, which was wide open.

'What are you doing there? The beer is running all over the cellar.'

'We were thinking what we should call the children that our daughter will have when she marries that young man. All the names in the calendar are taken already.'

'Well,' said the father, 'I will think about it with you.'

As neither mother nor daughter nor father came upstairs again, the suitor grew impatient and went down into the cellar to see what they could all be doing. He found them all three sitting on the stairs, while beside them the beer was running all over the ground from the tap, which was wide open.

'What in the world are you all doing that you don't come upstairs and that you let the beer run all over the cellar?'

'Yes, I know, my boy,' said the father, 'but if you marry our daughter what shall you call your children? All the names in the calendar are taken.'

When the young man heard this answer he replied, 'Well, good-bye, I am going away. When I shall have found three people sillier than you, I will come back and marry your daughter.'

So he continued his journey and, after walking a long way, he reached an orchard. Then he saw a man knocking down walnuts and trying to throw them into a cart with a fork.

'What are you doing there?' he asked.

'I want to load the cart with walnuts, but can not manage to do it.'

The young man advised him to get a basket and put the walnuts in it, so as to turn them into the cart.

'Well,' he said to himself, 'I have already found someone more foolish than those three.'

So he went on his way, and by-and-by he came to a wood. There he saw a man who wanted to give his pig some acorns to eat, and was trying with all his might to make him climb up the oak tree.

'What are you doing, my good man?' asked he.

'I want to make my pig eat some acorns, but I can't get him to go up the tree.'

'If you were to climb up and shake down the acorns the pig would pick them up.'

'Oh, I never thought of that.'

'Here is the second foolish one,' said the young man to himself.

Some way farther along the road he came upon a man who had never worn any trousers, and who was trying to put on a pair. So he had fastened them to a tree and was jumping with all his might up in the air and trying to hit the two legs of the trousers as he came down.

'It would be much better if you held them in your hands,' said the young man, 'and then put your legs in, one after the other.'

'Dear me, to be sure! You are sharper than I am, for that never occurred to me.'

And having found three people more foolish than his bride, or her father or her mother, the young man went back to marry the young lady. And in course of time they had a great many children.

[Story from Hainaut. M. Lemoine. *La Tradition*. No. 34]

Kari Woodengown

THERE WAS ONCE UPON
a time a king whose wife had died leaving one daughter. The
princess was so wise and so pretty that it was impossible for
anyone to be wiser or prettier. For a long time the king went
sorrowing for his wife, for he had loved her exceedingly, but
at last he grew tired of living alone, and married a widow.
She also had a daughter, as ill-favoured and wicked as the other
was good and beautiful. The stepmother and her daughter
were envious of the king's daughter because she was so pretty,
but so long as the king was at home they dared do her no
harm, because of his great love for her.

Then there came a time when he made war on another king
and went away to fight, and then the new queen thought
she could do what she liked; so she both starved and beat the
king's daughter and chased her about into every corner. At
last she thought that everything was too good for her, and set
her to looking after the cattle. So the princess went about with
the cattle, and herded them in the woods and in the fields. Of
food she got little and grew pale and thin and was nearly
always sad. Among the herd there was a great blue bull, which
always kept itself very smart and sleek. He often came to the

king's daughter and let her stroke him. So one day, when she was again crying and sorrowing, the bull came up to her and asked why she was always so full of care? She made no answer, but continued to weep.

'Well,' said the bull, 'I know what it is, though you will not tell me. You are weeping because the queen is unkind to you and because she wants to starve you to death. But you need be under no concern about food, for in my left ear there lies a cloth, and if you will but take it and spread it out, you can have as many dishes as you like.'

So the princess took the cloth and spread it out upon the grass, and then it was covered with the daintiest dishes anyone could desire, and there were mead and cake. And now she became brisk and well again, and grew so rosy and plump and fair that the queen and her scraggy daughter turned blue and white with vexation at it. The queen could not imagine how her stepdaughter could look so well on a little poor food, so she ordered one of her handmaidens to follow her into the wood and watch, for she thought some of the servants must be giving her food. So the maid followed her into the wood and watched and saw how the stepdaughter took the cloth out of the blue bull's ear and spread it out and how the cloth was then covered with the most delicate dishes, which the stepdaughter ate and regaled herself with. So the waiting maid went home and told the queen.

And now the king came home, and he had conquered the other king with whom he had been at war. So there was great gladness in the palace, but no one was happier than the king's daughter. The queen, however, pretended to be ill and gave the doctor much money to say she would never be well again unless she had some of the flesh of the blue bull to eat. The king's daughter and the people in the palace asked the doctor if there were no other means of saving her and begged for the bull's life, for they were all fond of him declaring there was no other such bull in the whole country. But it was all in vain, he was to be killed, and should be killed, and nothing else would serve.

When the king's daughter heard it she was full of sorrow, and went down to the byre to the bull. He too was standing there hanging his head and looking so downcast that she fell a-weeping over him.

'Why are you weeping?' said the bull.

So she told him that the king had come home again, and that the queen had pretended to be ill and had made the doctor say she could never be well again unless some of the flesh of the blue bull was given her to eat, and that now he was to be killed.

'When once they have taken my life they will soon kill you also,' said the bull. 'If you are of the same mind with me, we will take our departure this very night.'

The king's daughter thought it was bad to go and leave her father, but worse still to be with the queen, so she promised the bull she would come.

At night, when all the others had gone to bed, the king's daughter stole softly down to the byre and the bull took her on his back and ran out of the courtyard as quickly as he could.

So at cockcrow next morning, when the people came to kill the bull, he was gone, and when the king rose and asked for his daughter she was gone too. He sent forth messengers to all parts of the kingdom to search for them and published his loss in all the land, but no one had seen anything of them.

In the meantime the bull travelled through many lands with the king's daughter on his back, and one day they came to a great copper wood, where the trees and the branches and the leaves and the flowers and everything else were of copper.

The bull said to the king's daughter, 'When we enter this wood, you must take care not to touch a leaf of it, or all will be over both with me and with you, for a troll with three heads, who owns the wood, lives here.'

So she said she would be on her guard and not touch anything. And she was very careful and bent herself out of the way of the branches and put them aside with her hands; but it was so thickly wooded it was all but impossible to go forward, and do what she might, she somehow or other tore off a leaf which got into her hand.

'Oh! Oh! What have you done now?' said the bull. 'It will now cost us a battle for life or death, but do be careful to keep the leaf!'

Very soon afterward they came to the end of the wood, and the troll with three heads came rushing up to them.

'Who is touching my wood?' said the troll.

'The wood is just as much mine as yours!' said the bull.

'We shall have a tussle for that!' shrieked the troll.

'That may be,' said the bull.

So they rushed on each other and fought. The bull butted and kicked with all the strength of his body, but the troll fought quite as well as he did, and the whole day went by before the bull put an end to him, and then he himself was so full of wounds and so worn out he was scarcely able to move. So they had to wait a day, and the bull told the king's daughter to take the horn of ointment which hung at the troll's belt, and rub him with it. Then he was himself again, and the next day they set off once more.

And now they journeyed on for many, many days, and then after a long, long time they came to a silver wood. The trees and the boughs and the leaves and the flowers and everything else were of silver. Before the bull went into the wood, he said to the king's daughter:

'When we enter this wood you must, for Heaven's sake, be very careful not to touch anything at all, and not pluck off even so much as one leaf, or else all will be over both with you and with me. A troll with six heads owns the wood, and I do not think I should be able to overcome him.'

'Yes,' said the king's daughter, 'I will take good care not to touch what you do not wish me to touch.'

But the wood was so crowded, and the trees so close together, that they could scarcely go forward. She was as careful as she could be and bent out of the way of the branches and thrust them from her with her hands; but every instant a branch struck against her eyes, and in spite of all her care, she happened to pull off one leaf.

'Oh! Oh! What have you done now?' said the bull. 'It will cost us a battle for life or death, for this troll has six heads and is twice as strong as the other, but do be careful to keep the leaf.'

Just as he said this up came the troll. 'Who is touching my wood?' said he.

'It is just as much mine as yours!'

'We shall have a tussle for that!' screamed the troll.

'That may be,' said the bull, and rushed at the troll. He gored out his eyes and drove his horns right through him, but the troll fought just as well as he did, and it was three whole days before the bull had the life out of him. The bull was then so weak and worn out it was only with pain and effort he could move, and so covered with wounds was he that the blood streamed from him. He told the king's daughter to take the horn of ointment hanging at the troll's belt and anoint

At last they set forth on their way again, but the bull was still weak
and could not go quickly

him with it. She did this, and then he came to himself again, but they had to stay there and rest for a week before the bull was able to go any farther.

At last they set forth on their way again, but the bull was still weak, and at first could not go quickly. The king's daughter wished to spare him and said she was young and light of foot and would willingly walk, but he would not give her leave, and she seated herself on his back again. So they travelled for a long time, and through many lands, and the king's daughter did not at all know where he was taking her, but after a long, long time they came to a gold wood.

It was so golden that the gold dripped off it, and the trees and the branches and the flowers and the leaves were all of pure gold. Here all happened just as it had happened in the copper wood and silver wood. The bull told the king's daughter that on no account was she to touch it, for there was a troll with nine heads who was the owner, and as he was much larger and stronger than both the others put together, he did not believe he could overcome him. So she said she would take great care not to touch anything, and he should see that she did. But the wood was still thicker than the silver wood, and the farther into it they went, the worse it grew.

The wood became thicker and thicker, and closer and closer, and at last the king's daughter thought there was no way they could go forward. She was so terrified lest she should break anything off that she sat and twisted, and turned herself on this side and on that, to get out of the way of the branches and pushed them away from her with her hands. But every moment they struck against her eyes so she could not see what she was clutching, and before she knew what she was doing she had a golden apple in her hands. She was now in such terror that she began to cry, and wanted to throw it away, but the bull said she was to keep it and take the greatest care of it. He comforted her as well as he could, but he believed it would be a hard struggle and doubted whether it would go well with him.

Just then the troll with nine heads came, and he was so frightful that the king's daughter scarcely dared to look at him.

'Who is breaking my wood?' he screamed.

'It is as much mine as yours!' said the bull.

'We shall have a tussle for that!' screamed the troll.

'That may be,' said the bull. So they rushed at each other and fought, and it was such a dreadful sight that the king's daughter very nearly swooned. The bull gored the troll and ran his horns right through him, but the troll fought as well as he did, and when the bull had gored one head to death the other heads breathed life into it again, so it was a whole week before the bull was able to kill him. But then he himself was so worn out and weak he could not move at all. His body was all one wound, and he could not even so much as tell the king's daughter to take the horn of ointment out of the troll's belt and rub him with it. She did this without being told; so he came to himself again, but he had to lie there for three weeks and rest before he was in a state to move.

Then they journeyed onward by degrees, for the bull said they had still a little farther to go, and in this way they crossed many high hills and thick woods. This lasted for a while, and then they came upon the fells.

'Do you see anything?' asked the bull.

'No, I see nothing but the sky above and the wild fellside,' said the king's daughter.

Then they climbed up higher, where the fell grew more level so they could see farther around them.

'Do you see anything now?' said the bull.

'Yes, I see a small castle, far, far away,' said the princess.

'It is not so very little after all,' said the bull.

After a long, long time they came to a high hill, where there was a precipitous wall of rock.

'Do you see anything now?' said the bull.

'Yes, now I see the castle quite near, and it is much, much larger,' said the king's daughter.

'Thither shall you go,' said the bull. 'Immediately below the castle is a pigsty, where you shall dwell. There you will find a wooden gown, which you are to put on, and then go to the castle and say that you are called Kari Woodengown and that you are seeking a place. But now you must take out your little knife and cut off my head with it, and then you must flay me and roll up my hide and put it there under the rock, and beneath the hide you must lay the copper leaf and the silver leaf and the golden apple. Close beside the rock a stick is standing, and when you want me for anything you have only to knock at the wall of rock with that.'

At first she would not do it, but when the bull said it was the only reward he wished for all he had done for her, she could not do otherwise. So though she thought it very cruel, she slaved on and cut at the great animal with the knife till she had cut off his head and hide, and then she folded up the hide and laid it beneath the mountain wall and put the copper leaf, and the silver leaf, and the golden apple inside it.

Then she went away to the pigsty, but all the way she wept and was very sorrowful. Then she put on the wooden gown and walked to the king's palace. When she arrived she went into the kitchen and begged for a place, saying that her name was Kari Woodengown. The cook told her she might stay there and help wash up, for the girl who had done that before had just gone away.

'And as soon as you get tired of being here you will take yourself off too,' said he.

'No,' said she, 'that I shall certainly not.' And then she washed up, and did it very tidily.

On Sunday some strangers were coming to the king's palace, so Kari begged leave to carry up the water for the prince's bath, but the others laughed at her, and said, 'What do you want there? Do you think the prince will ever look at such a fright as you?'

She went on begging, however, until at last she was given leave. When she was going upstairs her wooden gown made such a clatter that the prince came out and said, 'What sort of creature may you be?'

'I was to take this water to you,' said Kari.

'Do you suppose that I will have any water that you bring?' said the prince, and emptied it over her.

She had to bear that, but then she asked permission to go to church. First she went to the rock and knocked at it with the stick which was standing there, as the bull had told her to do. Instantly a man came forth and asked what she wanted. The king's daughter said that she had no clothes to wear to church. So be brought her a gown, that was as bright as the copper wood, and a horse and saddle too. When she reached the church she was so pretty and so splendidly dressed that everyone wondered who she could be. The prince himself liked her so well he could not take his eyes off her for an instant. As she was walking out the prince followed her and shut the church door after her, and thus he kept one of her gloves in his hand. Then she mounted her horse again; the prince followed and asked whence she came.

'Oh, I am from Bath Land,' said Kari. And when the prince took out the glove and wanted to give it back to her, she said:

> 'Darkness behind me, but light on my way,
> That the prince may not see where I'm going today!'

The prince had never seen the equal of that glove, and he went far and wide, asking about the country of the proud lady, who rode away without her glove, but there was no one who could tell him where it lay.

Next Sunday someone had to take up a towel to the prince.

'Ah, may I have leave to go up with that?' said Kari.

'What would be the use of that?' said the others who were in the kitchen. 'You saw what happened last time.'

Kari went on begging leave till she got it, and then she ran up the stairs so that her wooden gown clattered again. Out came the prince, and when he saw that it was Kari, he snatched the towel from her and flung it right in her eyes.

'Be off at once, you ugly troll,' said he. 'Do you think I will have a towel that has been touched by your dirty fingers?'

After that the prince went to church, and Kari also asked leave to go. They all asked how she could want to go when she had nothing to wear but that wooden gown, which was so black and hideous. But Kari said she had so much benefit from what was said that at last she had leave to go.

She went to the rock and knocked, whereupon out came the man and gave her a gown which was much more magnificent than the first. It was embroidered all over with silver and it shone like the silver wood, and he gave her also a most beautiful horse, with housings embroidered with silver, and a bridle of silver too.

When the king's daughter reached the church all the people were standing outside upon the hillside, and all of them wondered who on earth she could be. The prince was on the alert in a moment and wanted to hold her horse while she alighted. But she jumped off and said there was no need for that, the horse was so well broken that it stood still when she bade it and came when she called it. So they all went into the church together, but scarcely anyone listened to what was said, for they were all looking far too much at her. The prince fell much more deeply in love with her than he had been before.

When the sermon was over and she went out to mount her horse, the prince again came and asked her where she came from.

'I am from Towel Land,' said the king's daughter, and as she spoke she dropped her riding whip. While the prince was stooping to pick it up she said:

'Darkness behind me, but light on my way,
That the prince may not see where I'm going today!'

And she was gone again, neither could the prince see what had become of her. He went far and wide to inquire, but there was no one who could tell him where her country lay, so he was forced to have patience once more.

Next Sunday someone had to go to the prince with a comb. Kari begged leave to take it to him. The others scolded her for wanting to let the prince see her when she was so black and ugly in her wooden gown. But she would not give up asking until they gave her leave to take the prince the comb. When she went clattering up the stairs again, out came the prince, took the comb and flung it at her, ordering her to be off as fast as she could.

After that the prince went to church, and Kari also begged for leave to go. Again they all asked what she would do there, as she had no clothes she could be seen in by other people. The prince or someone else might very easily catch sight of her, they said, and then both she and they would suffer for it; but Kari said they had something else to do than to look at her, and she never ceased begging until she had leave to go.

Now all happened just as it had happened twice before. She went to the rock and knocked at it with the stick. Then the man came out and gave her a gown much more magnificent than either of the others. It was almost entirely made of pure gold and diamonds, and he gave her a noble horse with housings embroidered with gold and a golden bridle.

When the king's daughter came to the church the people were all standing on the hillside waiting for her, and the prince ran up and wanted to hold the horse, but she jumped off, saying:

'No, thank you, there is no need. My horse is so well broken it will stand still when I bid it.'

So they all hastened into the church together, but no one listened to what was said, for they were looking far too much at her and wondering whence she came. And the prince was far more in love than he had been before, and he was mindful of nothing but of looking at her.

Then the sermon was over and the king's daughter was about to leave the church. The prince had ordered a firkin of tar emptied out in the porch in order that he might help her over it but she set her foot down in the middle of it and jumped over. Thus one of her gold shoes was left sticking in the tar. When she had seated herself on the horse the prince came running up and asked her whence she came.

'From Comb Land,' said Kari. But when the prince wanted to return her gold shoe, she said:

> *'Darkness behind me, but light on my way,*
> *That the prince may not see where I'm going today!'*

The prince did not know what had become of her, so he travelled for a long and wearisome time all over the world, asking where Comb Land was. But when no one could tell him, he caused it to be made known everywhere that he would marry any woman who could put on the gold shoe. So fair maidens and ugly came from all regions, but there was none who had a foot so small she could put on the gold shoe.

After a long, long while came Kari Woodengown's wicked stepmother with her daughter too, and the shoe fitted her. But she was so loathsome that the prince was very unwilling to do what he had promised. Nevertheless all was made ready for the wedding, and she was decked out as a bride, but as

they were riding to church a little bird sat upon a tree
and sang:

'A slice off her heel
And a slice off her toes,
Kari Woodengown's shoe
Fills with blood as she goes!'

And when they looked into it the bird had spoken the truth,
for blood was trickling out of the shoe. So all the waiting
maids, and all the womenkind in the castle, had to come and
try on the shoe, but there was not one whom it would fit.

'But where is Kari Woodengown, then?' asked the prince,
when all the others had tried on the shoe, for he understood
the song of birds and it came to his mind what the bird
had said.

'Oh, that creature!' said the others. 'It's not the least use for
her to come here, for she has feet like a horse!'

'That may be,' said the prince, 'but as all the others have
tried it, Kari may try it too.'

'Kari!' he called out through the door. And Kari came upstairs, her wooden gown clattering as if a whole regiment of
dragoons was coming up.

'Now, you are to try on the gold shoe and be a princess,'
said the other servants, and they laughed at her and mocked
her. Kari took up the shoe, put her foot into it as easily as
possible, and then threw off her wooden gown, and there she
stood in the golden gown which flashed like rays of sunshine,
and on her other foot she had the fellow to the gold shoe.
The prince knew her in a moment and was so glad that he
ran and took her in his arms and kissed her. And when he
heard that she was a king's daughter he was even more delighted. And then they had the wedding.

[From P. C. Asbjornsen.]

15

Drakestail

DRAKESTAIL WAS VERY little, that is why he was called Drakestail. But tiny as he was he had brains, and he knew what he was about, for having begun with nothing he ended by amassing a hundred crowns. Now the king of the country, who was very extravagant and never kept any money, having heard that Drakestail had some, went one day in his own person to borrow his hoard, and Drakestail was not a little proud of having lent money to the king.

But after the first and second year, seeing that he never even dreamed of paying the interest, Drakestail became uneasy, and, at last, he resolved to go and see his majesty himself, and get repaid. So one fine morning Drakestail, very spruce and fresh, took to the road, singing:

'Quack, quack, quack, when shall I get my money back?'

He had not gone far when he met friend fox, on his rounds that way.

'Good morning, neighbour,' said the friend. 'Where are you off to so early?'

'I am going to the king for what he owes me.'

'Oh, take me with you!'

Drakestail said to himself, 'One can't have too many friends'
. . . 'I will,' said he, 'but going on all fours you will soon be
tired. Make yourself quite small, get into my throat—go into
my gizzard and I will carry you.'

'Happy thought!' said friend fox.

He took bag and baggage and, presto! He was gone like a
letter into the post. And Drakestail was off again, all spruce
and fresh, still singing:

'Quack, quack, quack, when shall I have my money back?'

He had not gone far when he met his friend, ladder, leaning
on her wall. 'Good morning, my duckling,' said the ladder.
'Whither away so bold?'

'I am going to the king for what he owes me.'

'Oh, take me with you!'

Drakestail said to himself, 'One can't have too many friends'
. . . 'I will,' said he, 'but with your wooden legs you will soon
be tired. Make yourself quite small, get into my throat—go
into my gizzard and I will carry you.'

'Happy thought!' said my friend ladder, and nimbly, bag
and baggage, went to keep company with friend fox.

'Quack, quack, quack.' And Drakestail was off again, singing,
and spruce as before. A little farther he met his friend river,
wandering quietly in the sunshine.

'My cherub,' said she, 'whither so lonesome, with arching
tail, on this muddy road?'

'I am going to the king you know, for what he owes me.'

'Oh, take me with you!'

Drakestail said to himself, 'I can't have too many friends'
. . . 'I will,' said he, 'but you who sleep while you walk will
soon be tired. Make yourself quite small, get into my throat—
go into my gizzard and I will carry you.'

'Ah, happy thought!' said my friend river.

She took bag and baggage, and glou, glou, glou took her place between friend fox and my friend ladder.

'Quack, quack, quack.' And Drakestail was off again, singing.

A little farther on he met comrade wasp's nest, manœuvring his wasps. 'Well, good morning, friend Drakestail,' said comrade wasp's nest. 'Where are we bound for so spruce and fresh?'

'I am going to the king for what he owes me.'

'Oh, take me with you!'

Drakestail said to himself, 'One can't have too many friends' . . . 'I will,' said he, 'but with your battalion to drag along, you will soon be tired. Make yourself quite small, go down my throat—get into my gizzard and I will carry you.'

'By Jove! That's a good idea!' said comrade wasp's nest.

And left file! He took the same road to join the others with all his party. There was not much more room, but by closing up a bit they managed. And Drakestail was off again, singing.

He arrived thus at the capital and threaded his way straight up the High Street still running, and singing, 'Quack, quack, quack, when shall I get my money back?' to the great astonishment of the good folks, till he came to the king's palace.

He struck with the knocker, Toc! Toc!

'Who is there?' asked the porter, putting his head out of the wicket.

' 'Tis I, Drakestail. I wish to speak to the king.'

'Speak to the king! That's easily said. The king is dining and will not be disturbed.'

'Tell him that it is I, and I have come he well knows why.'

The porter shut his wicket and went up to say it to the king, who was just sitting down to dinner with all his ministers.

'Good, good!' said the king laughing. 'I know what it is!

Make him come in, and put him with the turkeys and chickens.'

The porter descended.

'Have the goodness to enter.'

'Good!' said Drakestail to himself. 'I shall now see how they eat at court.'

'This way, this way,' said the porter. 'One step farther. There, there you are!'

'How? What? In the poultry yard?'

How vexed Drakestail was!

'Ah, so that's it,' said he. 'Wait! I will compel you to receive me. Quack, quack, quack, when shall I get my money back?' But turkeys and chickens are creatures who don't like people who are not as themselves. When they saw the newcomer and how he was made, and when they heard him crying too, they began to give him black looks.

'What is it? What does he want?'

Finally they rushed at him all together, to overwhelm him with pecks.

'I am lost!' said Drakestail to himself, when by good luck he remembered his comrade, friend fox, and he cried:

'Reynard, Reynard, come out of your earth,
Or Drakestail's life is of little worth.'

Then friend fox, who was only waiting for these words, hastened out, threw himself on the wicked fowls, and quick! Quack! He tore them to pieces; at the end of five minutes there was not one left alive. And Drakestail, quite content, began to sing again:

'Quack, quack, quack, when shall I get my money back?'

When the king who was still at table heard this refrain, and the poultry woman came to tell him what had been going on in the yard, he was terribly annoyed. He ordered them to throw this tail of a drake into the well, to make an end of him.

And it was done as he commanded. Drakestail was in despair of getting himself out of such a deep hole, when he remembered his friend the ladder.

'Ladder, Ladder, come out of your hold,
Or Drakestail's days will soon be told.'

My friend ladder, who was only waiting for these words, hastened out, leaned her two arms on the edge of the well, then Drakestail climbed nimbly on her back, and hop! He was in the yard, where he began to sing louder than ever.

When the king, who was still at table and laughing at the good trick he had played his creditor, heard him again claiming his money, he became livid with rage. He commanded that the furnace should be heated, and this tail of a drake thrown into it, because he must be a sorcerer.

The furnace was soon hot, but this time Drakestail was not so afraid; he counted on his friend river.

'River, River, outward flow,
Or to death Drakestail must go.'

My friend river hastened out, and errouf! She threw herself into the furnace, which she flooded, with all the people who had lighted it; after which she flowed growling into the hall of the palace to the height of more than four feet. And Drakestail, quite content, began to swim, singing deafeningly:

'Quack, quack, quack, when shall I get my money back?'

He saw all the king's ministers, sword in hand

The king was still at table and thought himself quite sure of his game. But when he heard Drakestail singing again and they told him all that had passed, he became furious and got up from table brandishing his fists.

'Bring him here, and I'll cut his throat! Bring him here quick!' cried he.

And quickly two footmen ran to fetch Drakestail.

'At last,' said the poor chap, going up the great stairs, 'they have decided to receive me.'

Imagine his terror when on entering he saw the king as red as a turkey cock, and all his ministers attending him, sword in hand. He thought this time it was all up with him. Happily, he remembered there was still one remaining friend, and he cried with dying accents:

'Wasp's nest, Wasp's nest, make a sally,
Or Drakestail never more may rally.'

Hereupon the scene changed.

'Bs, bs, bayonet them!' The brave wasp's nest rushed out with all his wasps. They threw themselves on the infuriated king and his ministers and stung them so fiercely that they lost their heads and, not knowing where to hide themselves, they all jumped pell-mell from the window and broke their necks on the pavement.

Behold Drakestail much astonished, all alone in the big salon and master of the field. He could not get over it. Nevertheless, he remembered shortly why he had come to the palace, and improving the occasion, he set to work to hunt for his dear money. But in vain he rummaged in all the drawers; he found nothing. All had been spent.

Ferreting thus from room to room he came at last to the one

with the throne in it and, feeling fatigued, he sat himself down on it to think over his adventure. In the meanwhile the people had found their king and his ministers with their feet in the air on the pavement, and they had gone into the palace to know how it had occurred. On entering the throne room, when the crowd saw there was already someone on the royal seat, they broke out in cries of surprise and joy:

'The king is dead, long live the king!
Heaven has sent us down this thing.'

Drakestail, who was no longer surprised at anything, received the acclamations of the people as if he had never done anything else all his life.

A few of them certainly murmured that a Drakestail would make a fine king! Those who knew him replied that a knowing Drakestail was a more worthy king than a spendthrift like the one who was lying on the pavement. In short, they ran and took the crown off the head of the dead king and placed it on Drakestail, whom it fitted like wax.

Thus he became king.

'And now,' said he after the ceremony, 'ladies and gentlemen, let's go to supper. I am so hungry!'

[*Contes de* Charles Marelles.]

The Pied Piper

AVERY LONG TIME ago the town of Hamel in Germany was invaded by bands of rats, the like of which had never been seen before nor will ever be again. They were great black creatures that ran boldly in broad daylight through the streets, and swarmed so, all over the houses, that people at last could not put hand or foot down anywhere without touching one.

When dressing in the morning they found them in their breeches and petticoats, in their pockets and in their boots; and when they wanted a morsel to eat, the voracious horde had swept away everything from cellar to garret. The night was even worse. As soon as the lights were out, these untiring nibblers set to work. And everywhere, in the ceilings, in the floors, in the cupboards, at the doors, there was a chase and a rummage, and so furious a noise of gimlets, pincers and saws, that a deaf man could not have rested for one hour together.

Neither cats nor dogs, nor poison nor traps, nor prayers nor candles burnt to all the saints—nothing would do any good. The more they killed the more came. But one Friday there arrived in the town a man with a queer face, who played the bagpipes, and sang this refrain:

> *'Qui vivra verra:*
> *Le voilà,*
> *Le preneur des rats.'*

He was a great gawky fellow, dry and bronzed, with a crooked nose, a long rat-tail moustache, two great yellow piercing and mocking eyes, under a large felt hat set off by a scarlet cock's feather. He was dressed in a green jacket with a leather belt and red breeches, and on his feet were sandals fastened by thongs passed round his legs in the gypsy fashion. That is how he may be seen to this day, painted on a window of the cathedral of Hamel.

He stopped in the great market place before the town hall, turned his back on the church, and went on with his music. singing:

> *'Who lives shall see:*
> *This is he,*
> *The ratcatcher.'*

The town council had just assembled to consider once more this plague of Egypt, from which no one could save the town. The stranger sent word to the counsellors that if they would make it worth his while, he would rid them of all their rats before night, down to the very last.

'Then he is a sorcerer!' cried the citizens with one voice. 'We must beware of him.'

The town counsellor, who was considered clever, reassured them. He said, 'Sorcerer or no, if this bagpiper speaks the truth, it was he who sent us this horrible vermin he wants to rid us of today for money. Well, we must learn to catch the devil in his own snares. You leave it to me.'

'Leave it to the town counsellor,' said the citizens one to another.

And the stranger was brought before them.

'Before night,' said he, 'I shall have dispatched all the rats in Hamel if you will but pay me a *gros* a head.'

'A *gros* a head!' cried the citizens. 'But that will come to millions of florins!'

The town counsellor simply shrugged his shoulders and said to the stranger, 'A bargain! To work; the rats will be paid for one *gros* a head as you ask.'

The bagpiper announced he would begin that very evening when the moon rose. He added that the inhabitants should at that hour leave the streets free and content themselves with looking out of their windows at what was passing, and that it would be a pleasant spectacle.

When the people of Hamel heard of the bargain, they too exclaimed, 'A *gros* a head! But this will cost us a deal of money!'

'Leave it to the town counsellor,' said the town council with a malicious air. And the good people of Hamel repeated:

'Leave it to the town counsellor.'

Toward nine at night the bagpiper reappeared on the market place. As at first, he turned his back to the church, and the moment the moon rose on the horizon, *Trarira, trari!* the bagpipes resounded.

It was first a slow, caressing sound, then more and more lively and urgent, and so sonorous and piercing that it penetrated the farthest alleys and retreats of the town.

Soon from the bottom of the cellars, the top of the garrets, from under all the furniture, from all the nooks and corners of the houses, out came the rats, searching for the door, flinging themselves into the street, and trip, trip, trip, beginning to run

in file toward the front of the town hall, so squeezed together
they covered the pavement like the waves of a flooded torrent.

When the square was quite full the bagpiper faced about
and, still playing briskly, turned toward the river that runs at
the foot of the walls of Hamel.

Arriving there, he turned round; the rats were following.

'Hop! Hop!' he cried, pointing with his finger to the middle
of the stream, where the water whirled and was drawn down
as if through a funnel. And hop, hop, without hesitating, the

rats took the leap, swam straight to the funnel, plunged in head foremost and disappeared.

The plunging continued thus without ceasing till midnight. At last, dragging himself with difficulty, came a big rat, white with age, and stopped on the bank. It was the king of the band.

'Are they all there, Friend Blanchet?' asked the bagpiper.

'They are all there,' replied Friend Blanchet.

'And how many were they?'

'Nine hundred and ninety thousand, nine hundred and ninety-nine.'

'Well reckoned?'

'Well reckoned.'

'Then go and join them, old sire, and *au revoir.*'

Then the old white rat sprang in his turn into the river, swam to the whirlpool and disappeared.

When the bagpiper had thus concluded his business he went to bed at his inn. And for the first time during three months the people of Hamel slept quietly through the night.

The next morning, at nine o'clock, the bagpiper repaired to the town hall, where the town council awaited him.

'All your rats took a jump into the river yesterday,' said he to the counsellors, 'and I guarantee that not one of them comes back. They were nine hundred and ninety thousand, nine hundred and ninety-nine, at one *gros* a head. Reckon!'

'Let us reckon the heads first. One *gros* a head is one head the *gros*. Where are the heads?'

The piper did not expect this treacherous stroke. He paled with anger and his eyes flashed fire.

'The heads!' cried he. 'If you care about them, go and find them in the river.'

'So,' replied the town counsellor, 'you refuse to hold to the terms of your agreement? We ourselves could refuse you all payment. But you have been of use to us, and we will not let you go without a recompense,' and he offered him fifty crowns.

'Keep your recompense for yourself,' replied the piper proudly. 'If you do not pay me I will be paid by your heirs.' Thereupon he pulled his hat down over his eyes, went hastily out of the hall, and left the town without speaking to a soul.

When the people of Hamel heard how the affair had ended they rubbed their hands and, with no more scruple than their town counsellor, laughed over the bagpiper who, they said, was caught in his own trap. But what made them laugh above all was his threat of getting himself paid by their heirs. Ha! They wished they had only such creditors for the rest of their lives.

Next day, which was a Sunday, they all went gaily to church, thinking that afterward they would at last be able to eat some good thing the rats had not tasted before them. They never suspected the terrible surprise that awaited them on their return home. No children anywhere, they had all disappeared!

'Our children! Where are our poor children?' was the cry that was soon heard in all the streets.

Then through the east door of the town came three little boys, who cried and wept, and this is what they told:

While the parents were at church a wonderful music had resounded. Soon all the little boys and all the little girls who had been left at home had gone out, attracted by the magic sounds, and had rushed to the great market place. There they found the piper playing his bagpipes. Then the stranger had begun to walk quickly, and they had followed, running, singing and dancing to the sound of the music, as far as the foot of the mountain which one sees on entering Hamel. At their approach the mountain had opened a little, and the bagpiper had gone in with them, after which it had closed again.

Only the three little ones who told the adventure had remained outside, as if by a miracle. One was lame and could not run fast enough; the other, who had left the house in haste, one foot shod, the other bare, had hurt himself against a big stone and could not walk without difficulty; the third had arrived in time, but in hurrying to go in with the others had struck so violently against the wall of the mountain that he fell backward at the moment it closed upon his comrades.

At this story the parents redoubled their lamentations. They ran with pikes and mattocks to the mountain and searched till evening to find the opening by which their children had disappeared, without being able to find it. At last, the night falling, they returned desolate to Hamel.

But the most unhappy of all was the town counsellor, for he had lost three little boys and two pretty little girls, and to crown all, the people of Hamel overwhelmed him with reproaches, forgetting that the day before they had all agreed with him.

What had become of all these unfortunate children?

The parents always hoped they were not dead, and that the piper, who certainly must have come out of the mountain, would have taken them with him to his country. That is why for several years they sent in search of them to different countries, but no one ever found a trace of the poor little ones.

It was not till much later that anything was to be heard of them.

About one hundred and fifty years after the event, when there was no longer one left of the fathers, mothers, brothers or sisters of that day, there arrived one evening in Hamel some merchants of Bremen returning from the East, who asked to speak with the citizens. They told how, in crossing Hungary, they had sojourned in a mountainous country called Transylvania, where the inhabitants spoke only German, while all around them nothing was spoken but Hungarian. These people also declared that they came from Germany, but they did not know how they chanced to be in this strange country.

'Now,' said the merchants of Bremen, 'these Germans cannot be other than the descendants of the lost children of Hamel.'

The people of Hamel did not doubt it; and since that day they regard it as certain that the Transylvanians of Hungary are their countryfolk, whose ancestors, as children, were brought there by the bagpiper. There are more difficult things to believe than that.

[*Contes de* Charles Marelles.]

Little Golden Hood

Y OU KNOW THE TALE
of poor Little Red Riding-hood, whom the wolf deceived and
devoured, with her cake, her little butter can, and her grandmother; well, the true story happened quite differently, as we
know now. And first of all the little girl was called and is still
called Little Golden Hood; secondly, it was not she, nor the
good grandmother, but the wicked wolf who was, in the end,
caught and devoured.

There was once a little peasant girl, pretty and bright as a
star. Her real name was Blanchette, but she was more often
called Little Golden Hood, because of a wonderful little cloak
with a hood, gold and fire coloured, which she always wore.
This little hood was given her by her grandmother, who was
so old she did not know her age. It ought to bring the child
good luck, for it was made of a ray of sunshine, she said. And
as the good old woman was considered something of a witch,
everyone thought the little hood rather bewitched too.

One day the mother said to the child, 'Let us see, my Little
Golden Hood, if you can find your way by yourself. You shall
take this good piece of cake to your grandmother for her
Sunday treat tomorrow. You will ask her how she is, and come

back at once, without stopping to chatter on the way with people you don't know. Do you quite understand?'

'I quite understand,' replied Blanchette gaily. And off she went with the cake, quite proud of her errand.

But the grandmother lived in another village, and there was a big wood to cross before getting there. At a turn of the road under the trees, suddenly Blanchette cried, 'Who goes there?'

'Friend Wolf.'

He had seen the child start out alone, and was waiting to devour her, when at the same moment he perceived some wood-cutters who might observe him, and he changed his mind. Instead of falling upon Blanchette he came frisking up to her like a good dog.

' 'Tis you, my nice Little Golden Hood,' said he. So the little girl stopped to talk with the wolf who, for all that, she did not know in the least.

'You know me, then!' said she. 'What is your name?'

'My name is Friend Wolf. And where are you going, my pretty one, with your little basket on your arm?'

'I am going to my grandmother, to take her a good piece of cake for her Sunday treat.'

'And where does she live, your grandmother?'

'She lives at the other side of the wood, in the first house in the village, near the windmill.'

'Ah, yes! I know now,' said the wolf. 'Well, that's just where I'm going. I shall get there before you, no doubt, with your little bits of legs, and I'll tell her you're coming to see her; then she'll wait for you.'

Thereupon the wolf cut across the wood, and in five minutes arrived at the grandmother's house.

He knocked at the door, *toc, toc.*

No answer.

He knocked louder.

Was nobody at home?

Then he stood up, put his two forepaws on the latch and the door opened.

Not a soul was in the house.

The old woman had risen early to sell herbs in the town, and she had gone off in such haste that she had left her bed unmade, with her great nightcap on the pillow.

'Good,' said the wolf to himself, 'I know what I'll do.'

He shut the door, pulled on the grandmother's nightcap down to his eyes, then he lay down all his length in the bed and drew the curtains.

In the meantime the good Blanchette went quietly on her way, as little girls do, amusing herself here and there by picking Easter daisies, watching the little birds making their nests, and running after the butterflies which fluttered in the sunshine.

At last she arrived at the door.

Knock, knock.

'Who is there?' said the wolf, softening his rough voice as best he could.

'It's me, Granny, your Little Golden Hood. I'm bringing you a big piece of cake for your Sunday treat.'

'Press your finger on the latch, then push, and the door will open.'

'Why, you've got a cold, Granny,' said she, coming in.

'Ahem, a little, a little,' replied the wolf, pretending to cough. 'Shut the door well, my little lamb. Put your basket on the table, and then take off your frock and come and lie down by me. You shall rest a little.'

The good child undressed, but she kept her little hood upon her head. When she saw what a figure her granny was in bed, the poor little thing was much surprised.

'Oh,' cried she, 'how like you are to Friend Wolf, Grandmother!'

'That's on account of my nightcap, child,' replied the wolf.

'Oh, what hairy arms you have, Grandmother!'

'All the better to hug you, my child.'

'Oh, what a big tongue you have, Grandmother!'

'All the better for answering, child.'

'Oh, what a mouthful of great white teeth you have, Grandmother!'

'That's for crunching little children with!' And the wolf opened his jaws wide to swallow Blanchette.

But she put down her head crying, 'Mamma! Mamma!' and the wolf only caught her little hood.

Thereupon, oh, dear! Oh, dear! He drew back, crying and shaking his jaw as if he had swallowed red-hot coals.

It was the little fire-coloured hood that had burnt his tongue right down his throat. The little hood was one of those magic caps that they used to have, for making oneself invisible or invulnerable.

So there was the wolf with his throat burned, jumping off the bed and trying to find the door, howling and howling as if all the dogs in the country were at his heels.

Just at this moment the grandmother arrived, returning from the town with her long sack empty on her shoulder.

'Ah, brigand!' she cried. 'Wait a bit!' Quickly she opened her sack wide across the door, and the maddened wolf sprang in, head downward.

It was he now that was caught, for the brave old dame shut her sack, so; and she ran and emptied it into the well, where the wolf, still howling, tumbled in and was drowned.

'Ah, scoundrel! You thought you would crunch my little grandchild! Well, tomorrow we will make her a muff of your skin, and you yourself shall be crunched, for we will give your carcass to the dogs.'

Thereupon the grandmother hastened to dress poor Blanchette, who was still trembling with fear in the bed.

'Well,' she said to her, 'without my little hood where would you be now, darling?' And, to restore heart and legs to the child, she made her eat a good piece of her cake and drink a good draught of wine, after which she took her by the hand and led her back to her home.

And then, who was it who scolded her when she knew all that had happened? It was the mother. But Blanchette promised over and over again that she would never more stop to listen to a wolf, so that at last the mother forgave her.

And Blanchette, the Little Golden Hood, kept her word. And in fine weather she may still be seen in the fields with her pretty little hood, the colour of the sun.

But to see her you must rise early.

[*Contes de* Charles Marelles.]

The Golden Branch

ONCE UPON A TIME
there was a king who was so morose and disagreeable that he
was feared by all his subjects, and with good reason. For the
most trifling offences he would have their heads cut off. King
Grumpy, as he was called, had one son, who was as different
from his father as he could possibly be. No prince equalled him
in cleverness and kindness of heart, but unfortunately he was
terribly ugly. He had crooked legs and squinting eyes, a large
mouth all on one side and a hunchback. Never was there a
more beautiful soul in such a frightful little body, but in spite
of his appearance everybody loved him. The queen, his mother,
called him Curlicue, because it was a name she liked, and it
seemed to suit him.

King Grumpy, who cared a great deal more for his own
grandeur than for his son's happiness, wished to betroth the
prince to the daughter of a neighbouring king whose great
estates joined his own, for he thought that this alliance would
make him more powerful than ever, and as for the princess she
would do very well for Prince Curlicue, for she was as ugly as
himself. Indeed, though she was the most amiable creature in
the world, there was no concealing the fact that she was fright-

ful, and she always went about with a crutch, and people called her Princess Cabbage Stalk.

The king, having asked for and received a portrait of this princess, had it placed in his great hall under a canopy, and sent for Prince Curlicue, to whom he said that, as this was the portrait of his future bride, he hoped the prince found it charming.

The prince after one glance at it turned away with a disdainful air, which greatly offended his father.

'Am I to understand that you are not pleased?' he asked sharply.

'No, sire,' replied the prince. 'How could I be pleased to marry an ugly princess?'

'Certainly it becomes you to object to that,' said King Grumpy, 'since you are ugly enough to frighten anyone yourself.'

'That is the very reason,' said the prince, 'that I wish to marry someone lovely. I am tired enough of seeing myself.'

'I tell you that you shall marry her,' cried King Grumpy angrily.

And the prince, seeing that it was of no use to remonstrate, bowed and retired.

King Grumpy was not used to being contradicted and he was much displeased with his son and ordered him to be imprisoned in the tower that was kept for rebellious princes. But it had not been used for about two hundred years, because there had not been any. The prince thought all the rooms looked strangely old-fashioned, but as there was a good library he was pleased, for he was fond of reading. But when he looked at the books he found that they were written in a forgotten language, and he could not understand a single word, though he amused himself trying.

King Grumpy was so convinced that Prince Curlicue would soon get tired of prison, and so consent to marry the Princess Cabbage Stalk, that he sent ambassadors to her father proposing that she should be married to his son, who would make her perfectly happy.

The king was delighted to receive an offer for his unlucky daughter, though, to tell the truth, he found it impossible to admire the prince's portrait. However, he had it placed in as favourable a light as possible and sent for the princess, but the moment she caught sight of it she looked the other way and began to cry. The king, annoyed to see how greatly she disliked it, took a mirror, and holding it up before the unhappy princess, said:

'I see you do not think the prince handsome, but look at yourself. Have you any right to complain about that?'

'Sire,' she answered, 'I do not wish to complain, only I beg of you, do not make me marry at all. I had rather be the unhappy Princess Cabbage Stalk all my life than inflict the sight of my ugliness on anyone else.'

But the king would not listen to her and sent her away with the ambassadors.

In the meantime the prince was kept safely locked up in his tower and, that he might be as dull as possible, King Grumpy ordered that no one should speak to him and that they should give him next to nothing to eat. But all the prince's guards were so fond of him that they did everything they dared, in spite of the king, to make the time pass pleasantly.

One day, as the prince was walking up and down the great gallery, thinking how miserable it was to be so ugly and forced to marry an equally frightful princess, he looked up suddenly and noticed that the painted windows were particularly bright and beautiful. To change his sad thoughts he began to examine them attentively. He found that the pictures were scenes from the life of a man who appeared in every window, and the prince, fancying some resemblance to himself, began to be deeply interested. In the first window there was a picture of him in one of the turrets of the tower, farther on he was seeking something in a chink in the wall, in the next picture he was opening an old cabinet with a golden key, and so it went on through numbers of scenes, and presently the prince noticed that another figure occupied an important place in each scene. It was a tall handsome young man. Poor Prince Curlicue found it a pleasure to look at him, he was so straight and strong.

By this time it had grown dark, and the prince had to go back to his own room. To amuse himself he took up a quaint old book and began to look at the pictures. What was his surprise to find they represented the same scenes as the windows and, what was more, they seemed alive. In looking at pictures of musicians he saw their hands move and heard sweet sounds; there was a picture of a ball, and the prince could watch the little dancing people come and go. He turned a page, and there was an excellent smell of a savoury dinner, and one of the figures who sat at the feast looked at him and said:

'We drink your health, Curlicue. Try to give us our queen again, for if you do you will be rewarded; if not, it will be the worse for you.'

At these words the prince, who had been growing more and more astonished, was fairly terrified and, dropping the book with a crash, sank back insensible. The noise brought his guards to his aid, and as soon as he revived they asked him what was the matter. He answered that he was so faint and giddy with hunger he had imagined he saw and heard all sorts of strange things. Thereupon, in spite of the king's orders, the guards gave him an excellent supper. When he had eaten he again opened his book, but could see none of the wonderful pictures, which convinced him that he had been dreaming before.

However, when he went into the gallery next day and looked at the painted windows again, he found that they moved, and the figures came and went as if alive. After watching the one who was like himself find the key and open the old cabinet, he determined to go and examine the place himself, to find out what the mystery was. So he went up into the turret and began to search about and tap upon the walls, and all at once he came upon a place that sounded hollow. Taking a hammer he broke away a bit of the stone, and found behind it a little golden key. The next thing was to find the cabinet, and the prince soon came upon it, hidden away in a dark corner, though indeed it was so old and battered-looking he would never have noticed it of his own accord. At first he could not see any keyhole, but after a careful search he found one hidden in the carving. The golden key just fitted it, so the prince gave it a vigorous turn, and the doors flew open.

Ugly and old as the cabinet was outside, nothing could have been more rich and beautiful than what met the prince's astonished eyes. Every drawer was made of crystal, of amber, or of some precious stone, and was full of every kind of treasure. Prince Curlicue was delighted; he opened one after another, until at last he came to one tiny drawer which contained only an emerald key.

'I believe that this must open that little golden door in the middle,' said the prince to himself. And he fitted in the little key and turned it. The tiny door swung back and a soft crimson light gleamed over the whole cabinet. It came from

an immense glowing carbuncle, made into a box, which lay
before him. But what was his horror on opening it, to find that
it contained a man's hand, holding a portrait. His first thought
was to put back the terrible box and fly from the turret, but a
voice in his ear said:

'This hand belonged to one whom you can help and restore.
Look at this beautiful portrait, the original of which was the
cause of all my misfortunes, and if you wish to help me, go
without a moment's delay to the great gallery, notice where
the sun's rays fall most brightly, and if you seek there you
will find my treasure.'

The voice ceased, and though the prince in his bewilderment
asked various questions, he received no answer. So he put back
the box and locked up the cabinet again. Then having replaced
the key in the crack in the wall, he hastened down to the
gallery.

When he entered it, all the windows shook and clattered in
the strangest way; but the prince did not heed them, he was
looking so carefully for the place where the sun shone most
brightly. It seemed to him that it was upon the portrait of a
splendidly handsome young man.

He found that it rested against the ebony and gold panelling,
just like the other pictures in the gallery. He was puzzled, not
knowing what to do next until, looking at the nearest, he saw
a picture of himself lifting the picture from the wall.

The prince took the hint and, lifting aside the picture without difficulty, found himself in a marble hall adorned with
statues. From this he passed on through numbers of splendid
rooms, until at last he reached one all hung with blue gauze.
The walls were of turquoises, and upon a low couch lay a lovely
lady, who seemed asleep. Her hair, black as ebony, was spread

across the pillows, making her face look ivory white. She was restless, and when he softly advanced, fearing to wake her, he could hear her murmur:

'Ah! How dared you think to win my love by separating me from my beloved Florimond, and in my presence cutting off that dear hand that even you should have feared and honoured?'

And then the tears rolled slowly down the lovely lady's cheeks, and Prince Curlicue realized she was under an enchantment and that it was the hand of her lover he had found.

At this moment a huge eagle flew into the room, holding in its talons a Golden Branch, upon which were growing what looked like clusters of cherries, only every cherry was a single glowing ruby.

This he presented to the prince, who guessed by this time that he was in some way to break the enchantment of the sleeping lady. Taking the branch he touched her lightly with it, saying:

'Fair one, I know not by what enchantment you are bound, but in the name of your beloved Florimond I conjure you to come back to the life you have lost but not forgotten.'

Instantly the lady opened her lustrous eyes, and saw the eagle hovering near.

'Ah! Stay, dear love, stay,' she cried. But the eagle, uttering a dolorous cry, fluttered his broad wings and disappeared. Then the lady turned to Prince Curlicue, and said:

'I know it is to you I owe my deliverance from an enchantment which has held me for two hundred years. If I can do anything for you in return, you have only to tell me, and all my fairy power shall be used to make you happy.'

'Madam,' said Prince Curlicue, 'I wish to restore your beloved Florimond to his natural form, since I cannot forget the tears you shed for him.'

A huge eagle flew into the room, holding in its talons a Golden Branch

'That is very amiable of you, dear Prince,' said the fairy, 'but it is reserved for another person to do that. I cannot explain more at present. But is there nothing you wish for yourself?'

'Madam,' cried the prince, flinging himself down at her feet, 'only look at my ugliness. I am called Curlicue and am an object of derision. I entreat you to make me less ridiculous.'

'Rise, Prince,' said the fairy, touching him with the Golden Branch. 'Be as handsome as you are kind and accomplished and take the name of Prince Peerless, since that is the only title which will suit you now.'

Silent from joy, the prince kissed her hand to express his thanks, and when he rose and saw his new reflection in the mirrors which surrounded him, he understood that Curlicue was indeed gone forever.

'How I wish,' said the fairy, 'that I dared tell you what is in store for you and warn you of the traps which lie in your path, but I must not. Fly from the tower, Prince, and remember that the Fairy Douceline will be your friend always.'

When she finished speaking, the prince, to his great astonishment, found himself no longer in the tower, but set down in a thick forest at least a hundred leagues away from it.

When the guards found that the prince did not ask for his supper as usual, they went into his room. Not finding him there, they were very much alarmed and searched the tower from turret to dungeon, but without success. Knowing that the king would certainly have their heads cut off for allowing the prince to escape, they then agreed to say that he was ill. After making the smallest among them look as much like Prince Curlicue as possible, they put him in the prince's bed and sent to inform the king.

King Grumpy was delighted, for he thought he would all the sooner be brought to do as he wished, and marry the princess. So he sent back word that the prince was to be treated as severely as before, which was just what they had hoped he would say. In the meantime the Princess Cabbage Stalk had reached the palace, travelling in a litter.

King Grumpy went out to meet her, but when he saw her, with a skin like a tortoise's, her thick eyebrows meeting above her large nose, and her mouth from ear to ear, he could not help crying out:

'Well, I must say Curlicue is ugly enough, but I don't think you need have thought twice before consenting to marry him.'

'Sire,' she replied, 'I know too well what I am like to be hurt by what you say, but I assure you I have no wish to marry your son. I had rather be called Princess Cabbage Stalk than Queen Curlicue.'

This made King Grumpy very angry.

'Your father has sent you here to marry my son,' he said, 'and you may be sure that I am not going to offend him by altering his arrangements.'

At this juncture the guards, who were in great fear that they would be found out, sent to tell the king his son was dead, which annoyed him very much. He made up his mind it was the princess's fault and gave orders that she should be imprisoned in Prince Curlicue's place. The Princess Cabbage Stalk was astonished at this unjust proceeding and sent many messages of remonstrance to King Grumpy. But he was in such a temper no one dared to deliver them, or to send the letters which the princess wrote to her father. However, she lived in hope of soon going back to her own country and tried to amuse herself as well as she could until the time should come. Every day she walked up and down the long gallery, until she too was fascinated by the ever-changing pictures in the windows, and recognized herself in one of the figures.

'They seem to have taken great delight in painting me since I came to this country,' she said to herself. 'One would think that I and my crutch were put in on purpose to make that slim, charming young shepherdess in the next picture look prettier by contrast. Ah, how nice it would be to be as pretty as that!'

All at once she became aware that she was not alone, for behind her stood a tiny old woman in a cap, who was as ugly as herself and quite as lame.

'Princess,' she said, 'your regrets are so piteous that I come to offer you the choice of goodness or beauty. If you wish to be pretty you shall have your way, but you will also be vain, capricious and frivolous. If you remain as you are now, you shall be wise and amiable and modest.'

'Alas, madam!' cried the princess. 'Is it impossible to be at once wise and beautiful?'

'Child,' answered the old woman, 'it is decreed that you must choose between the two. See, I have brought with me my white and yellow muff. Breathe upon the yellow side and you will become like the pretty shepherdess you so much admire, and you will have won the love of the handsome shepherd whose picture you were studying with interest. Breathe upon the white side and your looks will not alter, but you will grow better and happier day by day. Now you may choose.'

'Ah, well,' said the princess, 'I suppose one can't have everything, and it's certainly better to be good than pretty.'

And she breathed upon the white side of the muff and thanked the old fairy, who immediately disappeared. The Princess Cabbage Stalk felt very forlorn when she was gone and began to think it was quite time her father sent an army to rescue her. If I could but get up into the turret, she thought, to see if anyone is coming!

But to climb up there seemed impossible. Nevertheless she presently hit upon a plan. The great clock was in the turret, as she knew, though the weights hung down into the gallery. Taking one of them off the rope, she tied herself on in its place, and when the clock was wound, up she went triumphantly into the turret. She looked out over the country the first thing, but seeing nothing she sat down to rest a little, and accidentally leaned back against the wall which Curlicue, or rather Prince Peerless, had so hastily mended. Out fell the broken stone and with it the golden key. The clatter it made upon the floor attracted the Princess Cabbage Stalk's attention.

She picked it up and after a moment's consideration decided that it must belong to the curious old cabinet in the corner, which had no visible keyhole. And then it was not long before she had it open and was admiring the treasures it contained as much as Prince Peerless had done before her, and at last she came to the carbuncle box. No sooner had she opened it than with a shudder of horror she tried to throw it down, but some mysterious power compelled her to hold it against her will. And at this moment a voice in her ear said softly:

'Take courage, Princess; upon this adventure your future happiness depends.'

'What am I to do?' asked the princess trembling.

'Take the box,' replied the voice, 'and hide it under your pillow, and when you see an eagle, give it to him without losing a moment.'

Terrified as the princess was, she did not hesitate to obey and hastened to put back all the other precious things precisely as she had found them. For three days nothing happened, but at last the princess heard something flutter against her window, and drawing back her curtains she saw in the moonlight that it was an eagle.

Limping across at her utmost speed she threw the window open, and the great eagle sailed in, beating his wings for joy. The princess lost no time in offering it the carbuncle box, which it grasped in its talons, and instantly disappeared, leaving in its place the most beautiful prince she had ever seen, who was splendidly dressed and wore a diamond crown.

'Princess,' said he, 'for two hundred years a wicked enchanter has kept me here. We both loved the same fairy, but she preferred me. He was more powerful than I, and succeeded, when for a moment I was off my guard, in changing me into an eagle, while my queen was left in an enchanted sleep. I knew that after two hundred years a prince would recall her to the light of day and a princess, in restoring to me the hand which my enemy had cut off, would give me back my natural form. Tell me, Princess, what is it you wish for most? Shall I make you as beautiful as you deserve to be?'

'Ah, if you only would!' cried the princess, and at the same moment she heard a crick-cracking in all her bones. She grew tall and straight and pretty, with eyes like shining stars and a skin as white as milk.

'Oh, wonderful! Can this really be my poor little self?' she exclaimed, looking down in amazement at her tiny worn-out crutch.

'Indeed, Princess,' replied Florimond, 'it is yourself, but you must have a new name, since the old one does not suit you now. Be called Princess Sunbeam, for you are bright and charming enough to deserve the name.'

And so saying he disappeared, and the princess, without knowing how she came there, found herself walking under shady trees by a clear river. Of course, the first thing she did was to look at her own reflection in the water, and she was surprised to find that she was exactly like the shepherdess she had so much admired and wore the same white dress and flowery wreath that she had seen in the painted windows. To complete the resemblance, her flock of sheep appeared, grazing round her, and she found a gay crook adorned with flowers upon the bank of the river.

Quite tired out by so many new and wonderful experiences, the princess sat down to rest at the foot of a tree, and there she fell fast asleep. Now it happened that it was in this very country that Prince Peerless had been set down, and while the Princess Sunbeam was still sleeping peacefully, he came strolling along in search of a shady pasture for his sheep.

The moment he caught sight of the princess he recognized her as the charming shepherdess whose picture he had seen so often in the tower, and as she was far prettier than he had remembered her, he was delighted that chance had led him that way.

He was still watching her admiringly when the princess opened her eyes, and as she also recognized him they were soon great friends. The princess asked Prince Peerless to tell her of some peasant who would give her a lodging, and he said he knew of an old woman whose cottage would be the very place for her. So they went there together, and the princess was charmed with the old woman and everything belonging to her. Supper was soon spread under a shady tree, and she invited the prince to share the cream and brown bread the old woman provided. This he was delighted to do, and having first fetched from his own garden all the strawberries, cherries, nuts and flowers he could find, they sat down together and were very merry.

After this they met every day as they guarded their flocks and were so happy that Prince Peerless begged the princess to marry him so they might never be parted again. Now Princess

Sunbeam never forgot that she was a real princess, and she was not at all sure she ought to marry a humble shepherd, though she knew she would like to do so very much.

So she resolved to consult an enchanter of whom she had heard, and without saying a word to anybody she set out to find the castle in which he lived with his sister, a powerful fairy. The way was long and lay through a thick wood, where the princess heard strange voices calling to her from every side, but she was in such a hurry that she stopped for nothing, and at last she came to the courtyard of the enchanter's castle.

The grass and briers were growing as high as if it were a hundred years since anyone had set foot there, but the princess got through at last, with a good many scratches by the way, and then she went into a dark, gloomy hall, where there was but one tiny hole through which daylight could enter. The hangings were all of bats' wings, and from the ceiling hung twelve cats, who filled the hall with their ear-piercing yells. Upon the long table twelve mice were fastened by the tail, and just in front of each one's nose, but quite beyond its reach, lay a tempting morsel of fat bacon.

The princess was looking at the poor creatures in dismay, when the enchanter suddenly entered, wearing a long black robe and with a crocodile upon his head. In his hand he carried a whip made of twenty long snakes, all alive and writhing, and the princess was so terrified at the sight that she heartily wished she had not come. Without saying a word she ran to the door, but it was covered with a thick spider's web, and when she broke it she found another and another and another. In fact, there was no end to them; the princess's arms ached with tearing them down, and yet she was no nearer to getting out. The wicked enchanter behind her laughed maliciously. At last he said:

'You might spend the rest of your life over that without doing any good, but as you are young, and quite the prettiest creature I have seen for a long time, I will marry you if you like, and I will give you those cats and mice you see there for your own. They are princes and princesses who have happened to offend me. They used to love one another as much as they now hate one another. Aha! It's a pretty little revenge to keep them like that.'

'Oh, if you would only change me into a mouse too,' cried the princess.

'Oh, so you won't marry me?' said he. 'Little simpleton, you should have everything heart can desire.'

'No, indeed; nothing could make me marry you; in fact, I don't think I shall ever love anyone,' cried the princess.

'In that case,' said the enchanter, touching her, 'you had better become neither fish nor fowl. You shall be light and airy, and as green as the grass you live in. Off with you, Madam Grasshopper.'

And the princess, rejoicing to find herself free once more, skipped out into the garden, the prettiest little green grasshopper in the world. But as soon as she was safely out she was rather sorry for herself.

'Certainly beauty is short-lived, and this funny little face and green crepe dress are a comical end to it. I had better have married my amiable shepherd. It must be for my pride that I am condemned to be a grasshopper, and sing day and night in the grass by this brook, when I feel far more inclined to cry.'

In the meantime Prince Peerless had discovered the princess's absence, and was lamenting it by the river bank, when he suddenly became aware of the presence of a little old woman. She was quaintly dressed in a ruff and farthingale, and a velvet hood covered her snow-white hair.

'You seem sorrowful, my son,' she said. 'What is the matter?'

'Alas, mother,' answered the prince, 'I have lost my sweet shepherdess, but I am determined to find her again, though I should have to traverse the whole world in search of her.'

'Go that way, my son,' said the old woman, pointing toward the path leading to the castle. 'I have an idea you will soon overtake her.'

The prince thanked her heartily and set out. As he met with no hindrance, he soon reached the enchanted wood and there he thought he saw the Princess Sunbeam gliding before him among the trees. Prince Peerless hastened after her, but could never get any nearer. Then he called to her:

'Sunbeam, my darling—only wait for me a moment.'

But the phantom did but fly the faster, and the prince spent the whole day in this vain pursuit. When night came he saw a castle before him all lighted up and, as he imagined the princess must be in it, he made haste to get there too. He entered without difficulty, and in the hall a terrible old fairy met him. She was so thin that the light shone through her, and her eyes glowed like lamps. Her skin was like a shark's, her arms were thin as laths, and her fingers like spindles. Nevertheless she wore rouge and patches, a mantle of silver brocade and a crown of diamonds, and her dress was covered with jewels and green and pink ribbons.

'At last you have come to see me, Prince,' said she. 'Don't waste another thought upon that little shepherdess, who is unworthy of your notice. I am the Queen of the Comets, and can bring you to great honour if you will marry me.'

'Marry you, madam,' cried the prince, in horror. 'No, I will never consent to that.'

Thereupon the fairy, in a rage, gave two strokes of her wand and filled the gallery with horrible goblins, against whom the prince had to fight for his life. Though he had only his dagger, he defended himself so well that he escaped without any harm, and presently the old fairy stopped the fray and asked the prince if he was still of the same mind. When he answered firmly that he was, she called up the appearance of the Princess Sunbeam to the other end of the gallery, and said:

'You see your beloved there? Take care what you are about, for if you again refuse to marry me she shall be torn in pieces by two tigers.'

The prince was distracted, for he fancied he heard his dear shepherdess weeping and begging him to save her. In despair he cried:

'Oh, Fairy Douceline, have you abandoned me after so many promises of friendship? Help! Help us now!'

Immediately a soft voice said in his ear, 'Be firm, happen what may, and seek the Golden Branch.'

Thus encouraged, the prince was firm in his refusal, and at length the old fairy in a fury cried, 'Get out of my sight, obstinate Prince. Become a cricket!'

And instantly the handsome Prince Peerless became a little black cricket, who luckily remembered the injunction to seek the Golden Branch. So he hastened to leave the fatal castle, and sought shelter in a hollow tree, where he found a forlorn-looking little grasshopper crouching in a corner, too miserable to sing.

Without in the least expecting an answer, the prince asked it, 'And where may you be going, Gammer Grasshopper?'

'Where are you going yourself, Gaffer Cricket?' replied the grasshopper.

'What! Can you speak?' said he.

'Why should I not speak as well as you? Isn't a grasshopper as good as a cricket?' said she.

'I can talk because I was a prince,' said the cricket.

'And for that very same reason I ought to be able to talk more than you, for I was a princess,' replied the grasshopper.

'Then you have met with the same fate I have,' said he. 'But where are you going now? Cannot we journey together?'

'I seemed to hear a voice in the air which said, "Be firm, happen what may, and seek the Golden Branch,"' answered the grasshopper, 'and I thought the command must be for me, so I started at once, though I don't know the way.'

At this moment they were interrupted by two mice who, breathless from running, flung themselves headlong through the hole into the tree, nearly crushing the grasshopper and the cricket, though they got out of the way as fast as they could.

'Ah, madam,' said the fatter of the two, 'I have such a pain in my side from running so fast. How does Your Highness find yourself?'

'I have pulled my tail off,' replied the younger mouse, 'but as I should still be on the sorcerer's table unless I had, I do not regret it. Are we pursued, think you? How lucky we were to escape!'

'I only trust that we may escape cats and traps, and reach the Golden Branch soon,' said the fat mouse.

'You know the way then?' said the other.

'Oh, dear, yes! As well as the way to my own house, madam. This Golden Branch is indeed a marvel, a single leaf from it makes one rich forever. It breaks enchantments, and makes all who approach it young and beautiful. We must set out for it at the break of day.'

'May we have the honour of travelling with you—this respectable cricket and myself?' said the grasshopper, stepping forward. 'We also are on a pilgrimage to the Golden Branch.'

The mice courteously assented, and after many polite speeches the whole party fell asleep. With the earliest dawn they were on their way, and though the mice were in constant fear of being overtaken or trapped, they reached the Golden Branch in safety.

It grew in the midst of a wonderful garden, all the paths of which were strewn with pearls as big as peas. The roses were crimson diamonds, with emerald leaves. The pomegranates were garnets, the marigolds topazes, the daffodils yellow diamonds, the violets sapphires, the cornflowers turquoises, the tulips amethysts, opals and diamonds, so that the garden borders blazed like the sun. The Golden Branch itself had become as tall as a forest tree and sparkled with ruby cherries to its topmost twig. No sooner had the grasshopper and the cricket touched it than they were restored to their natural forms, and their surprise and joy were great when they recognized each other. At this moment Florimond and the Fairy Douceline appeared in great splendour, and the fairy, as she descended from her chariot, said with a smile:

'So you two have found one another, I see, but I have still a surprise left for you. Don't hesitate, Princess, to tell your devoted shepherd how dearly you love him, as he is the very prince your father sent you to marry. Come here, both of you, and let me crown you, and we will have the wedding at once.'

The prince and princess thanked her with all their hearts and declared that to her they owed all their happiness, and then the two princesses, who had so lately been mice, came and begged the fairy to use her power to release their unhappy friends who were still under the enchanter's spell.

'Really,' said the Fairy Douceline, 'on this happy occasion I cannot find it in my heart to refuse you anything.'

And she gave three strokes of her wand upon the Golden Branch, and immediately all the prisoners in the enchanter's castle found themselves free and came with all speed to the wonderful garden, where one touch of the Golden Branch restored each one to his natural form, and they greeted one another with many rejoicings.

To complete her generous work the fairy presented them with the wonderful cabinet and all the treasures it contained, which were worth at least ten kingdoms. But to Prince Peerless and Princess Sunbeam she gave the palace and garden of the Golden Branch where, immensely rich and greatly beloved by all their subjects, they lived happily ever after.

[*Le Rameau d'Or,* par Madame d'Aulnoy.]

The Three Dwarfs

T HERE WAS ONCE UPON
a time a man who lost his wife, and a woman who lost her
husband; and the man had a daughter and so had the woman.
The two girls were great friends and used often to play
together. One day the woman turned to the man's daughter
and said:

'Go and tell your father that I will marry him, and then you
shall wash in milk and drink wine, but my own daughter shall
wash in water and drink it too.'

The girl went straight home and told her father what the
woman had said.

'What am I to do?' he answered. 'Marriage is either a success
or it is a failure.'

At last, being of an undecided character and not able to
make up his mind, he took off his boot and, handing it to
his daughter, said:

'Take this boot which has a hole in the sole, hang it up on
a nail in the hayloft, and pour water into it. If it holds water
I will marry again, but if it doesn't I won't.'

The girl did as she was told, but the water drew the hole
together and the boot filled up to the very top. So she told her

father the result. He went to see for himself, and when he saw that it was true and no mistake, he accepted his fate, proposed to the widow, and they were married at once.

On the morning after the wedding, when the two girls awoke, milk was standing for the man's daughter to wash in and wine for her to drink; but for the woman's daughter, only water to wash in and only water to drink. On the second morning, water to wash in and water to drink was standing for the man's daughter as well. And on the third morning, water to wash in and water to drink was standing for the man's daughter, and milk to wash in and wine to drink for the woman's daughter; and so it continued ever after.

The woman hated her stepdaughter from the bottom of her heart because the girl was so beautiful and charming, while her own daughter was both ugly and repulsive.

One winter's day when there was a hard frost, and mountain and valley were covered with snow, the woman made a dress of paper, and calling the girl to her said:

'There, put on this dress and go out into the wood and fetch me a basket of strawberries!'

'Now Heaven help us,' replied her stepdaughter; 'strawberries don't grow in winter. The earth is frozen and the snow has covered up everything. And why send me in a paper dress? It is so cold outside one's very breath freezes; the wind will whistle through my dress, and the brambles tear it from my body.'

'How dare you contradict me!' said her stepmother. 'Be off with you at once, and don't show your face again till you have filled the basket with strawberries.'

Then she gave her a hard crust of bread, saying, 'That will be enough for you today.' And she thought, the girl will certainly perish and I shan't be bothered with her any more.

The girl was so obedient that she put on the paper dress and set out with her little basket. There was nothing but snow far and near, not a green blade of grass to be seen anywhere. When she came to the wood she saw a little house, and out of it peeped three dwarfs. She wished them good day, and knocked modestly at the door. They called to her to enter, so she stepped in and sat down on a seat by the fire, wishing to warm herself and eat her crust. The dwarfs said at once:

'Give us some of your food!'

'Gladly,' she said, and breaking her crust in two, she gave them the half. Then they asked why she wore a paper dress in the depths of winter.

'Oh,' she answered, 'I have been sent to get a basketful of strawberries and daren't show my face again at home till I bring them with me.'

When she had finished her bread they gave her a broom

and told her to sweep away the snow from the back door. As soon as she left the room, the three little men considered what reward to give her for being so sweet and good and for sharing her last crust with them.

The first said, 'Every day she shall grow prettier.'

The second said, 'Every time she opens her mouth a piece of gold shall fall out.'

And the third said, 'A king shall come and marry her.'

The girl in the meantime was sweeping the snow away from the back door, and what do you think she found there? Heaps of fine ripe strawberries that showed dark red against the white snow! She joyfully picked enough to fill her basket, thanked the little men for their kindness, shook hands with them and ran home to her stepmother with the strawberries. When she walked in and said, 'Good evening,' a piece of gold fell out of her mouth. Then she told what had happened to her in the wood, and at every word pieces of gold dropped from her mouth, and the room was soon covered with them.

'She surely has more money than wit to throw gold about like that,' said her stepsister, but in her secret heart she determined that she too would go to the wood and look for strawberries. But her mother refused to let her go, saying:

'My dear child, it is far too cold; you might freeze to death.'

The girl, however, left her mother no peace, so at last she gave in, but she insisted on her putting on a beautiful fur cloak, and she gave her bread and butter and cakes to eat on the way.

The girl went straight to the little house in the wood, and as before the three little men were looking out of the window. She took no notice of them, and without as much as 'By your leave,' she flounced into the room, sat herself down at the fire, and began to eat her bread and butter and cakes.

'Give us some,' cried the dwarfs.

18

But she answered, 'No, I won't, it is hardly enough for myself; so catch me giving you any.'

When she had finished eating they said, 'There's a broom for you, go and clear up our back door.'

'Do it yourselves. I'm not your servant,' she answered rudely.

When they did not give her anything, she left the house in no amiable frame of mind. Then the three little men consulted together. What should they do to her, since she was so bad and had such an evil, covetous heart that she grudged everybody good fortune?

The first said, 'She shall grow uglier every day.'

The second said, 'Every time she speaks a toad shall jump out of her mouth.'

And the third said, 'She shall die a most miserable death.'

The girl searched for strawberries, but she found none and returned home in a very bad temper. When she opened her mouth to tell her mother what had befallen her in the wood, a toad jumped out, and everyone was disgusted with her.

Then the stepmother did nothing but plot mischief against the man's daughter who was daily growing more and more beautiful. At last, one day the wicked woman took a large pot, put it on the fire and boiled some yarn in it. When it was well scalded she hung it round the poor girl's shoulder and, giving her an axe, bade her break a hole in the frozen river and rinse the yarn in it. Her stepdaughter obeyed as usual and broke a hole in the ice. She was in the act of wringing out the yarn when a magnificent carriage passed, and the king sat inside. The carriage stood still, and the king asked her:

'My child, who are you, and what in the world are you doing here?'

'I am only a poor girl,' she answered, 'and am rinsing my yarn in the river.'

Then the king was sorry for her and, when he saw how beautiful she was, he said, 'Will you come away with me?'

'Most gladly,' she replied, for she knew how willingly she would leave her stepmother and sister, and how gladly they would be rid of her.

So she stepped into the carriage and drove away with the king, and when they reached his palace the wedding was celebrated with much splendour. So all turned out just as the three little dwarfs had said.

After a year the queen had a little son. When her stepmother heard of her good fortune she came to the palace with her daughter and took up her abode there. Now one day, when the king was out and nobody else near, the wicked woman took the queen by her head, and the daughter took her by the heels, and they dragged her from her bed and flung her out of the window into the stream which flowed beneath it. Then the stepmother laid her ugly daughter in the queen's place. When the king came home and wished to speak to his wife the woman called out:

'Quietly, quietly! This will never do. Your wife is very ill, you must let her rest all today.'

The king suspected no evil and didn't come again till next morning. When he spoke to his wife and she answered him, instead of the usual piece of gold a toad jumped out of her mouth. Then he asked what it meant, and the old woman told him it was nothing but weakness, and that she would soon be all right again.

But that same evening the scullion noticed a duck swimming in the stream, saying as it passed:

'What does the king, I pray you tell,
Is he awake or sleeps he well?'

and receiving no reply, it continued:

> *'And all my guests, are they asleep?'*

and the scullion answered:

> *'Yes, one and all they slumber deep.'*

Then the duck went on:

> *'And what about my baby dear?'*

and he answered:

> *'Oh, it sleeps soundly, never fear.'*

Then the duck assumed the queen's shape, went up to the child's room, tucked him up comfortably in his cradle, and then swam back down the stream again, in the likeness of a duck. This was repeated for two nights, and on the third the duck said to the scullion:

'Go and tell the king to swing his sword three times over me on the threshold.'

The scullion did as she bade him, and the king came with his sword and swung it three times over the duck, and lo and behold! His wife stood before him once more, alive, and as blooming as ever.

The king rejoiced greatly, but he kept the queen in hiding till the Sunday on which the child was to be christened. After the christening he said:

'What punishment does that person deserve who drags another out of bed and throws him into the water?'

Then the wicked old stepmother answered, 'No better fate than to be put into a barrel lined with sharp nails and to be rolled in it down the hill into the water.'

'You have pronounced your own doom,' said the king.

[Jakob and Wilhelm Grimm.]

The Enchanted Canary

Once upon a time
in the reign of King Cambrinus, there lived at Avesnes one of
his lords, who was the finest man—by which is meant the
fattest—in the whole country of Flanders. He ate four meals a
day, slept twelve hours out of the twenty-four, and the only
thing he ever did was to shoot at small birds with his bow
and arrow.

Still, with all his practice he shot very badly, he was so fat
and heavy. And as he grew daily fatter, he was at last obliged
to give up walking, and had to be dragged about in a wheel-
chair. The people made fun of him and gave him the name of
my Lord Tubby.

Now, the only trouble that Lord Tubby had was with his
son, whom he loved very much, although they were not in
the least alike, for the young prince was as thin as a cuckoo.
And what vexed him more than all was, that though the young
ladies throughout all his lands did their best to make the prince
fall in love with them, he would have nothing to say to any of
them, and told his father he did not wish to marry.

Instead of chatting with them in the dusk, he wandered
about the woods, whispering to the moon. No wonder the

young ladies thought him very odd, but they liked him all the better for that; and as he had received at his birth the name of Désiré, they all called him Amour Désiré.

'What is the matter with you?' his father often said to him. 'You have everything you can possibly wish for: a good bed, good food, and tuns of good mead. The only thing you lack in order to become as fat as a pig, is a wife who can bring you broad, rich lands. So marry, and you will be perfectly happy.'

'I ask nothing better than to marry,' replied Désiré, 'but I have never seen a woman who pleases me. All the girls here are pink and white, and I am tired to death of their eternal lilies and roses.'

'My faith!' cried Tubby.

'Father, there must be women somewhere in the world who are neither pink nor white, and I tell you, once for all, that I will never marry until I have found one exactly to my taste.'

Some time afterward, the prior of the Abbey of Saint Amand sent to the Lord of Avesnes a basket of oranges, with a beautifully written letter saying that these golden fruit, then unknown in Flanders, came straight from a land where the sun always shone.

That evening Tubby and his son ate the golden oranges at supper and thought them delicious.

Next morning as the day dawned, Désiré went down to the stable and saddled his pretty white horse. Then he went, all dressed for a journey, to the bedside of Tubby, and found him smoking his first pipe.

'Father,' he said gravely, 'I have come to bid you farewell. Last night I dreamed that I was walking in a wood, where the trees were covered with golden oranges. I gathered one of them, and when I opened it out came a lovely princess with a golden skin. That is the wife I want, and I am going to look for her.'

The Lord of Avesnes was so much astonished that he let his pipe fall to the ground. Then he became so diverted at the notion of his son marrying a woman inside an orange that he burst into fits of laughter.

Désiré waited to bid him good-bye until he was quiet again; but as his father went on laughing and showed no signs of stopping, the young man took his hand, kissed it tenderly, opened the door, and in the twinkling of an eye was at the bottom of the staircase. He jumped lightly on his horse and was a mile from home before Tubby had ceased laughing.

'A golden wife! He must be mad! Fit for a straight-waistcoat!' cried the good man, when he was able to speak. 'Here! Quick! Bring him back to me.'

The servants mounted their horses and rode after the prince; but they went all ways except the right one and, instead of bringing him back, they returned themselves when it grew dark, their horses worn out and covered with dust.

When Désiré thought they could no longer catch him, he pulled his horse into a walk, like a prudent man who knows he has far to go. He travelled in this way for many weeks, passing by villages, towns, mountains, valleys and plains, but always pushing south, where every day the sun seemed hotter and more brilliant.

At last, one day at sunset, Désiré felt the sun so warm that he thought he must now be near the place of his dream. He was at that moment close to the corner of a wood where stood a little hut, before the door of which his horse stopped of its own accord. An old man with a white beard was sitting on the doorstep enjoying the fresh air. The prince got down from his horse and asked leave to rest.

'Come in, my young friend,' said the old man; 'my house is not large, but it is big enough to hold a stranger.'

The traveller entered, and his host put before him a simple meal. When his hunger was satisfied the old man said to him:

'If I do not mistake, you come from far. May I ask where you are going?'

'I will tell you,' answered Désiré, 'though most likely you will laugh at me. I dreamed that in the land of the sun there was a wood full of orange trees, and that in one of the oranges I should find a beautiful princess who is to be my wife. It is she I am seeking.'

'Why should I laugh?' asked the old man. 'Madness in youth is true wisdom. Go, young man, follow your dream, and if you do not find the happiness you seek, at any rate you will have had the happiness of seeking it.'

The next day the prince arose early and took leave of his host.

'The wood you saw in your dream is not far from here,' said the old man. 'It is in the depths of the forest, and this road will lead you there. You will come to a vast park surrounded by high walls. In the middle of the park is a castle, where dwells a horrible witch who allows no living being to enter the doors. Behind the castle is the orange grove. Follow the wall till you come to a heavy iron gate. Don't try to press it open, but oil the hinges with this.' And the old man gave him a small bottle.

'The gate will open of itself,' he continued, 'and a huge dog which guards the castle will come to you with his mouth wide open, but just throw him this oat cake. Next, you will see a woman leaning over her heated oven. Give her this brush. Lastly, you will find a well on your left; do not forget to take the cord of the bucket and spread it in the sun. When you have done this, do not enter the castle, but go round it and enter the orange grove. Then gather three oranges and get back to the gate as fast as you can. Once out of the gate, leave the forest by the opposite side.

'Now, attend to this: whatever happens, do not open your oranges till you reach the bank of a river or a fountain. Out of each orange will come a princess, and you can choose which you like for your wife. Your choice once made, be very careful never to leave your bride for an instant. And remember that the danger which is most to be feared is never the danger we are most afraid of.'

Désiré thanked his host warmly, and took the road he pointed out. In less than an hour he arrived at the wall, which was very high indeed. He sprang to the ground, fastened his horse to a tree and soon found the iron gate. Then he took out his bottle and oiled the hinges, when the gate opened of itself, and he saw an old castle standing inside. The prince entered boldly into the courtyard.

Suddenly he heard fierce howls, and a dog as tall as a donkey, with eyes like billiard balls, came toward him, showing his teeth, which were like the prongs of a fork. Désiré flung him the oat cake, which the great dog instantly snapped up, and the young prince passed quietly on.

A few yards farther he saw a huge oven, with a wide, red-hot gaping mouth. A woman as tall as a giant was leaning over the oven. Désiré gave her the brush, which she took in silence.

Then he went on to the well, drew up the cord, which was half-rotten, and stretched it out in the sun.

Lastly he went round the castle, and plunged into the orange grove. There he gathered the three most beautiful oranges he could find and turned to go back to the gate.

But just at this moment the sun was darkened, the earth trembled, and Désiré heard a voice crying:

'Baker, baker, take him by his feet and throw him into the oven!'

'No,' replied the baker. 'A long time has passed since I first began to scour this oven with my own flesh. You never cared to give me a brush; but he has given me one, and he shall go in peace.'

'Rope, O rope!' cried the voice again, 'twine yourself round his neck and strangle him.'

'No,' replied the rope. 'You have left me for many years past to fall to pieces with the damp. He has stretched me out in the sun. Let him go in peace.'

'Dog, my good dog,' cried the voice, more and more angry, 'jump at his throat and eat him up.'

'No,' replied the dog. 'Though I have served you long, you

never gave me any bread. He has given me as much as I want. Let him go in peace.'

'Iron gate, iron gate,' cried the voice, growling like thunder, 'fall on him and grind him to powder.'

'No,' replied the gate. 'It is a hundred years since you left me to rust, and he has oiled me. Let him go in peace.'

Once outside, the young adventurer put his oranges into a bag that hung from his saddle, mounted his horse and rode quickly out of the forest.

Now he was longing to see the princesses, and he was very anxious to come to a river or a fountain, but, though he rode for hours, a river or fountain was nowhere to be seen. Still his heart was light, for he felt that he had come through the most difficult part of his task, and the rest was easy.

About midday he reached a sandy plain, scorching in the sun. Here he was seized with dreadful thirst; he took his gourd and raised it to his lips.

But the gourd was empty; in the excitement of his joy he had forgotten to fill it. He rode on, struggling with his sufferings, but at last he could bear it no longer.

He let himself slide to the earth and lay down beside his horse, his throat burning, his chest heaving, and his head going round. Already he felt that death was near him, when his eyes fell on the bag where the oranges peeped out.

Poor Désiré, who had braved so many dangers to win the lady of his dreams, would have given at this moment all the princesses in the world, were they pink or golden, for a single drop of water.

'Ah,' he said to himself, 'if only these oranges were real fruit—fruit as refreshing as what I ate in Flanders! And, after all, who knows?'

This idea put some life into him. He had the strength to

lift himself up and put his hand into his bag. He drew out an orange and opened it with his knife.

Out of it flew the prettiest little canary that ever was seen.

'Give me something to drink, I am dying of thirst,' said the golden bird.

'Wait a minute,' replied Désiré, so much astonished that he forgot his own sufferings; and to satisfy the bird he took a second orange and opened it without thinking what he was doing. Out of it flew another canary, and she too began to cry:

'I am dying of thirst; give me something to drink.'

Then Tubby's son saw his folly, and while the two canaries flew away he sank on the ground where, exhausted by his last effort, he lay unconscious.

When he came to himself, he had a pleasant feeling of freshness all about him. It was night, the sky was sparkling with stars, and the earth was covered with a heavy dew.

The traveller, having recovered, mounted his horse, and at the first streak of dawn he saw a stream dancing in front of him and stooped down and drank his fill.

He hardly had courage to open his last orange. Then he remembered that the night before he had disobeyed the orders of the old man. Perhaps his terrible thirst was a trick of the cunning witch, and suppose, even though he opened the orange on the banks of the stream, that he did not find in it the princess he sought?

He took his knife and cut it open. Alas! Out of it flew a little canary, just like the others, who cried:

'I am thirsty; give me something to drink.'

Great was the disappointment of Désiré. However, he was determined not to let this bird fly away; so he took up some water in the palm of his hand and held it to its beak.

Scarcely had the canary drunk when she became a beautiful

girl, tall and straight as a poplar tree, with black eyes and a golden skin. Désiré had never seen anyone half so lovely, and he stood gazing at her in delight.

On her side she seemed quite bewildered, but she looked about her with happy eyes and was not at all afraid of her deliverer.

He asked her name. She answered that she was called the Princess Zizi; she was about sixteen years old, and for ten years of that time the witch had kept her shut up in an orange, in the shape of a canary.

'Well, then, my charming Zizi,' said the young prince, who was longing to marry her, 'let us ride away quickly so as to escape from the wicked witch.'

He mounted his horse and took her in front of him, and holding her carefully in his arms, they began their journey.

Everything the princess saw was new to her, and in passing through mountains, valleys and towns, she asked a thousand questions. Désiré was charmed to answer them. It is so delightful to teach those one loves!

Once she inquired what the girls in his country were like.

'They are pink and white,' he replied, 'and their eyes are blue.'

'Do you like blue eyes?' said the princess; but Désiré thought it was a good opportunity to find out what was in her heart, so he did not answer.

'And no doubt,' went on the princess, 'one of them is your intended bride?'

Still he was silent, and Zizi drew herself up proudly.

'No,' he said at last. 'None of the girls of my own country are beautiful in my eyes, and that is why I came to look for a wife in the land of the sun. Was I wrong, my lovely Zizi?'

This time it was Zizi's turn to be silent.

When they were about four stone-throws from the gates of the castle they dismounted in the forest, by the edge of a fountain.

'My dear Zizi,' said Tubby's son, 'we cannot present ourselves before my father like two common people who have come back from a walk. We must enter the castle with more ceremony. Wait for me here, and in an hour I will return with carriages and horses fit for a princess.'

'Don't be long,' replied Zizi, and she watched him go with wistful eyes.

Suddenly she heard a noise among the trees. Fearing lest it should be a wolf, she hid herself in the hollow trunk of a willow tree which hung over the fountain. It was big enough to hold her altogether, but she peeped out, and her pretty head was reflected in the clear water.

Then there appeared, not a wolf, but a creature quite as wicked and quite as ugly.

Not far from the fountain there lived a family of bricklayers. Now, fifteen years before this time, the father in walking through the forest had found a little girl, who had been deserted by the gypsies. He carried her home to his wife, and the good woman was sorry for her and brought her up with her own sons. As she grew older, the little girl became much more remarkable for strength and cunning than for sense or beauty. She had a low forehead, a flat nose, thick lips, coarse hair and a skin not golden like Zizi's, but the colour of clay.

As she was always being teased, she grew as noisy and cross as a titmouse. So they used to call her Titty.

Titty was often sent to fetch water from the fountain, and as she was very proud and lazy she disliked this very much. It was she who had frightened Zizi by appearing with her pitcher on her shoulder. Just as she was stooping to fill her pitcher, she saw reflected in the water the lovely image of the princess.

'What a pretty face!' she exclaimed, 'Why, it must be mine! How in the world can they call me ugly? I am certainly much too pretty to be their water carrier!'

So saying, she broke her pitcher and went home.

'Where is your pitcher?' asked her father.

'Well, what do you expect? The pitcher may go many times to the well—'

'But at last it is broken. Well, here is a bucket that will not break."

Titty returned to the fountain, and addressing once more the image of Zizi, she said, 'No; I don't mean to be a beast of burden any longer.' And she flung the bucket so high in the air that it stuck in the branches of an oak.

'I met a wolf,' she told her father, 'and I broke the bucket across his nose.'

He asked her no more questions, but took down a broom and gave her such a beating that her pride was humbled a little. Then he handed her an old copper milk can, and said:

'If you don't bring it back full, your bones shall suffer for it.'

Titty went off rubbing her sides; but this time she did not dare to disobey, and in a very bad temper stooped down over the well. It was not at all easy to fill the milk can, which was large and round. It would not go down into the well, and she had to try again and again.

At last her arms grew so tired that when she did manage to get the can properly under the water she had no strength to pull it up, and it rolled to the bottom.

On seeing the can disappear, she made such a miserable face that Zizi, who had been watching her all this time, burst into fits of laughter. Titty perceived the mistake she had made and made up her mind to be revenged at once.

'What are you doing there, you lovely creature?' she said to Zizi.

'I am waiting for my prince,' Zizi replied. And then, with a simplicity natural in a girl so lately a canary, she told all her story.

Titty had often seen the young prince pass by, when he was going hunting. He never had noticed her, but Titty on her side had admired him, though she thought he might well have been a little fatter.

'Dear, dear!' she said to herself. 'So he likes yellow women! Why, I am yellow too, and if I could only think of a way—'

It was not long before she did think of it.

'What,' cried the sly Titty, 'they are coming with great pomp to fetch you! Would you show yourself to so many fine lords and ladies with your hair down like that? Get down at once, my poor child, and let me dress your hair for you!'

The innocent Zizi came down at once, and stood by Titty, who began to comb her long brown locks. Suddenly she drew a pin from her stays, and just as the titmouse digs its beak into the heads of linnets and larks, Titty dug the pin into the head of Zizi.

No sooner did Zizi feel the prick of the pin than she became a bird again and, spreading her wings, she flew away.

'That was neatly done. The prince will be clever if he finds his bride.' And, arranging her dress, Titty seated herself on the grass to await Désiré.

Meanwhile the prince was coming as fast as his horse could carry him. He was so impatient that he was always full fifty yards in front of the lords and ladies sent by Tubby to bring back Zizi.

19

At the sight of the hideous girl he was struck dumb with surprise and horror.

'Ah me,' said Titty, 'so you don't know your poor Zizi? While you were away the wicked witch came and turned me into this. But if you only have the courage to marry me I shall get back my beauty.' And she began to cry bitterly.

Now the good-natured Désiré was as soft-hearted as he was brave. 'Poor girl,' he said to himself. 'It is not her fault, after all, that she has grown so ugly, it is mine. Oh! Why did I not follow the old man's advice? Why did I leave her alone? Besides, it depends on me to break the spell, and I love her too much to let her remain like this.'

So he presented her to the lords and ladies of the court, explaining to them the terrible misfortune which had befallen his beautiful bride.

They all pretended to believe it, and the ladies at once put on the false princess the rich dresses they had brought for Zizi. She was then perched on the top of a magnificent ambling palfrey, and they set forth to the castle. But unluckily the rich dress and jewels only made Titty look uglier still, and Désiré could not help feeling hot and uncomfortable when he made his entry with her into the city.

Bells were pealing, chimes ringing, and the people filling the streets and standing at their doors to watch the procession go by, and they could hardly believe their eyes as they saw what a strange bride their prince had chosen.

In order to do her more honour, Tubby came to meet her at the foot of the great marble staircase. At the sight of the hideous creature he almost fell backward.

'What!' he cried. 'Is this the wonderful beauty?'

'Yes, Father,' replied Désiré with a sheepish look. 'But she

'What,' he cried, 'is this the wonderful beauty?'

has been bewitched by a wicked sorceress, and will not regain her beauty until she is my wife.'

'Does she say so? Well, if you believe that, you may drink cold water and think it bacon,' the unhappy Tubby answered crossly.

But all the same, as he adored his son, he gave Titty his hand and led her to the great hall, where the bridal feast was spread. The feast was excellent, but Désiré hardly touched anything. However, to make up, the other guests ate greedily and, as for Tubby, nothing ever took away his appetite.

When the moment arrived to serve the roast goose, there was a pause, and Tubby took the opportunity to lay down his knife and fork for a little. But as the goose gave no sign of appearing, he sent his head carver to find out what was the matter in the kitchen.

Now this was what had happened. While the goose was turning on the spit, a beautiful little canary hopped on to the sill of the open window.

'Good morning, my fine cook,' she said in a silvery voice to the man who was watching the roast.

'Good morning, lovely golden bird,' replied the chief of the scullions, who had been well brought up.

'I pray that Heaven may send you to sleep,' said the golden bird, 'and that the goose may burn, so there may be none left for Titty.'

And instantly the chief of the scullions fell fast asleep, and the goose was burned to a cinder.

When he awoke he was horrified and gave orders to pluck another goose, to stuff it with chestnuts and put it on the spit. While it was browning at the fire, Tubby inquired for his goose a second time. The master cook himself mounted to the hall to make his excuses and to beg his lord to have a little patience. Tubby showed his impatience by abusing his son.

'As if it wasn't enough,' he grumbled between his teeth, 'that the boy should pick up a hag without a penny, but the goose must go and burn now. It isn't a wife he has brought me, it is Famine herself.'

While the master cook was upstairs, the golden bird came again to perch on the window sill, and called in her clear voice to the scullion, who was watching the spit:

'Good morning, my fine scullion!'

'Good morning, lovely golden bird,' replied the scullion, whom the master cook had forgotten in his excitement to warn.

'I pray Heaven,' went on the canary, 'that it will send you to sleep, and that the goose may burn, so that there may be none left for Titty.'

And the scullion fell fast asleep, and when the master cook came back he found the goose as black as the chimney. In a fury he woke the scullion, who in order to save himself from blame told the whole story.

'That accursed bird,' said the cook; 'it will end by getting me sent away. Come, some of you, and hide yourselves, and if it comes again, catch it and wring its neck.'

He spitted a third goose, lit a huge fire, and seated himself by it. The bird appeared a third time, and said:

'Good morning, my fine cook.'

'Good morning, lovely golden bird,' replied the cook, as if nothing had happened, and at the moment that the canary was beginning, 'I pray Heaven that it may send,' a scullion who was hidden outside rushed out and shut the shutters.

The bird flew into the kitchen. Then all the cooks and scullions sprang after it, knocking at it with their aprons. At length one of them caught it just at the very moment that

Tubby entered the kitchen, waving his sceptre. He had come to see for himself why the goose had never made its appearance. The scullion stopped at once, just as he was about to wring the canary's neck.

'Will some one be kind enough to tell me the meaning of all this?' cried the Lord of Avesnes.

'Your Excellency, it is the bird,' replied the scullion, and he placed it in his hand.

'Nonsense! What a lovely bird!' said Tubby, and in stroking its head he touched a pin that was sticking between its feathers. He pulled it out, and lo! The canary at once became a beautiful girl with a golden skin who jumped lightly to the ground.

'Gracious! What a pretty girl!' said Tubby.

'Father! It is Zizi!' exclaimed Désiré, who entered at this moment.

And he took her in his arms, crying, 'My darling Zizi, how happy I am to see you once more!'

'Well, and the other one?' asked Tubby.

The other one was stealing quietly to the door.

'Stop her!' called Tubby. 'We will judge her cause at once.' And he seated himself solemnly on the oven, and condemned Titty to be burned alive. After which the lords and cooks formed themselves in lines, and Tubby betrothed Désiré to Zizi.

The marriage took place a few days later. All the boys in the countryside were there, armed with wooden swords and decorated with epaulets made of gilt paper. And Zizi obtained Titty's pardon and she was sent back to her home.

On the evening of the wedding day all the larders, cellars, cupboards and tables of the people, whether rich or poor, were loaded as if by enchantment with bread, wine, beer, cakes and tarts, roast larks, and even geese, so Tubby could not complain any more that his son had married Famine.

Since that time there has always been plenty to eat in that country, and since that time, too, you see in the midst of the fair-haired blue-eyed women of Flanders a few beautiful girls, whose eyes are black and whose skins are the colour of gold. They are the descendants of Zizi.

[*Contes du Roi Gambrinus,* par Charles Deulin.]

The Twelve Brothers

THERE WAS ONCE UPON a time a king and a queen who lived happily together, and they had twelve children, all of whom were boys. One day the king said to his wife, 'If our thirteenth child is a girl, all her twelve brothers must die, so that she may be very rich and the kingdom hers alone.'

Then he ordered twelve coffins to be made, and he filled them with shavings and placed a little pillow in each. These he put away in an empty room and, giving the key to his wife, he bade her tell no one of it.

The queen grieved and refused to be comforted; so much so that the youngest boy, Benjamin, who was always with her said to her one day:

'Dear Mother, why are you so sad?'

'My child,' she answered, 'I may not tell you the reason.'

But he left her no peace, till she unlocked the room and showed him the twelve coffins filled with shavings, and with the little pillow laid in each. Then she said:

'My dearest Benjamin, your father has ordered that if I bring a girl into the world you are all to be buried in them.' She wept bitterly as she spoke, but her son comforted her and said:

'Don't cry, dear Mother. We'll manage to escape somehow and will fly for our lives.'

'Yes,' replied the queen, 'that is what you must do. Go with your eleven brothers out into the wood, and let one of you always sit on the highest tree you can find, keeping watch on the tower of the castle. If I have another little son I will wave a white flag, and then you may safely return. But if I have a little daughter I will wave a red flag, which will warn you to fly away as quickly as you can, and may the kind Heaven have pity on you. Every night I will get up and pray for you, in winter that you may always have a fire to warm yourselves by, and in summer that you may not languish in the heat.'

Then she blessed her sons and they set out into the wood. They found a very high oak tree, and there they sat, turn about, keeping their eyes always fixed on the castle tower. On the twelfth day, Benjamin noticed a flag waving in the air, but alas! It was not white, but blood red! When the brothers heard this they were very angry and said:

'Shall we forsooth suffer death for the sake of a girl? Let us swear vengeance, and vow that wherever and whenever we shall meet a girl, she shall die at our hands.'

Then they went their way deeper into the wood, and where it was thickest and darkest, they came upon a little enchanted house which stood empty.

'Here,' they said, 'let us take up our abode, and you, Benjamin, you shall stay at home and keep house for us. We others will go out and fetch food.'

So they went forth into the wood, and shot hares and roe deer, birds and wood pigeons, and any other game they came across. They always brought their spoils home to Benjamin, who soon learned to make them into dainty dishes. So they lived for ten years in this little house, and the time slipped merrily away.

In the meantime their little sister at home was growing up quickly. She was kind-hearted and of a fair countenance, and she had a gold star right in the middle of her forehead. One day a big washing was going on at the palace, and the girl, looking down from her window, saw twelve men's shirts hanging up to dry, and asked her mother:

'Who in the world do these shirts belong to? Surely they are far too small for my father?'

And the queen answered sadly, 'Dear child, they belong to your twelve brothers.'

'But where are my twelve brothers?' said the girl. 'I have never even heard of them.'

'Heaven alone knows in what part of the wide world they are wandering,' replied her mother. Then she proceeded to tell her all that had happened, and when she had finished her daughter said:

'Do not cry, dearest Mother. I will go and seek my brothers till I find them.'

So she took the twelve shirts and went on straight into the middle of the big wood. She walked all day long, and came in the evening to the little enchanted house. She stepped in and found a youth who, marvelling at her beauty, at the royal robes she wore and the golden star on her forehead, asked her where she came from and whither she was going.

'I am a princess,' she answered, 'and am seeking for my twelve brothers. I mean to wander as far as the blue sky stretches over the earth till I find them.'

Then she showed him the twelve shirts which she had taken with her, and Benjamin saw that it must be his sister, and said:

'I am Benjamin, your youngest brother.'

So they wept for joy, and kissed and embraced each other again and again. After a time Benjamin said:

'Dear sister, there is still a little difficulty, for we had all agreed that any girl we met should die at our hands, because it was for the sake of a girl that we had to leave our kingdom.'

'But,' she replied, 'I will gladly die if by that means I can restore my twelve brothers to their own.'

'No,' he answered, 'there is no need for that. Only go and hide under that tub till our eleven brothers come in, and I'll soon make matters right with them.'

She did as she was bid, and soon the others came home from the chase and sat down to supper.

'Well, Benjamin, what's the news?' they asked.

But he replied, 'I like that. Have you nothing to tell me?'

'No,' they answered.

Then he said, 'Well, now, you've been out in the wood all the day and I've stayed quietly at home, and all the same I know more than you do.'

'Then tell us!' they cried.

But he answered, 'Only on condition that you promise faithfully that the first girl we meet shall not be killed.'

'She shall be spared,' they promised. 'Only tell us the news.'

Then Benjamin said, 'Our sister is here!' And he lifted up the tub, and the princess stepped forward, in her royal robes, and with the golden star on her forehead, looking so lovely and sweet and charming that they all fell in love with her on the spot.

They arranged that she should stay at home with Benjamin and help him in the housework, while the rest of the brothers went out into the wood and shot hares and roe deer, birds and wood pigeons. Benjamin and his sister cooked their meals for them. She gathered herbs to cook with the vegetables, fetched the wood, and watched the pots on the fire, and always when her eleven brothers returned she had their supper ready for them. Besides this, she kept the house in order, tidied all the rooms, and made herself so generally useful that her brothers were delighted, and they all lived happily together.

Now there was a little garden round the enchanted house, in which grew twelve tall lilies. The girl, wishing to please her brothers, plucked the twelve flowers, meaning to present one to each of them as they sat at supper. But hardly had she plucked the flowers when her brothers were turned into twelve ravens, who flew croaking over the wood, and the house and garden vanished also. So the poor girl found herself left all alone in the wood, and as she looked round her she noticed an old woman standing close beside her, who said:

'My child, what have you done? Why didn't you leave the flowers alone? They were your twelve brothers. Now they are changed forever into ravens.'

The girl asked, sobbing, 'Is there no means of setting them free?'

'No,' said the old woman, 'there is only one way in the whole world, and that is so difficult that you won't free them by it, for you would have to be dumb and not laugh for seven years, and if you spoke a single word, though but an hour were wanting to the time, your silence would all have been in vain, and that one word would slay your brothers.'

Then the girl said to herself, 'If that is all, I am quite sure I can free my brothers.' So she searched for a high tree, and when she had found one she climbed up it and spun all day long, never laughing or speaking one word.

Now it happened one day that a king was hunting in the wood with a large greyhound, who ran sniffing to the tree on which the girl sat and jumped round it, yelping and barking

furiously. The king's attention was attracted and, when he looked up and beheld the beautiful princess with the golden star on her forehead, he was so enchanted by her beauty that he asked her on the spot to be his wife. She gave no answer, but nodded slightly with her head. Then he climbed up the tree himself, lifted her down, put her on his horse and bore her home to his palace.

The marriage was celebrated with much pomp and ceremony, but the bride neither spoke nor laughed.

When they had lived a few years happily together, the king's mother, who was a wicked old woman, began to slander the young queen, and said to the king:

'She is only a low-born beggar maid that you have married. Who knows what mischief she is up to? If she is deaf and can't speak, she might at least laugh; depend upon it, those who don't laugh have a bad conscience.'

At first the king paid no heed to her words, but the old woman harped so long on the subject, and accused the young queen of so many bad things, that at last he let himself be talked over, and condemned his beautiful wife to death.

So a great fire was lit in the courtyard of the palace, where she was to be burned. The king watched the proceedings from an upper window, crying bitterly the while, for he still loved his wife dearly. But just as she had been bound to the stake, and the flames were licking her garments with their red tongues, the very last moment of the seven years had come.

Then a sudden rushing sound was heard in the air, and twelve ravens were seen flying overhead. They swooped downward, and as soon as they touched the ground they turned into her twelve brothers, and she knew that she had freed them.

They quenched the flames and put out the fire and, unbinding their dear sister from the stake, they kissed and embraced her again and again. And now that she was able to open her mouth and speak, she told the king why she had been dumb and not able to laugh.

The king rejoiced greatly when he heard she was innocent, and they all lived happily ever afterward.

[Jakob and Wilhelm Grimm.]

Rapunzel

ONCE UPON A TIME
a man and his wife were very unhappy because they had no
children. These good people had a little window at the back
of their house, which looked into the most lovely garden, full
of all manner of beautiful flowers and vegetables; but the
garden was surrounded by a high wall, and no one dared to
enter it, for it belonged to a witch of great power, who was
feared by the whole world. One day the woman stood at the
window overlooking the garden and saw there a bed full of
the finest rampion. The leaves looked so fresh and green that
she longed to eat them. The desire grew day by day, and just
because she knew she couldn't possibly get any, she pined away
and became pale and wretched. Then her husband grew
alarmed and said:

'What ails you, dear wife?'

'Oh,' she answered, 'if I don't get some rampion to eat out of
the garden behind the house, I know I shall die.'

The man, who loved her dearly, said to himself, 'Come!
Rather than let your wife die you shall fetch her some rampion,
no matter the cost.' So at dusk he climbed over the wall into
the witch's garden and, hastily gathering a handful of rampion

leaves, he returned with them to his wife. She made them into a salad, which tasted so good that her longing for the forbidden food was greater than ever. If she were to know any peace of mind, there was nothing for it but that her husband should climb over the garden wall again and fetch her some more. So at dusk over he went, but when he reached the other side he drew back in terror, for there, standing before him, was the old witch.

'How dare you,' she said, with a wrathful glance, 'climb into my garden and steal my rampion like a common thief? You shall suffer for your foolhardiness.'

'Oh,' he implored, 'pardon my presumption; necessity alone drove me to the deed. My wife saw your rampion from her window and had such a desire for it that she would certainly have died if her wish had not been gratified.'

Then the witch's anger was a little appeased, and she said, 'If it's as you say, you may take as much rampion away with you as you like, but on one condition only—that you give me the child your wife will shortly bring into the world. All shall go well with it and I will look after it like a mother.'

The man in his terror agreed to everything she asked. As soon as the child was born the witch appeared and, having given it the name of Rapunzel, which is the same as rampion, she carried it off with her.

Rapunzel was the most beautiful child under the sun. When she was twelve years old the witch shut her up in a tower, in the middle of a great wood, and the tower had neither stairs nor doors, only high up at the very top a small window. When the old witch wanted to get in she stood underneath and called out:

> 'Rapunzel, Rapunzel,
> Let down your golden hair.'

20

For Rapunzel had wonderful long hair, and it was as fine as spun gold. Whenever she heard the witch's voice she unloosed her plaits, and let her hair fall down out of the window, and the old witch climbed up by it.

After they had lived like this for a few years, it happened one day that a prince was riding through the wood and passed by the tower. As he drew near it he heard someone singing so sweetly that he stood still spellbound, and listened. It was Rapunzel in her loneliness trying to while away the time by letting her sweet voice ring out into the wood. The prince longed to see the owner of the voice, but he sought in vain for a door in the tower. He rode home, but he was so haunted by the song he had heard that he returned every day to the wood and listened. One day, when he was standing thus behind a tree, he saw the old witch approach and heard her call out:

> 'Rapunzel, Rapunzel,
> Let down your golden hair.'

Then Rapunzel let down her plaits and the witch climbed up by them.

'So that's the staircase, is it?' said the prince. 'Then I too will climb it and try my luck.'

So on the following day, at dusk, he went to the foot of the tower and cried:

> 'Rapunzel, Rapunzel,
> Let down your golden hair.'

And as soon as she had let it down the prince climbed up.

At first Rapunzel was terribly frightened when a man came in, for she had never seen one before. But the prince spoke to

Rapunzel was frightened when a man came in, for she had never seen
one before

her kindly and told her at once that his heart had been so touched by her singing he felt he should know no peace of mind till he had seen her. Very soon Rapunzel forgot her fear, and when he asked her to marry him she consented at once.

For, she thought, he is young and handsome, and I'll certainly be happier with him than with the old witch. So she put her hand in his and said:

'Yes, I will gladly go with you, only how am I to get down out of the tower? Every time you come to see me you must bring a skein of silk with you, and I will make a ladder of them, and when it is finished I will climb down by it, and you will take me away on your horse.'

They arranged that, till the ladder was ready, he was to come to her every evening, because the old woman was with her during the day. The old witch, of course, knew nothing of what was going on, till one day Rapunzel, not thinking of what she was about, turned to the witch and said:

'How is it, good mother, that you are so much harder to pull up than the young prince? He is always with me in a moment.'

'Oh, you wicked child,' cried the witch. 'What is this I hear? I thought I had hidden you safely from the whole world and in spite of it you have managed to deceive me.'

In her wrath she seized Rapunzel's beautiful hair, wound it round and round her left hand, and then grasping a pair of scissors in her right, snip snap, off it came, and the beautiful plaits lay on the ground. And, worse than this, she was so hard-hearted that she took Rapunzel to a lonely desert place and there left her to live in loneliness and misery.

But on the evening of the day in which she had driven poor Rapunzel away, the witch fastened the plaits on to a hook in the window, and when the prince came and called out:

'Rapunzel, Rapunzel,
Let down your golden hair.'

she let them down, and the prince climbed up as usual. But instead of his beloved Rapunzel he found the old witch, who fixed her evil, glittering eyes on him, and cried mockingly:

'Ah, ah! You thought to find your lady love, but the pretty bird has flown and its song is dumb. The cat caught it and will scratch out your eyes too. Rapunzel is lost to you forever—you will never see her more.'

The prince was beside himself with grief, and in his despair he jumped right down from the tower and, though he escaped with his life, the thorns among which he fell pierced his eyes. Then he wandered, blind and miserable, through the wood, eating nothing but roots and berries and weeping and lamenting the loss of his lovely bride.

So he wandered about for some years, as wretched and unhappy as he could well be, and at last he came to the desert place where Rapunzel was living. Of a sudden he heard a voice which seemed strangely familiar to him. He walked eagerly in the direction of the sound, and when he was quite close, Rapunzel recognized him and fell on his neck and wept. Two of her tears touched his eyes, and in a moment they became quite clear again, and he saw as well as ever he had. Then he led her to his kingdom, where they were received and welcomed with great joy, and they lived happily ever after.

[Jakob and Wilhelm Grimm.]

Mother Holle

ONCE UPON A TIME there was a widow who had two daughters; one of them was pretty and clever, the other ugly and lazy. But as the ugly one was her own daughter, the pretty one had to do all the work of the house, and was in fact the maid of all work. Every day she had to sit by a well on the high road and spin till her fingers were so sore they bled. One day some drops of blood fell on her spindle, so she dipped it into the well to wash it. But, as luck would have it, it dropped from her hand and fell right in. She ran weeping to her stepmother and told her what had happened.

She scolded her harshly, and was so merciless in her anger that she said, 'Well, since you've dropped the spindle down, you must go after it. And don't let me see your face again until you bring it with you.'

Then the poor girl returned to the well and, not knowing what she was about in the despair and misery of her heart, she sprang into the well and sank to the bottom. For a time she lost all consciousness. When she came to herself she was lying in a lovely meadow, with the sun shining brightly overhead and a thousand flowers blooming at her feet. She rose and

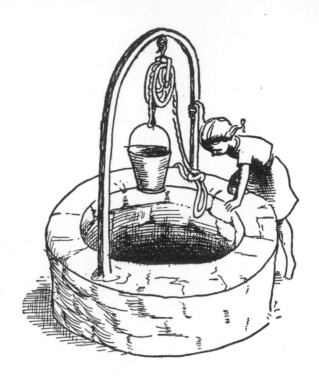

wandered through this enchanted place, till she came to a
baker's oven full of bread, and the bread called out to her as
she passed:

'Oh, take me out, take me out, or I shall be burnt to a cinder.
I am quite done enough.'

So she stepped up quickly to the oven and took out all the
loaves, one after the other. Then she went on a little farther
and came to a tree laden with beautiful rosy-cheeked apples,
and as she passed by it called out:

'Oh, shake me, shake me! My apples are all quite ripe.'

She did as she was asked and shook the tree till the apples
fell like rain and none were left hanging. When she had

gathered them all up into a heap she went on her way again, and came at length to a little house, at the door of which sat an old woman. The old dame had such large teeth that the girl felt frightened and wanted to run away, but the old woman called after her:

'What are you afraid of, dear child? Stay with me and be my little maid, and if you do your work well I will reward you handsomely. But you must be very careful how you make my bed. You must shake it well till the feathers fly; then people in the world below say it snows, for I am Mother Holle.'

She spoke so kindly that the girl took heart and readily entered her service. She did her best to please the old woman, and shook her bed with such a will that the feathers flew about like snowflakes. So she led a very easy life, was never scolded, and lived on the fat of the land. But after some time with Mother Holle she grew sad and depressed, and at first she hardly knew herself what was the matter. At last she knew she was homesick, so she went to Mother Holle and said:

'I know I am a thousand times better off here than ever I was before. But I have a great longing to go home, in spite of all your kindness to me. I can remain with you no longer, but must return to my own people.'

'Your desire to go home pleases me,' said Mother Holle, 'and because you have served me so faithfully, I will show you the way back to the world myself.'

So she took her by the hand and led her to an open door. As the girl passed through it a heavy shower of gold fell over her, till she was covered from top to toe.

'That's a reward for being such a good little maid,' said Mother Holle, and she gave her back the spindle that had fallen into the well. Then she shut the door, and the girl found herself back in the world again, not far from her own house. When she came to the courtyard the old hen, who sat on the top of the wall, called out:

> *'Click, clock, clack,*
> *Our golden maid's come back.'*

Then she went in to her stepmother, and as she had returned covered with gold she was welcomed home. She told all that had happened to her, and when the mother heard how she had come by her riches, she was most anxious to secure the same luck for her own idle daughter. So she told her to sit at the well and spin. She stuck her hand into a hedge of thorns and pricked her finger. Then she threw the spindle into the well and jumped in after it. Like her sister she came to the beautiful meadow and followed the same path. When she reached the baker's oven the bread called out as before:

'Oh, take me out, take me out, or I shall be burnt to a cinder! I am quite done enough.'

But the good-for-nothing girl answered, 'A pretty joke, indeed; just as if I should dirty my hands for you!'

And on she went. Soon she came to the apple tree, which cried:

'Oh, shake me, shake me! My apples are all quite ripe.'

'I'll see myself farther,' she replied, 'one of them might fall on my head.'

And so she pursued her way. When she came to Mother Holle's house she wasn't the least afraid, and she readily agreed to become her maid. The first day she worked very hard, and did all her mistress told her, for she thought of the gold she would give her. But on the second day she began to be lazy, and on the third she wouldn't even get up in the morning. She didn't make Mother Holle's bed as she should have done, and never shook it enough to make the feathers fly.

So her mistress soon grew weary of her and dismissed her, much to the lazy creature's delight. For now, she thought, the shower of golden rain will come.

Mother Holle led her to the same door as she had done her sister, but when she passed through it, instead of the gold rain a kettleful of pitch came showering over her.

'That's a reward for your service,' said Mother Holle, and she closed the door behind her.

So the lazy girl came home all covered with pitch, and when the old hen on the top of the wall saw her, it called out:

'Click, clock, clack,
Our dirty girl's come back.'

The pitch remained sticking to her, and never as long as she lived could it be scrubbed off.

[Jakob and Wilhelm Grimm.]

Minnikin

THERE WAS ONCE UPON
a time a couple of needy folk who lived in a wretched hut, where
was nothing but black want. They had neither enough food to
eat nor wood to burn. But if they had next to nothing of all
else they had the blessing of God so far as children were concerned, and every year brought them one more.

The man was always going about grumbling and growling
and saying that it seemed to him there might be too many of
these good gifts; so shortly before another baby came he went
away into the wood for some firewood, saying that he did not
want to see the new child; he would hear him quite soon
enough when he began to squall for some food.

As soon as he was born, this baby began to look about the
room. 'Ah, my dear Mother,' said he, 'give me some of my
brothers' old clothes and food enough for a few days, and I
will go out into the world and seek my fortune, for you have
children enough.'

'Heaven help you, my son!' said the mother. 'That will never
do; you are still far too small.'

But the little creature was determined and begged and
prayed so long that the mother was forced to let him go. Then

gaily and happily he went out into the world. But almost before he was out of the house another boy was born, and he too looked about him, and said:

'Ah, my dear Mother, give me some of my brothers' old clothes and food for some days, and then I will go out into the world and find my brother, for you have children enough.'

'Heaven help you, little creature! You are far too little for that,' said the woman; 'it would never do.'

But she spoke to no purpose, for the boy begged until he had a bundle of provisions, and then he set out manfully into the world to find his brother.

When the younger had walked for some time he caught sight of his brother a short distance in front of him, and called to him and bade him stop.

'Wait a minute,' he said. 'You are walking as if for a wager, but you should have stayed to see your younger brother before you hurried off into the world.'

So the elder stood still and looked back, and when the younger had come up to him, he said:

'Now let us sit down and see what kind of food our mother has given us.' And that they did.

'What will you be called?' asked the elder.

'I will be called Minnikin,' answered the second. 'And you, what will you be called?'

'I will be called King Pippin,' answered the elder.

They then went onward. When they had walked for some time they came to a crossway, and there they agreed to part, and each take his own road. This they did, but no sooner had they walked a short distance than they met again. So they parted once more, and each took his own road, but in a very short time the same thing happened again—they met each other before they were at all aware, and so it happened the third time also. Then they arranged that one should go east and the other west.

'But if ever you fall into any want or trouble,' said the elder, 'call me thrice, and I will come and help you. Only you must not call me until you are in the utmost need.'

'In that case we shall not see each other for some time,' said Minnikin. So they bade farewell to each other, and Minnikin went east and King Pippin went west.

When Minnikin had walked a long way alone, he met an old, old woman, who had only one eye. Minnikin took it.

'Oh, oh!' cried the old woman. 'What has become of my eye?'

'What will you give me to get your eye back?' said Minnikin.

'I will give you a sword which is such a sword that it can conquer a whole army, let it be ever so great,' replied the woman.

'Let me have it, then,' said Minnikin.

The old woman gave him the sword in return for her eye. Then Minnikin went onward, and when he had wandered on for some time he again met an old, old woman who had only one eye. Minnikin took it before she was aware.

'Oh, oh! What has become of my eye?' cried the old woman.

'What will you give me to get your eye back?' said Minnikin.

'I will give you a ship which can sail over fresh water and salt water, over high hills and deep dales,' answered the old woman.

'Let me have it then,' said Minnikin.

So the old woman gave him a little ship which was no bigger than he could put in his pocket, and then he gave her eye back, and she went her way and Minnikin his. When he had walked on for a long time, he met for the third time an old, old woman who had only one eye. This eye also Minnikin took, and when the woman screamed and lamented, and asked what had become of her eye, Minnikin said:

'What will you give me to get your eye back?'

'I will give you the art to brew a hundred lasts of malt in one brewing.'

So, for teaching that art, the old woman got her eye back, and they both went away by different roads.

But when Minnikin had walked a short distance, he thought he would see what his ship could do. So he took it out of his pocket, and no sooner had he put one foot into the ship than it became much larger, and when he set the other foot into it, it grew as large as ships that sail on the sea. Then Minnikin said:

'Now go over fresh water and salt water, over high hills and deep dales, and do not stop until you come to the king's palace.' And in an instant the ship went away as swiftly as any bird in the air until it was just below the king's palace, and there it stood still.

From the windows of the king's palace many persons had seen Minnikin come sailing thither and had stood to watch him. They were so astounded to see a ship come sailing through the air! But while they were running down from the king's palace, Minnikin got out of the ship and put it in his pocket again, for the moment he was out of it, it once more became as small as it had been when he got it from the old woman. Those who came from the palace could see nothing but a ragged boy standing down by the seashore. The king asked where he had come from, but the boy did not tell him. He begged very earnestly for a place in the king's palace. If there was nothing else for him to do, he said he would fetch wood and water for the kitchenmaid; and that he obtained leave to do.

When Minnikin went up to the king's palace he saw that everything was hung with black; so he asked the kitchenmaid what that meant.

'Oh, I will tell you that,' answered the kitchenmaid. 'The king's daughter was long ago promised to three trolls, and next Thursday evening one of them is to come to fetch her. Ritter Red said he can set her free, but who knows? So you may easily imagine what grief and distress we are in here.'

When Thursday evening came, Ritter Red accompanied the princess to the seashore, where she was to meet the troll. Ritter Red was to stay with her and protect her. He, however, was very unlikely to do the troll much injury, for no sooner had the princess seated herself than Ritter Red climbed up into a great tree and hid himself among the branches.

The princess begged him most earnestly not to leave her; but Ritter Red did not concern himself about that.

He was terrible to see and he had five heads

'It is better that one should die than two,' said he.

In the meantime Minnikin begged the kitchenmaid very prettily to give him leave to go down to the strand for a short time.

'Oh, what could you do down at the strand?' said the kitchenmaid. 'You have nothing to do there.'

'Oh yes, my dear, just let me go,' said Minnikin. 'I should so like to go and amuse myself with the other children.'

'Well, well, go then!' said the kitchenmaid. 'But don't let me find you staying over the time when the pan has to be set on the fire for supper, and the roast put on the spit. And mind you bring back a good big armful of wood for the kitchen.'

Minnikin promised this and ran down to the seashore, where the king's daughter was sitting, just as the troll came rushing up with a great whistling and whirring. He was so big and stout that he was terrible to see, and he had five heads.

'Fire!' screeched the troll.

'Fire yourself!' said Minnikin.

'Can you fight?' roared the troll.

'If not, I can learn,' said Minnikin.

So the troll struck at him with a great iron bar which he had in his fist. The sods flew five yards up in the air.

'Fie!' said Minnikin. 'That was not much of a blow. Now you shall see one of mine.'

So he grasped the sword which he had received from the old woman and slashed at the troll so that all five heads went flying away over the sands. When the princess saw that she was delivered she was so delighted she skipped and danced.

'Come and rest a bit with your head in my lap,' she said to Minnikin. And as he slept she put a golden dress on him.

But when Ritter Red saw there was no longer any danger, he lost no time in creeping down from the tree. He threatened the princess, until she promised to say it was he who had rescued her. Then he took the troll's lungs and tongues and put them in his handkerchief, and led the princess back to the king's palace. Whatsoever had been lacking to him in the way of honour before was lacking no longer, for the king could not exalt him enough, and always set him on his own right hand at table.

As for Minnikin, first he went out on the troll's ship and took a great quantity of gold and silver hoops away with him, and then he trotted back to the king's palace. When the kitchen-maid caught sight of all this gold and silver she was quite amazed, and said:

'My dear friend Minnikin, where did you get all that?' She was half afraid he had not come by it honestly.

'Oh,' answered Minnikin, 'I have been home a while, and these hoops had fallen off some of our buckets, so I brought them away with me for you.'

When the kitchenmaid heard that they were for her, she asked no more questions about the matter. She thanked Minnikin, and everything was right again at once.

Next Thursday evening everyone was full of grief and afflic-tion, but Ritter Red said that he had been able to deliver the king's daughter from one troll, he could very easily deliver her from another, and he led her down to the seashore. But when the troll was expected, he said as he had said before, 'It is better that one should die than two.' And he climbed up into the tree again.

Minnikin once more begged leave to go down to the sea-shore for a short time.

'Oh, what can you do there?' said the kitchenmaid.

'My dear, do let me go!' said Minnikin; 'I should so like to amuse myself a little with the other children.'

So this time also she said he should have leave to go, but he must first promise that he would be back by the time the joint was turned and would bring a great armful of wood with him.

No sooner had Minnikin got down to the strand than the troll came rushing along with a great whistling and whirring, and he was twice as big as the first troll, and he had ten heads.

'Fire!' shrieked the troll.

'Fire yourself!' said Minnikin.

'Can you fight?' roared the troll.

'If not, I can learn,' said Minnikin.

So the troll struck at him with his iron club—which was still bigger than the club the first troll had had—so that the earth flew ten yards up in the air.

'Fie!' said Minnikin. 'That was not much of a blow. Now you shall see one of my blows.'

Then he grasped his sword and struck at the troll so that all his ten heads danced away over the sands.

And again the king's daughter said to him, 'Rest a while on my lap.' And while Minnikin slept she drew some silver raiment over him.

As soon as Ritter Red saw there was no longer any danger afoot, he crept down from the tree and threatened the princess. At last she was again forced to promise to say that it was he who had rescued her. After which he took the tongues and the lungs of the troll and put them in his handkerchief, and then he conducted the princess back to the palace. There was joy and gladness in the palace, as may be imagined, and the king did not know how to show enough honour and respect to Ritter Red.

Minnikin, however, took home with him an armful of gold and silver hoops from the troll's ship. When he came back to the king's palace the kitchenmaid clapped her hands and wondered where he could have found all that gold and silver. But Minnikin answered that he had been home for a short time, and that it was only the hoops which had fallen off some pails, and that he had brought them away for the kitchenmaid.

When the third Thursday evening came, everything happened exactly as it had happened before. Everything in the king's palace was hung with black, and everyone was sorrowful and distressed. But Ritter Red said that he did not think they had much reason to be afraid—he had delivered the king's daughter from two trolls, so he could easily deliver her from the third as well. He led her down to the strand, but when the time drew near for the troll to come, he climbed up into the tree again and hid himself.

The princess wept and entreated him to stay, but all to no purpose. He stuck to his old speech, 'It is better that one life should be lost than two.'

This evening also, Minnikin begged for leave to go down to the seashore.

'Oh, what can you do there?' asked the kitchenmaid.

However, he begged until at last he had leave to go, but he promised to be back again in the kitchen when the roast had to be turned.

Almost immediately the troll came, with a great whizzing and whirring, and he was much, much bigger than either of the former trolls, and he had fifteen heads.

'Fire!' roared the troll.

'Fire yourself!' said Minnikin.

'Can you fight?' screamed the troll.

'If not, I can learn,' said Minnikin.

'I will teach you,' yelled the troll, and struck at him with his iron club and the earth flew up fifteen yards into the air.

'Fie!' said Minnikin. 'That was not much of a blow. Now I will let you see one of my blows.'

So saying he grasped his sword and cut at the troll in such a way that all his fifteen heads danced away over the sands. Then the princess was freed, and she thanked Minnikin and blessed him for saving her.

'Rest a while now on my lap,' said she. And while he slept she put a garment of brass upon him. 'But how shall it be made known it was you who saved me?'

'That I will tell you,' answered Minnikin. 'When Ritter Red has taken you home again, and said that it was he who rescued you, he will, as you know, have you to wife and half the kingdom. But when they ask you on your wedding day whom you will have to be your cupbearer, you must say, "I will have the ragged boy who is in the kitchen and carries wood and water for the kitchenmaid." And when I am filling your cups for you, I will spill a drop upon his plate but none upon yours, and then he will be angry and strike me, and this will take place thrice. But the third time you must say, "Shame on you thus to smite the beloved of my heart. It is he who delivered me from the trolls, and he is the one I will have."'

Then Minnikin went on board the troll's ship and took a great quantity of gold and silver and other precious things, and out of these he once more gave to the kitchenmaid a whole armful of gold and silver hoops.

No sooner did Ritter Red see that all danger was over than he crept down from the tree, and threatened the king's daughter till she promised to say that he had rescued her. Then he conducted her back to the king's palace, and if honour enough had not been done him before it was certainly done now, for the king had no other thought than how to make much of the man who had saved his daughter from the three trolls. And it was settled then that Ritter Red should marry her and receive half the kingdom.

On the wedding day, however, the princess begged that she might have the boy, who was in the kitchen and carried wood and water for the kitchenmaid, to fill the wine cups at the wedding feast.

'Oh, what can you want with that ragged boy?' said Ritter Red, but the princess insisted on having him as cupbearer and would have no one else. And at last everything was done as had been agreed on between the princess and Minnikin. He spilled a drop on Ritter Red's plate but none upon hers, and each time that he did it Ritter Red fell into a rage and struck him.

At the first blow all the ragged garments fell off Minnikin, at the second blow the brass garments fell off, and at the third the silver raiment, and there he stood in the golden raiment, which was so bright and splendid that light flashed from it. Then the king's daughter said:

'Shame on you thus to smite the beloved of my heart. It is he who delivered me from the trolls, and he is the one I will marry.'

Ritter Red insisted he was the man who had saved her, but the king said, 'He who delivered my daughter must have some token in proof of it.'

So Ritter Red ran off at once for his handkerchiefs with the lungs and tongues, and Minnikin brought all the gold and silver and precious things which he had taken out of the trolls' ships. And they laid these tokens before the king.

'He who has such precious things in gold and silver and diamonds,' said the king, 'must be the one who killed the trolls, for such things are not to be had anywhere else.'

One day the king went out walking with Minnikin, and

Minnikin asked him if he had never had any other children.

'Yes,' said the king, 'I had another daughter, but the troll carried her away because there was no one who could save her. You are going to have one daughter of mine, but if you set the other free, who has been taken by the troll, you shall willingly have the other half of the kingdom as well.'

'I may as well make the attempt,' said Minnikin, 'but I must have an iron cable which is five hundred ells long, and then I must have five hundred men with me and provisions for five weeks, for I have a long voyage before me.'

So the king said he should have these things, but the king was afraid that he had no ship large enough to carry them all.

'But I have a ship of my own,' said Minnikin, and he took the one which the old woman had given him out of his pocket. The king laughed and thought it was only one of his jokes, but Minnikin begged him to give him what he had asked for. All was brought as Minnikin asked. First he ordered them to lay the cable in the ship, but there was no one who was able to lift it, and there was only room for one or two men at a time in the little ship. Then Minnikin himself took hold of the cable and laid one or two links of it in the ship, and it grew bigger and bigger, and at last the ship was so large that the cable, the five hundred men, and provisions, and Minnikin himself, had room enough.

'Now go over fresh water and salt water, over hill and dale, and do not stop until you come to where the king's daughter is,' said Minnikin to the ship. And off it went in a moment over land and water till the wind whistled and moaned all about it. When they had sailed thus a long, long way, the ship stopped short in the middle of the sea.

'Ah, now we are here,' said Minnikin, 'but how we are to get back again is a very different thing.'

Then he took the cable and tied one end of it round his body. 'Now I must go to the bottom,' he said, 'but when I give a good jerk to the cable and want to come up again, you must all pull like one man, or there will be an end of life both for you and for me.'

So saying he sprang into the water, and the bubbles rose up all around him. He sank lower and lower, and at last he came to the bottom. There he saw a large hill with a door in it. When he was inside he found the other princess sewing, but when she saw Minnikin she clapped her hands.

'Ah, Heaven be praised!' she cried. 'I have not seen a Christian man since I came here.'

'I have come for you,' said Minnikin.

'Alas! You will not be able to take me,' said the king's daughter. 'It is no use even to think of that; if the troll catches sight of you he will take your life.'

'You had better tell me about him,' said Minnikin. 'Where has he gone? It would be amusing to see him.'

So the king's daughter told Minnikin that the troll was out trying to find someone who could brew a hundred lasts of malt at one brewing, for there was to be a feast.

'I can do that,' said Minnikin.

'Ah, if only the troll were not so quick-tempered I might have told him that,' answered the princess, 'but he will tear you to pieces, I fear, as soon as he comes in. However, I will try to find some way. Hide yourself here in the cupboard, and then we will see what happens.'

And almost before Minnikin had crept into the cupboard and hidden himself, in came the troll.

'Huf! What a smell of Christian man's blood!' said the troll.

'Yes, a bird flew over the roof with a man's bone in his bill, and let it fall down our chimney,' answered the princess. 'I made haste enough to get it away again, but it must be that which smells so.'

'Yes, it must be that,' said the troll.

Then the princess asked if he had found anyone who could brew a hundred lasts of malt at one brewing.

'No, there is no one who can do it,' said the troll.

'A short time since there was a man here who said he could do it,' said the king's daughter.

'How clever you always are!' said the troll. 'How could you let him go away? You must have known I wanted a man of that kind.'

'Well, I didn't let him go, after all,' said the princess, 'but hid him in the cupboard. However, if you have not found anyone, then the man is still here.'

'Let him come out,' said the troll.

When Minnikin came, the troll asked if it were true that he could brew a hundred lasts of malt at one brewing.

'Yes,' said Minnikin, 'it is.'

'It is well then that I have found you,' said the troll. 'Fall to work this very minute, but Heaven help you if you do not brew the ale strong.'

'Oh, it shall taste well,' said Minnikin, and at once set himself to brew the malt.

'But I must have more trolls to help carry what is wanted,' said Minnikin. 'These that I have are good for nothing.'

So he got more and more until there was a swarm of them, and then the brewing went on. When the sweetwort was ready they were all, of course, anxious to taste it, first the troll himself and then the others. But Minnikin had brewed the wort so strong that they all fell down dead like so many flies as soon as they had drunk any of it. At last there was no one left but one wretched old troll lying behind the stove.

'Oh, poor old creature,' said Minnikin, 'you shall have a taste of the wort too like the rest.' So he went away and scooped up a little from the bottom of the brewing vat and gave it to her, and then he was quit of the whole of them.

While Minnikin was now looking about him, he cast his eye on a large chest. He filled it with gold and silver, and then he tied the cable round himself and the princess and the chest, and tugged at the rope with all his might, whereupon his men drew them up safe and sound. As soon as Minnikin had all safely on his ship, he said:

'Now go over salt water and fresh water, over hill and dale, and do not stop until you come to the king's palace.'

And in a moment the ship went off so fast that the yellow foam rose up all about it. When those who were in the king's palace saw the ship, they lost no time in going to meet Minnikin with song and music, and with great rejoicings. But the gladdest of all was the king, for now he had his other daughter safe again.

But Minnikin was not happy, for both the princesses wanted to marry him, and he wanted to have none other than the one he had first saved, and she was the younger. For this cause he was continually walking back and forth, thinking how he could contrive to marry her, and yet not be unkind to her sister.

One day when he was walking about and thinking of this, it came into his mind that if he only had his brother with him, who was so like himself that no one could distinguish the one from the other, he could let him have the elder princess and half the kingdom. As for himself, he thought, the other half was quite enough. As soon as this occurred to him he went outside the palace and called for King Pippin, but no one came. So he called a second time, and a little louder, but no! Still no one came. So Minnikin called for the third time, and with all his might, and there stood his brother by his side.

'I told you not to call me unless you were in the utmost need,' he said to Minnikin, 'and there is not even so much as a midge here who can do you any harm!' And with that he gave Minnikin such a blow that he rolled over on the grass.

'Shame on you to strike me!' said Minnikin. 'First have I won one princess and half the kingdom, and then the other princess and the other half of the kingdom. And now, when I was thinking I would give you one of the princesses and half of the kingdom, do you think you have any reason to give me such a blow?'

When King Pippin heard that he begged his brother's pardon, and they were reconciled at once and became good friends.

'Now, as you know,' said Minnikin, 'we are so like each other that no one can tell one of us from the other. So just change clothes with me and go up to the palace, and then the princesses will think that I am coming in, and the one who kisses you first shall be yours, and I will have the other.' For he could very well guess how things would go.

King Pippin at once agreed to this. He changed clothes with his brother, and went into the palace. When he entered the princesses' apartments they believed that he was Minnikin, and both of them ran up to him at once. But the elder, who was bigger and stronger, pushed her sister aside, and threw her arms round King Pippin's neck and kissed him. So he got her to wife, and Minnikin the younger sister. It will be easy to understand that two weddings took place, and they were so magnificent that they were heard of and talked about all over seven kingdoms.

[From J. E. Moe.]

Bushy Bride

THERE WAS ONCE ON A
time a widower who had a son and a daughter by his first wife.
They were both good children and loved each other with all
their hearts. After some time had gone by the man married
again, and he chose a widow with one daughter who was ugly
and wicked, and her mother was ugly and wicked too. From
the very day the new wife came into the house there was no
peace for the man's children, and not a corner to be found
where they could get any rest. So the boy thought the best
thing he could do was to go out into the world and try to earn
his own bread.

When he had roamed about for some time he came to the
king's palace, where he obtained a place under the coachman.
Very brisk and active he was, and the horses that he looked
after were so fat and sleek they shone again.

But his sister, who was still at home, fared worse and worse.
Both her stepmother and her stepsister were always finding
fault with her, whatsoever she did and whithersoever she went,
and they scolded her and abused her so that she never had an
hour's peace. They made her do all the work, and hard words
fell to her lot early and late, but little enough food accompanied
them.

One day they sent her to the brook to fetch some water, and an ugly and horrible head rose up out of the water.

'Wash me, girl!' it said.

'Yes, I will wash you with pleasure,' said the girl, and began to wash and scrub the ugly face, but she couldn't help thinking that it was an unpleasant piece of work. When she had done it, and done it well, another head rose up out of the water, and this one was uglier still.

'Brush me, girl!' said the head.

'Yes, I will brush you with pleasure,' said the girl, and set to work with the tangled hair and, as may be easily imagined, this too was by no means pleasant work.

When she had that done, another and much more ugly and horrible head rose up out of the water.

'Kiss me, girl!' said the head.

'Yes, I will kiss you,' said the man's daughter, and she did it, but she thought it was the worst bit of work she had ever had to do in her life. Then the heads all began to talk to each other, and to ask what they should do for this girl who was so full of kindliness.

'She shall be the prettiest girl that ever was, and fair and bright as the day,' said the first head.

'Gold shall drop from her hair whenever she brushes it,' said the second.

'Gold shall drop from her mouth whenever she speaks,' said the third head.

So when the man's daughter went home, looking as beautiful and bright as day, the stepmother and her daughter grew more ill-tempered, and it was worse still when she began to talk, and they saw that golden coins dropped from her mouth. The stepmother fell into such a passion that she drove the man's daughter into the pigsty—she might stay there with her fine show of gold, the stepmother said, but she should not be permitted to set foot in the house.

It was not long before the mother wanted her own daughter to go to the stream to fetch some water. When she got there with her pails, the first head rose up out of the water close to the bank.

'Wash me, girl!' it said.

'Wash yourself!' answered the woman's daughter.

Then the second head appeared. 'Brush me, girl!' said the head.

'Brush yourself!' said the woman's daughter.

So down it went to the bottom, and the third head came up. 'Kiss me, girl!' said the head.

'As if I would kiss your ugly mouth!' said the girl.

So again the heads talked together about what they should do for this girl who was so ill-tempered and full of her own importance, and they agreed that she should have a nose that was four ells long, a jaw that was three ells and a fir bush in the middle of her forehead, and every time she spoke ashes should fall from her mouth.

When she came back to the cottage door with her pails, she called to her mother who was inside, 'Open the door!'

'Open the door yourself, my own dear child!'

'I can't get near, because of my nose,' said the daughter.

When the mother came and saw her, she screamed and lamented, but neither the nose nor the jaw grew any the less for that.

Now the brother, who was in service in the king's palace, had painted a portrait of his sister, which he carried with him, and every morning and evening he knelt down before it and prayed for his sister, so dearly did he love her.

The other stableboys had heard him doing this, so they

peeped through the keyhole into his room, and saw that he was kneeling there before a picture. So they told everyone that every morning and evening the youth knelt down and prayed to an idol. At last they went to the king himself and begged that he too would peep through the keyhole and see for himself what the youth did. At first the king would not believe this, but after a long, long time, they prevailed, and he crept on tiptoe to the door, peeped through, and saw the youth on his knees, with his hands clasped together before a picture hanging on the wall.

'Open the door!' cried the king. But the youth did not hear. So the king called to him again, but the youth was praying so fervently he did not hear him this time either.

'Open the door, I say!' cried the king again. 'I want to come in.'

So the youth sprang to the door and unlocked it, but in his haste he forgot to hide the picture. When the king saw it, he stood still as if he could not stir from the spot.

'There is nowhere on earth so beautiful a woman as this!' said the king.

But the youth told him she was his sister, and that he had painted her, and if she was not prettier than the picture she was at all events not uglier.

'Well, if she is as beautiful as that, I will have her for my queen,' said the king, and he commanded the youth to go home and fetch her without a moment's delay. The youth promised to make all the haste he could, and set forth from the king's palace.

When the brother arrived at home to fetch his sister, her stepmother and stepsister would go too. So they all set out together, and the man's daughter took with her a casket, in which she kept her gold, and a dog which was called Little Snow. These two things were all that she had inherited from her mother. When they had travelled for some time they had to cross the sea, and the brother sat down at the helm, and the mother and the two sisters went to the fore part of the vessel, and they sailed a long, long way. At last they came in sight of land.

'Look at that white strand there; that is where we shall land,' said the brother, pointing across the sea.

'What is my brother saying?' inquired the man's daughter.

'He says you are to throw your casket out into the sea,' answered the stepmother.

'Well, if my brother says so, I must do it,' said the man's daughter, and she flung her casket into the sea.

When they had sailed for some time longer, the brother once more pointed over the sea. 'There you may see the palace for which we are bound,' said he.

'What is my brother saying?' asked the man's daughter.

'Now he says that you are to throw your dog into the sea,' answered the stepmother.

The man's daughter wept, and was sorely troubled, for Little Snow was the dearest thing she had on earth, but at last she threw him overboard.

'If my brother says that, I must do it, but Heaven ' ~ ow unwilling I am to throw you out, Little Snow!' sa

So they sailed onward a long way farther.

'There you may see the king coming out to meet us, the brother, pointing to the seashore.

'What is my brother saying?' asked his sister again.

'Now he says that you are to make haste and throw yourself overboard,' answered the stepmother.

She wept and she wailed, but as her brother had said that, she thought she must do it. So she leaped into the sea.

But when they arrived at the palace, and the king beheld the ugly bride with a nose four ells long, a jaw three ells, and a forehead that had a bush in the middle of it, he was very wroth, and none can blame him for that. So he caused the brother to be thrown into a pit full of snakes.

On the first Thursday night after this, a beautiful maiden came into the kitchen of the palace, and begged the kitchen-maid, who slept there, to lend her a brush. She begged very prettily, and then she brushed her hair, and the gold dropped from it. A little dog was with her, and she said to it:

'Go out, Little Snow, and see if it will soon be day.'

This she said thrice, and the third time that she sent out the dog to see, it was very near dawn. Then she was forced to depart, but as she went she said:

> 'Out on thee, ugly Bushy Bride,
> Sleeping so soft by the young king's side,
> On sand and stones my bed I make,
> And my brother sleeps with the cold snake,
>   Unpitied and unwept.

'I shall come twice more, and then never again.'

In the morning the kitchenmaid related what she had seen and heard, and the king said that next Thursday night he himself would watch in the kitchen and see if this were true, and when it had begun to grow dark he went out into the kitchen. But though he rubbed his eyes and did everything he could to keep himself awake it was all in vain, for the Bushy Bride crooned and sang till his eyes were fast closed, and when the beautiful young maiden came he was sound asleep and snoring.

This time also, as before, she borrowed a brush and brushed her hair with it, and the gold dropped down as she did it. And again she sent the dog out three times, and when day dawned she departed, but as she was going she said as she had said before, 'I shall come once more, and then never again.'

On the third Thursday night the king once more insisted on keeping watch. Then he set two men to hold him; each to shake him and jerk him by the arm whenever he seemed to fall asleep; and he set two men to watch his Bushy Bride. But as the night wore on the Bushy Bride again began to croon and sing, so that his eyes closed and his head drooped.

Then came the lovely maiden, took the brush and brushed her hair till the gold dropped from it, and then she sent her Little Snow out to see if it would soon be day, and this she did three times. The third time it was just beginning to grow light, and then she said:

'Out on thee, ugly Bushy Bride,
Sleeping so soft by the young king's side,
On sand and stones my bed I make,
And my brother sleeps with the cold snake,
Unpitied and unwept.

'Now I shall never come again,' she said, and turned to go. But the two men who were holding the king by the arms seized his hands and forced a knife into his grasp, and then made him cut her little finger just enough to make it bleed.

Thus the true bride was freed. The brother was at once taken out of the snake pit—the snakes had never touched him— and the mother and the Bushy Bride were flung down instead of him.

And now the real wedding was held, and in such a way that it was heard of and spoken about all over seven kingdoms. The king and his bride drove to church, and Little Snow was in the carriage too. When the blessing was given they went home again, and after that I saw no more of them.

[From J. E. Moe.]

Snowdrop

ONCE UPON A TIME, in the middle of winter when the snowflakes were falling like feathers on the earth, a queen sat at a window framed in black ebony and sewed. And as she sewed and gazed out on the white landscape, she pricked her finger with the needle, and three drops of blood fell on the snow outside. Because the red showed out so well against the white she said to herself:

'Oh, what would I not give to have a child as white as snow, as red as blood, and as black as ebony!'

And her wish was granted, for not long afterward a little daughter was born to her, with a skin as white as snow, lips and cheeks as red as blood, and hair as black as ebony. They called her Snowdrop, and not long after her birth the queen died.

After a year the king married again. His new wife was a beautiful woman, but so proud and overbearing that she could not stand any rival to her beauty. She possessed a magic mirror, and when she used to stand before it, gazing at her own reflection, and ask:

'Mirror, mirror, hanging there,
Who in all the land's most fair?'

it always replied:

'You are most fair, my Lady Queen,
None fairer in the land, I ween.'

Then she was quite happy, for she knew the mirror always spoke the truth.

But Snowdrop was growing prettier and prettier every day, and when she was seven years old she was as beautiful as she could be, and fairer even than the queen herself. One day when the queen asked her mirror the usual question, it replied:

'My Lady Queen, you are fair, 'tis true,
But Snowdrop is fairer far than you.'

Then the queen flew into the most awful passion and turned every shade of green in her jealousy. From this hour she hated poor Snowdrop, and every day her envy, hatred and malice grew, for envy and jealousy are like evil weeds which spring up and choke the heart. At last she could endure Snowdrop's presence no longer and, calling a huntsman to her, she said:

'Take the child out into the wood and never let me see her face again. You must kill her, and bring me back her lungs and heart, that I may know for certain she is dead.'

The huntsman did as he was told and led Snowdrop out into the wood, but as he was in the act of drawing out his knife to slay her, she said:

'Oh, dear huntsman, spare my life, and I will promise to fly forth into the wide wood and never to return home again.'

Because she was so young and pretty the huntsman had pity on her, and said, 'Well, run along, poor child.' For he thought the wild beasts would soon eat her up.

And his heart felt lighter because he hadn't had to do the deed himself. As he turned away a young boar came running past, so he shot it, and brought its lungs and heart home to the queen as a proof that Snowdrop was really dead. And the wicked woman had them stewed in salt, and ate them, thinking she had made an end of Snowdrop forever.

Now when the poor child found herself alone in the big wood the very trees seemed to take strange shapes, and she felt so frightened she didn't know what to do. Over the sharp stones and through the bramble bushes she stumbled, and the wild beasts ran past her, but they did her no harm. She ran as far as her legs would carry her, and as evening drew in she saw a little house and stepped inside to rest.

Everything was very small in the little house, but very clean and neat. In the middle of the room there stood a little table, covered with a white tablecloth and seven little plates and forks and spoons and knives and tumblers. Side by side against the wall there were seven little beds, covered with snow-white counterpanes. Snowdrop felt so hungry and so thirsty she ate a bit of bread and a little porridge from each plate and drank a drop of wine out of each tumbler. Then feeling tired and sleepy, she lay down on one of the beds, but it wasn't comfortable. Then she tried all the others in turn, but one was too long, another too short, and it was only when she tried the seventh that she found one to suit her exactly. So she lay down upon it, said her prayers like a good child, and fell fast asleep.

When it was quite dark the masters of the little house returned. They were seven dwarfs who worked in the mines, deep down in the heart of the mountain. They lighted their seven little lamps, and as soon as their eyes were accustomed to the glare they saw that someone had been in the room, for all was not in the same order as they had left it.

The first said, 'Who has been sitting on my little chair?'

The second said, 'Who has been eating my little loaf?'

The third said, 'Who has been tasting my porridge?'

The fourth said, 'Who has been eating out of my little plate?'

The fifth said, 'Who has been using my little fork?'

The sixth said, 'Who has been cutting with my little knife?'

The seventh said, 'Who has been drinking out of my little tumbler?'

Then the first dwarf looked round and saw a little hollow in his bed, and he asked, 'Who has been lying on my bed?' The others came running round, and cried when they saw their beds, 'Somebody has lain on ours too.'

But when the seventh came to his bed, he started back in amazement, for there he beheld Snowdrop fast asleep. Then he called the others, who turned their little lamps full on the bed, and when they saw Snowdrop lying there they nearly fell down with surprise.

'Goodness gracious,' they cried, 'what a beautiful child!'

They were so enchanted by her beauty that they did not wake her but let her sleep on in the little bed. The seventh dwarf slept with his companions one hour in each bed, and in this way he managed to pass the night.

In the morning Snowdrop awoke, but when she saw the seven little dwarfs she felt frightened. But they were so friendly, and asked her what her name was in such a kind way, that she replied:

'I am Snowdrop.'

'Why did you come to our house?' continued the dwarfs.

Then she told them how her stepmother had wished her put to death, and how the huntsman had spared her life, and how she had run the whole day till she had come to their little house. The dwarfs, when they had heard her sad story, asked her:

'Will you stay and keep house for us, cook, make the beds, do the washing, sew and knit? If you keep everything neat and clean, you shall want for nothing.'

'Yes,' answered Snowdrop, 'I will gladly do all you ask.'

And so she lived happily with them. Every morning the dwarfs went into the mountain to dig for gold, and in the evening when they returned home, Snowdrop always had their supper ready for them. But during the day she was left quite alone, so the good dwarfs warned her, saying:

'Beware of your stepmother. She will soon find out you are here, and whatever you do don't let anyone into the house.'

Now the queen never dreamed but that she was once more

the most beautiful woman in the world; so stepping before her mirror one day she said:

> *'Mirror, mirror, hanging there,*
> *Who in all the land's most fair?'*

and the mirror replied:

> *'My Lady Queen, you are fair, 'tis true,*
> *But Snowdrop is fairer far than you.*
> *Snowdrop, who dwells with the seven little men,*
> *Is as fair as you, as fair again.'*

When the queen heard these words she was nearly struck dumb with horror, for the mirror always spoke the truth. She knew now that the huntsman must have deceived her and Snowdrop was still alive. She pondered day and night how she might destroy her, for her jealous heart left her no rest. At last she hit upon a plan. She stained her face and dressed herself up as an old pedlar wife, so that she was quite unrecognizable. In this guise she went over the seven hills till she came to the house of the seven dwarfs. There she knocked at the door, calling out at the same time:

'Fine wares to sell, fine wares to sell!'

Snowdrop peeped out of the window, and called, 'Good day, mother, what have you to sell?'

'Good wares, fine wares,' she answered, 'laces of every shade and description.' And she held one up that was made of some gay-coloured silk.

'Surely I can let the honest woman in,' said Snowdrop; so she unbarred the door and bought the pretty lace.

'Good gracious, child,' said the old woman, 'what a figure you have! Come! I'll lace you up properly for once.'

Snowdrop, suspecting no evil, stood before her and let her lace up her bodice but the old woman laced her so quickly and so tightly that it took Snowdrop's breath away, and she fell down as if dead.

'Now you are no longer the fairest,' said the wicked old woman, and then she hastened away.

In the evening the seven dwarfs came home, and what a fright they had when they saw their dear Snowdrop lying on the floor, as still and motionless as a dead person. They lifted her up tenderly, and when they saw how tightly laced she was they cut the lace, and she began to breathe a little and gradually came back to life. When the dwarfs heard what had happened, they said:

'Depend upon it, the old pedlar wife was none other than the queen. In future you must be sure to let no one in, if we are not at home.'

As soon as the wicked old queen reached home she went straight to her mirror, and said:

> 'Mirror, mirror, hanging there,
> Who in all the land's most fair?'

and the mirror answered as before:

> 'My Lady Queen, you are fair, 'tis true,
> But Snowdrop is fairer far than you.
> Snowdrop, who dwells with the seven little men,
> Is as fair as you, as fair again.'

When she heard this the queen became as pale as death, because she saw at once that Snowdrop must be alive again. 'This time,' she said to herself, 'I will think of something that will make an end of her once and for all.'

And by the witchcraft which she understood so well she made a poisonous comb. Then she dressed herself up in the form of another old woman. So she went over the seven hills till she reached the house of the seven dwarfs, and knocking at the door she called out:

'Fine wares for sale.'

Snowdrop looked out of the window and said, 'You must go away, for I may not let anyone in.'

'But surely you are not forbidden to look out?' asked the old woman, and she held up the poisonous comb for her to see.

It pleased the girl so much that she opened the door. When they had settled their bargain the old woman said:

'Now I'll comb your hair properly for you.'

Poor Snowdrop suspected no evil, but hardly had the comb touched her hair than the poison worked and she fell down unconscious.

'Now, my fine lady, you're really done for this time,' said the wicked woman, and she made her way home as fast as she could.

Fortunately it was now near evening and the seven dwarfs came home. When they saw Snowdrop lying as if dead on the ground, they at once suspected that the wicked queen had been at work again. So they searched till they found the poisonous comb, and the moment they pulled it out of her hair Snowdrop came to herself again, and told them what had happened. Then they warned her once more to open the door to no one.

As soon as the queen was home she went straight to her mirror, and asked:

> 'Mirror, mirror, hanging there,
> Who in all the land's most fair?'

and it replied as before:

'My Lady Queen, you are fair, 'tis true,
But Snowdrop is fairer far than you.
Snowdrop, who dwells with the seven little men,
Is as fair as you, as fair again.'

When she heard these words she literally shook with rage. 'Snowdrop shall die!' she cried. 'Yes, though it cost me my own life.'

Then she went to a secret chamber, which no one knew of but herself, and there she made a poisonous apple. Outwardly it looked beautiful, white with red cheeks, so anyone who saw it would long to eat it. When the apple was finished, she stained her face and dressed herself up as a peasant, and so she went over the seven hills to the seven dwarfs. She knocked at the door, as usual, but Snowdrop put her head out of the window and called out:

'I may not let anyone in, the seven dwarfs have forbidden me to do so.'

'Are you afraid of being poisoned?' asked the old woman. 'See, I will cut this apple in half. I'll eat the white cheek and you can eat the red.'

The apple was so cunningly made that only the red cheek was poisonous. Snowdrop longed to eat the tempting fruit, and when she saw that the peasant woman was eating it herself, she couldn't resist the temptation any longer and, stretching out her hand, she took the poisonous half. But hardly had the first bite passed her lips than she fell down dead on the ground. Then the eyes of the cruel queen sparkled, and laughing aloud, she cried:

'As white as snow, as red as blood, and as black as ebony, this time the dwarfs won't be able to bring you back to life.'

When she reached home she asked the mirror:

'Mirror, mirror, hanging there,
Who in all the land's most fair?'

and this time it replied:

'You are most fair, my Lady Queen,
None fairer in the land, I ween.'

Then her jealous heart was at rest—at least, as much at rest as a jealous heart can ever be.

When the little dwarfs came home in the evening they found Snowdrop lying on the ground, and she neither breathed nor stirred. They lifted her up and looked everywhere to see if they could find anything poisonous about. They unlaced her bodice, combed her hair, washed her with water and wine, but all in vain: the child was dead and remained dead. Then they placed her on a bier, and all the seven dwarfs sat round it, weeping and sobbing for three whole days. At last they made up their minds to bury her, but she looked as blooming as a living being, and her cheeks were still such a lovely colour, that they said: 'We cannot hide her away in the dark ground.'

So they had a coffin made of transparent glass, and they laid her in it and wrote on the lid in golden letters that she was a royal princess. Then they put the coffin on the top of the mountain, and one of the dwarfs always remained beside it and kept watch over it. And the very birds of the air came and bewailed Snowdrop's death, first an owl, and then a raven, and last of all a little dove.

Snowdrop lay a long time in the coffin, and she always looked the same, just as if she were fast asleep, and she remained as white as snow, as red as blood, and her hair as black as ebony.

Now it happened one day that a prince came to the wood

and passed by the dwarfs' house. He saw the coffin on the hill, with the beautiful Snowdrop inside it, and when he had read what was written on it in golden letters, he said to the dwarf:

'Give me the coffin. You shall have whatever you like for it.'

But the dwarf said, 'No, we wouldn't part with it for all the gold in the world.'

'Well, then.' he replied, 'give it to me, because I cannot live without Snowdrop. I will cherish and love it as my dearest possession.'

He spoke so sadly that the good dwarfs had pity on him and gave him the coffin, and the prince made his servants bear it away on their shoulders. Now it happened that as they were going down the hill they stumbled over a bush, and jolted the coffin so violently that the poisonous bit of apple fell out of Snowdrop's mouth. She opened her eyes, lifted up the lid of the coffin, and sat up alive and well.

'Oh, dear me, where am I?' she cried.

The prince answered joyfully, 'You are with me.' He told her all that had happened, adding, 'I love you better than anyone in the whole wide world. Will you come with me to my father's palace and be my wife?'

Snowdrop consented, and went with him, and the marriage was celebrated with great pomp and splendour.

Now Snowdrop's wicked stepmother was one of the guests invited to the wedding feast. When she had dressed herself very gorgeously for the occasion, she went to the mirror, and said:

> *'Mirror, mirror, hanging there,*
> *Who in all the land's most fair?'*

and the mirror answered:

'My Lady Queen, you are fair, 'tis true,
But Snowdrop is fairer far than you.'

When the wicked woman heard these words she was beside herself with rage and mortification. At first she didn't want to go to the wedding at all, but at the same time she felt she would never be happy till she had seen the young queen. As she entered, Snowdrop recognized her and nearly fainted with fear. But red-hot iron shoes had been prepared for the wicked old queen, and she was made to get into them and dance till she fell down dead.

[Jakob and Wilhelm Grimm.]

The Golden Goose

THERE WAS ONCE A MAN
who had three sons. The youngest of them was called Dullhead,
and was sneered and jeered at and snubbed on every possible
opportunity. One day it happened that the eldest son wished to
go into the forest to cut wood, and before he started his mother
gave him a fine rich cake and a bottle of wine so that he might
be sure not to suffer from hunger or thirst.

When he reached the forest he met a little old gray man
who wished him 'Good morning,' and said, 'Do give me a
piece of that cake you have, and a draught of your wine—I am
so hungry and thirsty.'

But this clever son replied, 'If I give you my cake and wine
I shall have none left for myself; you just go your own way.'
And he left the little man standing there and went farther on
into the forest. There he began to cut down a tree, but before
long he made a false stroke with his axe, and cut his own arm
so badly that he was obliged to go home and have it bound up.

Then the second son went to the forest, and his mother gave
him a good cake and a bottle of wine as she had to his elder
brother. He too met the little old gray man, who begged him
for a morsel of cake and a draught of wine.

He marched before the princess with the goose and its appendages

But the second son spoke most sensibly too, and said, 'Whatever I give to you I deprive myself of. Just go your own way, will you?' Not long afterward his punishment overtook him, for no sooner had he struck a couple of blows with his axe, than he cut his leg so badly that he had to be carried home.

Then the youngest son said, 'Father, let me go out and cut wood.'

But his father answered, 'Both your brothers have injured themselves. You had better not; you know nothing about it.'

But the boy begged so hard to be allowed to go that at last his father said, 'Very well, then—go! Perhaps when you have hurt yourself, you may learn to know better.' His mother gave him only a very plain cake made with water and baked in the cinders and a bottle of sour beer.

When he came to the forest, he too met the little gray old man, who greeted him and said, 'Give me a piece of your cake and a draught from your bottle. I am so hungry and thirsty.'

The boy replied, 'I have only a cinder-cake and some sour beer, but if you care to have that, let us sit down and eat.'

So they sat down, and when the boy brought out his cake he found it had turned into a fine rich cake, and the sour beer into excellent wine. Then they ate and drank, and when they had finished, the little man said:

'Now I will bring you luck, because you have a kind heart and are willing to share what you have with others. There stands an old tree. Cut it down, and amongst its roots you'll find something.'

With that the little man took his leave.

Then the boy fell to at once to hew down the tree, and when it fell he found amongst its roots a goose, whose feathers were all of pure gold. He lifted it out, carried it off, and took it with him to an inn where he meant to spend the night.

Now the landlord of the inn had three daughters, and when they saw the goose they were filled with curiosity about this wonderful bird, and each longed to have one of its golden feathers.

The eldest said to herself, 'No doubt I shall soon find a good opportunity to pluck out one of its feathers,' and the first time Dullhead happened to leave the room she caught hold of the goose by its wing. But, lo and behold! Her fingers seemed to stick fast to the goose and she could not take her hand away. Soon afterward the second daughter came in and thought to pluck a golden feather for herself too; but hardly had she touched her sister than she stuck fast as well. At last the third sister came with the same intentions, but the other two cried out, 'Keep off! For Heaven's sake, keep off!'

The youngest sister could not imagine why she was to keep off, and thought, if they are both there, why should not I be there too? So she sprang to them; but no sooner had she touched one of them than she stuck fast to her. So they all three had to spend the night with the goose.

Next morning the boy tucked the goose under his arm and went off, without in the least troubling himself about the three girls who were hanging on to it. They just had to run after him right or left as best they could. In the middle of a field they met the parson, and when he saw this procession he cried:

'For shame, you bold girls! What do you mean by running after a young fellow through the fields like that?'

And with that he caught the youngest girl by the hand to draw her away. But directly he touched her he hung on himself and had to run along with the rest of them.

Not long afterward the clerk came that way and was much surprised to see the parson following the footsteps of the three girls. 'Why, where is your reverence going so fast?' cried he. And he ran after him, caught him by the sleeve, and hung on to it himself.

As the five of them trotted along in this fashion one after the other, two peasants were coming from their work with their hoes. On seeing them the parson called out and begged them to come and rescue him and the clerk. But no sooner did they touch the clerk than they stuck on too, and so there were seven of them running after Dullhead and his goose.

After a time they all came to a town where a king reigned whose daughter was so serious and solemn that no one could ever manage to make her laugh. So the king had decreed that whoever should succeed in making her laugh should marry her.

When Dullhead heard this he marched before the princess with his goose and its appendages, and as soon as she saw these seven people continually running after each other, she burst out laughing and could not stop herself. Then he claimed her as his bride, but the king, who did not much fancy him as a son-in-law, made all sorts of objections, and told him he must first find a man who could drink up a whole cellarful of wine.

Dullhead bethought him of the little gray man, who could, he felt sure, help him. So he went off to the forest, and on the very spot where he had cut down the tree he saw a man with a most dismal expression of face.

He asked the man what he was taking so much to heart, and the man answered, 'I don't know how I am ever to quench this terrible thirst I am suffering from. Cold water doesn't suit me at all. To be sure I've emptied a whole barrel of wine, but what is one drop on a hot stone?'

'I think I can help you,' said the boy. 'Come with me, and you shall drink to your heart's content.'

So he took him to the king's cellar, and the man sat down

before the huge casks and drank and drank till he drank up the whole contents of the cellar before the day closed.

Then Dullhead asked once more for his bride, but the king felt vexed at the idea of a stupid fellow whom people called 'Dullhead' carrying off his daughter, and he began to make fresh conditions. He required Dullhead to find a man who could eat a mountain of bread. The boy did not wait to consider long but went straight off to the forest, and there on the same spot sat a man who was drawing in a strap as tight as he could round his body, and making a most woeful face the while. Said he:

'I've eaten up a whole oven full of loaves, but what's the good of that to anyone who is as hungry as I am? I declare my stomach feels quite empty, and I must draw my belt tight if I'm not to die of starvation.'

Dullhead was delighted, and said, 'Get up and come with me, and you shall have plenty to eat,' and he brought him to the king's court.

Now the king had given orders to have all the flour in his kingdom brought together and to have a huge mountain baked of it. But the man from the wood just took up his stand before the mountain and began to eat, and in one day it had all vanished.

For the third time Dullhead asked for his bride, but again the king tried to make some evasion, and demanded a ship which could sail on land or water. 'When you come sailing in such a ship,' said he, 'you shall have my daughter without further delay.'

Again the boy started off to the forest, and there he found the little old gray man with whom he had shared his cake, and who said:

'I have eaten and I have drunk for you, and now I will give

you the ship. I have done all this for you because you were kind and merciful to me.'

Then he gave him a ship which could sail on land or water, and when the king saw it he felt he could no longer refuse him his daughter. So they celebrated the wedding with great rejoicings, and after the king's death Dullhead succeeded to the kingdom, and lived happily with his wife for many years after.

[Jakob and Wilhelm Grimm.]

The Seven Foals

THERE WAS ONCE UPON
a time a couple of poor folks who lived in a wretched hut, far
away from everyone else, in a wood. They only just managed
to live from hand to mouth and had great difficulty in doing
even so much as that. They had three sons, and the youngest of
them was called Cinderlad, for he did nothing else but lie and
poke about among the ashes.

One day the eldest lad said that he would go out to earn his
living. He soon had leave to do that and set out on his way
into the world. He walked on and on for the whole day, and
when night was beginning to fall he came to a royal palace.
The king was standing outside on the steps and asked where
he was going.

'Oh, I am going about seeking a place, my father,' said the
youth.

'Will you serve me, and watch my seven foals?' asked the
king. 'If you can watch them for a whole day and tell me at
night what they eat and drink, you shall have the princess and
half my kingdom, but if you cannot, I will cut three red stripes
on your back.'

344

The youth thought it would be easy work to watch the foals and that he could do it well enough.

Next morning, when day was beginning to dawn, the king's Master of the Horse let out the seven foals, and they ran away, and the youth after them just as it chanced, over hill and dale, through woods and bogs. When the youth had run thus for a long time he began to be tired, and when he had held out a little longer he was heartily weary of watching at all, and at the same moment he came to a cleft in a rock where an old woman sat spinning, with her distaff in her hand.

As soon as she caught sight of the youth, who was running after the foals till the perspiration streamed down his face, she cried, 'Come hither, come hither, my handsome son, and let me comb your hair for you.'

The lad was willing enough, so he sat down in the cleft of the rock beside the old woman, and laid his head on her knees, and she combed his hair all day while he lay there and gave himself up to idleness.

When evening was drawing near, the youth wanted to go. 'I may just as well go straight home again,' said he, 'for it is no use to go to the king's palace.'

'Wait till it is dusk,' said the old woman, 'and then the king's foals will pass here again, and you can run home with them. No one will ever know that you have been lying here all day instead of watching the foals.'

So when they came she gave the lad a bottle of water and a bit of moss and told him to show these to the king and say that this was what his seven foals ate and drank.

'Have you watched faithfully and well the whole day long?' asked the king, when the lad came into his presence in the evening.

'Yes, that I have!' said the youth.

'Then you are able to tell me what it is that my seven foals eat and drink,' said the king.

So the youth produced the bottle of water and the bit of moss which had been given him by the old woman, saying:

'Here you see their meat, and here you see their drink.'

Then the king knew how his watching had been done and fell into such a rage that he ordered his people to chase the youth back to his own home at once, but first they were to cut three red stripes in his back.

When the youth reached home again, what a state of mind he was in! He had gone out once to seek a place, he said, but never would he do such a thing again.

Next day the second son said that he would now go out into the world to seek his fortune. His father and mother said 'No,' and bade him look at his brother's back, but the youth would not give up his design and stuck to it. After a long, long time he was given leave to go and set forth on his way.

When he had walked all day he too came to the king's palace, and the king was standing outside on the steps and asked where he was going. And when the youth replied that he was going about in search of a place, the king said that he might enter into his service and watch his seven foals. The king promised him the same punishment and the same reward that he had promised his brother. The youth at once consented to this and entered into the king's service, for he thought he could easily watch the foals and inform the king what they ate and drank.

In the gray light of dawn the Master of the Horse let out the seven foals, and off they went again over hill and dale, and off went the lad after them. But all went with him as it had with his brother. When he had run after the foals for a long,

long time and was hot and tired, he passed by a cleft in the rock where an old woman sat spinning with a distaff, and she called to him:

'Come hither, come hither, my handsome son, and let me comb your hair.'

The youth liked the thought of this, let the foals run where they chose, and seated himself in the cleft of the rock by the side of the old woman. So there he sat with his head on her lap, taking his ease the livelong day.

The foals came back in the evening, and then he too was given a bit of moss and a bottle of water, which he was to show to the king. But when the king asked the youth, 'Can you tell me what my seven foals eat and drink?' and the youth showed him the bit of moss and the bottle of water, and said, 'Yes, here may you behold their meat, and here their drink,' the king once more became wroth and commanded that three red stripes should be cut on the lad's back, and that he should then be chased back to his own home. So when the youth reached home again he too related all that had happened to him, and he too said that he had gone out in search of a place once, but that never would he do it again.

On the third day Cinderlad wanted to set out. He had a fancy to try to watch the seven foals himself, he said. The two others laughed at him and mocked him.

'What! When all went so ill with us, do you suppose you are going to succeed? You look like succeeding—you who have never done anything else but poke about among the ashes!' said they.

'Yes, I will go too,' said Cinderlad, 'for I have taken it into my head.'

The two brothers laughed at him, and his father and mother begged him not to go, but all to no purpose, and Cinderlad set out on his way. When he had walked the whole day, he too came to the king's palace as darkness began to fall.

There stood the king outside on the steps, and he asked whither he was bound.

'I am walking about in search of a place,' said Cinderlad.

'From whence do you come, then?' inquired the king, for by this time he wanted to know a little more about the men before he took any of them into his service.

So Cinderlad told him whence he came, and that he was brother to the two who had watched the seven foals for the king, and then he inquired if he might watch them on the following day.

'Oh, shame on them!' said the king, for it enraged him even to think of them. 'If you are brother to those two, you are not good for much. I have had enough of such fellows.'

'But as I have come, you might just give me leave to make the attempt,' said Cinderlad.

'Oh, very well, if you are determined to have your back flayed, you may have your own way,' said the king.

'I would much rather have the princess,' said Cinderlad.

Next morning, in the gray light of dawn, the Master of the Horse let out the seven foals again, and off they set over hill and dale, through woods and bogs, and off went Cinderlad after them. When he had run thus for a long time, he too came to the cleft in the rock. There the old woman was once more, spinning from her distaff, and she cried to Cinderlad:

'Come hither, come hither, my handsome son, and let me comb your hair for you.'

'Come to me, then; come to me!' said Cinderlad, as he passed by jumping and running, and keeping tight hold of one of the foals' tails.

When he had got safely past the cleft in the rock, the youngest foal said, 'Get on my back, for we have still a long way to go.' So the lad did this. And thus they journeyed onward a long, long way.

'Do you see anything now?' asked the foal.

'No,' said Cinderlad.

So they journeyed onward a good bit farther.

'Do you see anything now?' asked the foal.

'Oh, no,' said the lad.

When they had gone thus for a long, long way, the foal again asked, 'Do you see anything now?'

'Yes, now I see something that is white,' said Cinderlad. 'It looks like the trunk of a great birch tree.'

'Yes, that is where we are to go in,' said the foal.

When they came to the tree, the eldest foal broke it down on one side, and then they saw a door where the trunk had been standing. Inside this was a small room in which there was scarcely anything but a small fireplace and a couple of benches. But behind the door hung a great rusty sword and a small pitcher.

'Can you wield that sword?' asked the foal.

Cinderlad tried, but could not do it; so he had to take a draught from the pitcher, and then one more, and after that still another, and then he was able to wield the sword with perfect ease.

'Good,' said the foal; 'and now you must take the sword away with you, and with it shall you cut off the heads of all seven of us on your wedding day. Then we shall become princes again as we were before. For we are brothers of the princess whom you are to have when you can tell the king what we eat and drink, but there is a mighty troll who has cast a spell over us. When you have cut off our heads, you must take the greatest care to lay each head at the tail of the body to which it belonged before, and then the spell which the troll has cast upon us will lose all its power.'

Cinderlad promised to do this, and then they went on farther. When they had travelled a long, long way, the foal said:

'Do you see anything?'

'No,' said Cinderlad.

So they went on a great distance farther.

'And now?' inquired the foal. 'See you nothing now?'

'Alas, no!' said Cinderlad.

So they travelled onward again, for many and many a mile, over hill and dale.

'Now, then,' said the foal, 'do you not see anything now?'

'Yes,' said Cinderlad; 'now I see something like a blue streak, far, far away.'

'That is a river,' said the foal, 'and we have to cross it.'

There was a long, handsome bridge over the river, and when they had reached the other side of it they again travelled on a long, long way, and then once more the foal inquired if Cinderlad saw anything. Yes, this time he saw something that looked black, far, far away, and was rather like a church tower.

'Yes,' said the foal, 'we shall go into that.'

When the foals went into the churchyard they turned into men again and looked like the sons of a king, and their clothes were so magnificent that they shone with splendour. They went into the church and received bread and wine and a blessing. Cinderlad went in too. When the princes went out again, Cinderlad went out too, but he took with him a flask of wine and some consecrated bread. No sooner had the seven princes come out into the churchyard than they became foals again, and Cinderlad got upon the back of the youngest, and they returned by the way they had come, only they went much, much faster.

First they went over the bridge, and then past the trunk of the birch tree, and then past the old woman who sat in the cleft of the rock spinning, and they went by so fast that Cinderlad could not hear what she screeched after him, but just heard enough to understand she was terribly enraged.

It was all but dark when they came back to the king at nightfall, and he himself was standing in the courtyard waiting for them.

'Have you watched well and faithfully the whole day?' the king asked Cinderlad.

'I have done my best,' replied Cinderlad.

'Then you can tell me what my seven foals eat and drink?' asked the king.

So Cinderlad pulled out the bread and the flask of wine, and showed them to the king. 'Here may you behold their meat and here their drink,' said he.

'Yes, diligently and faithfully have you watched,' said the king. 'You shall have the princess and half the kingdom.'

So all was made ready for the wedding, and the king said that it was to be so stately and magnificent that everyone

24

should hear of it, and everyone inquire about it. But when they sat down to the marriage feast, the bridegroom arose and went down to the stable, for he said that he had forgotten something he must look to. Then he did what the foals had bidden him, and cut off the heads of all the seven. First the eldest, and then the second, and so on according to their age, and he was extremely careful to lay each head at the tail of the foal to which it had belonged, and when that was done, all the foals became princes again. When he returned to the marriage feast with the seven princes, the king was so joyful that he both kissed Cinderlad and clapped him on the back, and his bride was still more delighted with him than she had been before.

'Half my kingdom is yours already,' said the king, 'and the other half shall be after my death, for my sons can get countries and kingdoms for themselves now that they have become princes again.'

Therefore, as all may well believe, there was joy and merriment at that wedding.

[From J. E. Moe.]

The Story of Sigurd

ONCE UPON A TIME
there was a king in the North who had won many wars, but
now he was old. Yet he took a new wife, and then another
prince, who had wanted to marry her, came against him with
a great army. The old king went out and fought bravely,
but at last his sword broke, and he was wounded and his men
fled. But in the night, when the battle was over, his young wife
came out and searched for him among the slain. At last she
found him, and asked him whether he might be healed. But he
said 'No,' his luck was gone, his sword was broken, and he
must die.

And he told her that she would have a son, who would be
a great warrior and would avenge him on the other king, his
enemy. He bade her keep the broken pieces of the sword, to
make a new sword for his son, and that blade should be called
Gram. Then he died. And his wife called her maid to her
and said:

'Let us change clothes, and you shall be called by my name,
and I by yours, lest the enemy finds us.'

So this was done, and they hid in a wood, but there some
strangers met them and carried them off in a ship to Denmark.

And when they were brought before the king, he thought the maid looked like a queen, and the queen like a maid. So he asked the queen:

'How do you know in the dark of night whether the hours are wearing to the morning?'

And she said, 'I know because, when I was younger, I used to have to rise and light the fires, and still I waken at the same time.'

A strange queen to light the fires, thought the king. Then he asked the queen, who was dressed like a maid:

'How do you know in the dark of night whether the hours are wearing near the dawn?'

'My father gave me a gold ring,' said she, 'and always, ere the dawning, it grows cold on my finger.'

'A rich house where the maids wore gold,' said the king. 'Truly you are no servant, but a king's daughter.'

So he treated her royally, and as time went on she had a son called Sigurd, a beautiful boy and very strong. He had a tutor to be with him, and once the tutor bade him go to the king and ask for a horse.

'Choose a horse for yourself,' said the king.

Sigurd went to the wood, and there he met an old man with a white beard, and said, 'Come, help me in horse choosing.'

Then the old man said. 'Drive all the horses into the river, and choose the one that swims across.'

So Sigurd drove them, and only one swam across. Sigurd chose him. His name was Grani, and he came of Sleipnir's breed, and was the best horse in the world. For Sleipnir was the horse of Odin, the God of the North, and was as swift as the wind.

But a day or two later his tutor said to Sigurd, 'There is a great treasure of gold hidden not far from here and it would become you to win it.'

But Sigurd answered, 'I have heard stories of that treasure, and I know that the dragon Fafnir guards it, and he is so huge and wicked that no man dares to go near him.'

'He is no bigger than other dragons,' said the tutor, 'and if you were as brave as your father you would not fear him.'

'I am no coward,' said Sigurd. 'Why do you want me to fight with this dragon?'

Then his tutor, whose name was Regin, told him that all this great hoard of red gold had once belonged to his own father. And his father had three sons—the first was Fafnir, the dragon; the next was Otter, who could put on the shape of an otter when he liked; and the next was himself, Regin, and he was a great smith and maker of swords.

Now at that time a dwarf, called Andvari, lived in a pool beneath a waterfall, and there he had hidden a great hoard of gold. And one day Otter had been fishing there and had killed a salmon and eaten it, and was sleeping, like an otter, on a stone. Then someone came by and threw a stone at the otter and killed it, flayed off the skin and took it to the house of Otter's father. Then he knew his son was dead, and to punish the person who had killed him he said he must have the otter's skin filled with gold and covered all over with red gold, or it should go worse with him. Then the person who had killed Otter went down and caught the dwarf who owned all the treasure and took it from him.

Only one ring was left, which the dwarf wore, and even that was taken from him. The poor dwarf was very angry and prayed that the gold might never bring any but bad luck to all the men who might own it, forever. Then the otter skin was filled with gold and covered with gold, all but one hair, and that was covered with the poor dwarf's last ring.

But it brought good luck to nobody. First Fafnir, the dragon, killed his own father, and then he went and wallowed in the gold and would let his brother have none, and no man dared go near it.

When Sigurd heard the story he said to Regin, 'Make me a good sword that I may kill this dragon.'

So Regin made a sword, and Sigurd tried it with a blow on a lump of iron, and the sword broke.

Another sword he made, and Sigurd broke that too.

Then Sigurd went to his mother and asked for the broken pieces of his father's blade and gave them to Regin. And he hammered and wrought them into a new sword, so sharp that fire seemed to burn along its edges.

Sigurd tried this blade on the lump of iron, and it did not break, but split the iron in two. Then he threw a lock of wool into the river, and when it floated down against the sword it was cut into two pieces. So Sigurd said that sword would do. But before he went against the dragon he led an army to fight the men who had killed his father, Sigmund, and he slew their king and took all his wealth and went home.

When he had been at home a few days, he rode out with Regin one morning to the heath where the dragon used to lie. Then he saw the track which the dragon made when he went to a cliff to drink, and the track was as if a great river had rolled along and left a deep valley.

Then Sigurd went down into that deep place and dug many pits in it, and in one of the pits he lay hidden with his sword drawn and there he waited. Presently the earth began to shake with the weight of the dragon as he crawled to the water, and a cloud of venom flew before him as he snorted and roared so that it would have been death to stand before him.

Sigurd waited till half of him had crawled over the pit, and then he thrust the sword *Gram* right into his very heart. Then the dragon lashed with his tail till stones broke and trees crashed about him. Then he spoke, as he died, and said:

'Whoever you are who has slain me, this gold shall be your ruin, and the ruin of all who own it.'

Sigurd said, 'I would touch none of it, if by losing it I should never die. But all men die, and no brave man lets death frighten him from his desire. Die, Fafnir!' And then Fafnir died.

After that Sigurd was called Fafnir's Bane, and Dragon Slayer.

Then Sigurd rode back and met Regin, and Regin asked him to roast Fafnir's heart and let him taste of it. So Sigurd put the heart of Fafnir on a stake and roasted it. But it chanced that he touched it with his finger and it burned him. Then he put his finger in his mouth and so he tasted the heart of Fafnir. Then immediately he understood the language of birds, and he heard the woodpeckers say:

'There is Sigurd roasting Fafnir's heart for another, when he should taste of it himself and learn all wisdom.'

The next bird said, 'There lies Regin, ready to betray Sigurd, who trusts him.'

The third bird said, 'Let him cut off Regin's head, and keep all the gold himself.'

The fourth bird said, 'That let him do, and then ride over Hindfell, to the place where Brynhild sleeps.'

When Sigurd heard all this, and how Regin was plotting to betray him, he cut off Regin's head with one blow of the sword *Gram*. Then all the birds broke out singing:

'We know a fair maid,
A fair maiden sleeping;
Sigurd be not afraid,
Sigurd, win thou the maid
Fortune is keeping.

'High over Hindfell
Red fire is flaming,
There doth the maiden dwell,
She that should love thee well
Meet for thy taming.

'There must she sleep till thou
Comest for her waking;
Rise up and ride, for now
Sure she will swear the vow
Fearless of breaking.'

Then Sigurd remembered how the story went that some-where, far away, there was a beautiful lady enchanted. She was under a spell and must always sleep in a castle surrounded by flaming fire; there she must sleep forever till there came a knight who would ride through the fire and waken her. There he determined to go, but first he rode right down the horrible trail of Fafnir. The dragon had lived in a cave with iron doors, a cave dug deep down in the earth and full of gold bracelets and crowns and rings; and there, too, Sigurd found the Helm of Dread, a golden helmet which made its wearer invisible. All these he piled on the back of the good horse Grani, and then he rode south to Hindfell.

Now it was night, and on the crest of the hill Sigurd saw a red fire blazing up into the sky, and within the flame a castle with a banner on the topmost tower. Then he set the

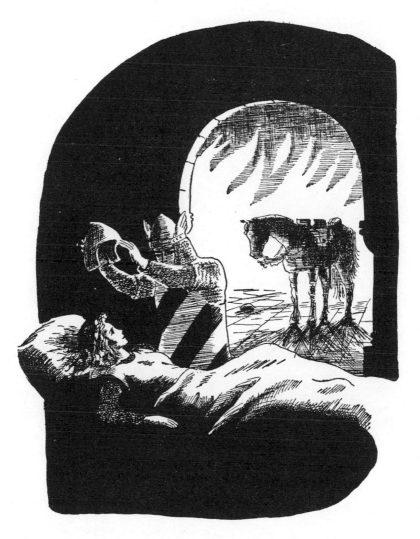

'Ah, is it Sigurd who comes to waken me at last?'

horse Grani at the fire, and he leaped through it lightly, as if it had been through the heather. So Sigurd went within the castle door, and there he saw someone sleeping, clad all in armour. Then he took the helmet off the head of the sleeper, and behold, she was a most beautiful lady. She wakened and said:

'Ah, is it Sigurd, Sigmund's son, who has broken the curse and comes here to waken me at last?'

This curse came upon her when the thorn of the tree of sleep ran into her hand long ago as a punishment because she had displeased Odin the God of the North. Long ago, too, she had vowed never to marry a man who knew fear, and dared not ride through the fence of flaming fire. For she was a warrior maid herself and went armed into the battle like a man. But now she and Sigurd loved each other and promised to be true to each other, and he gave her a ring, and it was the last ring taken from the dwarf Andvari.

Then Sigurd rode away, and he came to the house of a king who had a fair daughter. Her name was Gudrun, and her mother was a witch. Now Gudrun fell in love with Sigurd, but he was always talking of Brynhild, how beautiful she was and how dear. So one day Gudrun's mother put poppy and forgetful drugs in a magical cup, and bade Sigurd drink to her health, and he drank, and instantly he forgot poor Brynhild and loved Gudrun, and they were married with great rejoicings.

Now the witch, the mother of Gudrun, wanted her son Gunnar to marry Brynhild, and she bade him ride out with Sigurd and woo her. So forth they rode to her father's house, for Brynhild had quite gone out of Sigurd's mind by reason of the witch's brew, but she remembered him and loved him still. Then Brynhild's father told Gunnar that she would marry

none but him who could ride the flame in front of her enchanted tower. Thither they rode, and Gunnar set his horse
at the flame, but he could not face it. Then Gunnar tried
Sigurd's horse Grani, but he would not move with Gunnar
on his back.

Then Gunnar remembered witchcraft his mother had taught
him, and by his magic he made Sigurd look exactly like himself, and he looked exactly like Gunnar. Then Sigurd in the
shape of Gunnar and in his mail mounted on Grani, and Grani
leaped the fence of fire. Sigurd went in and found Brynhild,
but he did not remember her yet, because of the forgetful
medicine in the cup of the witch's wine.

Now Brynhild had no help but to promise she would be his
wife, the wife of Gunnar as she supposed, for Sigurd wore
Gunnar's shape and she had sworn to wed whoever should
ride the flame. And he gave her a ring, and she gave him back
the ring he had given her before in his own shape as Sigurd,
and it was the last ring of that poor dwarf Andvari. Then he
rode out again, and he and Gunnar changed shapes, and each
was himself again, and they went home to the witch queen,
where Sigurd gave the dwarf's ring to his wife, Gudrun. And
Brynhild went to her father, and said that a king had come
called Gunnar and had ridden the fire, and she must
marry him.

'Yet I thought,' she said, 'that no man could have done this
deed but Sigurd, Fafnir's Bane, who was my true love. But he
has forgotten me, and my promise I must keep.'

So Gunnar and Brynhild were married, though it was not
Gunnar but Sigurd in Gunnar's shape who had ridden the fire.
And when the wedding was over and all the feast, then the
magic of the witch's wine went out of Sigurd's brain, and he
remembered all.

He remembered how he had freed Brynhild from the spell, and how she was his own true love, and how he had forgotten and had married another woman and won Brynhild to be the wife of another man. But he was brave, and he spoke not a word of it to the others to make them unhappy.

Still he could not keep away the curse which was to come on everyone who owned the treasure of the dwarf Andvari and his fatal golden ring. And the curse soon came upon all of them. For one day, when Brynhild and Gudrun were bathing, Brynhild waded farthest out into the river and said she did that to show she was Gudrun's superior. For her husband, she said, had ridden through the flame when no other man dared face it.

Then Gudrun was very angry and said that it was Sigurd, not Gunnar, who had ridden the flame and had received from Brynhild that fatal ring, the ring of the dwarf Andvari. Then Brynhild saw the ring which Sigurd had given to Gudrun, and she knew it and knew all, and she turned as pale as a dead woman and went home. All that evening she never spoke.

Next day she told Gunnar, her husband, that he was a coward and a liar, for he had never ridden the flame, but had sent Sigurd to do it for him and pretended that he had done it himself. And she said he would never see her glad in his hall, never drinking wine, never playing chess, never embroidering with golden thread, never speaking words of kindness. Then she rent all her needlework asunder and wept aloud so that everyone in the house heard her. For her heart was broken, and her pride was broken in the same hour. She had lost her true love, Sigurd, the slayer of Fafnir, and she was married to a man who was a liar.

Then Sigurd came and tried to comfort her, but she would not listen and said she wished the sword stood fast in his heart.

'Not long to wait,' he said, 'till the bitter sword stands fast in my heart, and you will not live long when I am dead. But, dear Brynhild, live and be comforted and love Gunnar your husband, and I will give you all the gold, the treasure of the dragon Fafnir.'

Brynhild said, 'It is too late.'

Then Sigurd was so grieved and his heart so swelled in his breast that it burst the steel rings of his shirt of mail.

Sigurd went out and Brynhild determined to slay him. She mixed serpent's venom and wolf's flesh and gave them in one dish to her husband's younger brother, and when he had tasted them he was mad and went into Sigurd's chamber while he slept and pinned him to the bed with a sword. But Sigurd woke and caught the sword *Gram* and threw it at the man as he fled and the sword cut him in twain. Thus died Sigurd, Fafnir's Bane, whom no ten men could have slain in fair fight.

Then Gudrun wakened and saw him dead and she moaned aloud, and Brynhild heard her and laughed. But the kind horse Grani lay down and died of very grief. And then Brynhild fell a-weeping till her heart broke. So they attired Sigurd in all his golden armour and built a great pile of wood on board his ship, and at night laid on it the dead Sigurd and the dead Brynhild, and the good horse, Grani, and set fire to it and launched the ship. And the wind bore it blazing out to sea, flaming into the dark. So there were Sigurd and Brynhild burned together, and the curse of the dwarf Andvari was fulfilled.

[The *Volsunga Saga*]